CW00872111

Ruin's Entrance

a novel

Ray Stickle

Books by RAY STICKLE

The Footnotes
Ruin's Entrance
Stay, Illusion

Copyright © 2015 Ray Stickle
California Times Publishing, Los Angeles

www.californiatimespublishing.com

For Chris
Thank you. For the literature, the rich discussions, all of that. You know
what I mean.

Yonder house is haunted by a band that never leaves
it, a choir that sing in unison indeed, but harshly, for
their song is not of blessing. Lo, emboldened with
draughts of human blood, that revel-rout of Furies
inborn in the race, abide within there, not to be
exorcised. Fast clinging to the mansion, they hymn the
primordial crime.

- Aeschylus, *Agamemnon*

His gashed stabs looked like a breach in nature
For ruin's wasteful entrance.

- Shakespeare, *Macbeth*

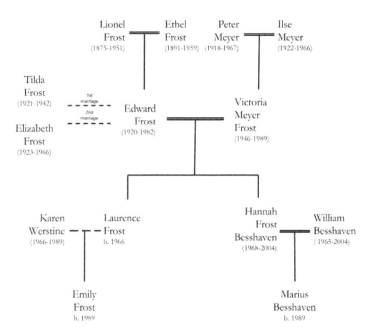

I
The Frost Estate

Chapter 1

WHAT DO YOU do when your adult life feels like the falling action in a penny-dreadful? The only possible resolution is death, but who knows when. The rest is just a sorting out, and not a very good one. I don't know who I am. I mean in the general sense. Here I'm the Ohio State professor talking about planets, born from stardust. Here I'm the schlub on the sofa with three empty bottles of wine and Beethoven on the stereo. I can name the opus number but I can't stand up.

And here I'm the vacationing dreamer in the cold desert at night with an eye to the lens of a telescope, knowing the faces in the far-off furnaces above burning all white and still and eternal. There's Miriam Reis. And Sara Feld. And David Pensak. And Mary Leiber. And the faces of Majdanek.

That's what it always leads back to, doesn't it?

I can't get it all straight and Emily's book hasn't helped. It came out last week but I've had a copy for over a month now, sitting on the coffee table like an urn, a halo of bare wood around it, all no-go, keep a wide circumference.

Heinrich Scherer seemed enamored with the efficiency of the semi-automatic weapons, the Zyklon B, the crematory ovens, the mass-burial pits. Before he got more intimate and more personal and started using a blade.

That's what it all leads back to, right? Our family's own Night of the Long Knives.

I suppose the person who's writing this is who I am. Now. In this moment. And if I'm lucky, the next. But I don't know. I don't know. Maybe our great-grandfather's fascination with the efficiency of twentieth-century mass murder led to my uncle's disavowal of all technology outside of the electric light, the internal combustion engine. Who can blame him? I seem to follow in his footsteps as much as I do anyone else's. I barely knew Laurence Frost. I barely knew my parents. Maybe I can make sense of it all if I write down what happened ten years ago. And before. I've tried. And given up. The crucible of planets is where I operate.

But then there's this falling action. The sorting out. I rather feel like I need to sort it out.

So where did it begin?

Chapter 2

THEY DIED IN a car accident. Late at night. My father behind the wheel. He'd been drinking, but that wasn't why they went off the road and into the steel utility pole going over sixty on a winding canyon road. It was my mother. In one of her moods again.

I didn't know this right away, of course. I was asleep in my room in our house north of Indianapolis. They were in Los Angeles. For one of her causes. Work assistance for war veterans. Educational opportunities for refugees—Somalis, Afghanis, Iraqis. I don't know. It was ultimately another charity. A place for her to spend her money and feel good about herself. Never mind she had a fourteen-year-old child at home with an au pair.

If they had died in Indianapolis I might have missed the next day of school. That would have been good.

***

"Marius Besshaven fucks flocks of ravens."

An October morning. 2003. I tried to sit near the windows, staring at the Canadian maples outside, their cardinal red leaves shivering in the breeze. These boys in their blue blazers in the warm classroom filled with the amped-up smell of new adolescence. They found a new rhyme for me each day.

"Fucks his mother too."

Fucks his mother. Yeah. I hardly knew what she looked like. Thin-almond eyes, like mine–mine gray, hers brown. Black hair, like mine. And what else? Slender, diminutive. Like me, like me.

"Fucks your mother, more like it."

"He doesn't have dick enough."

I watched the trees instead of responding to the taunts and this upset them. One of them—I can't remember his name. I can't remember any of their names. One of them used his size as a weapon. He had a back like a barn door. Body odor like a farm animal. I felt his abdomen against my shoulder.

"Hey, Marius, I've got dick enough for you."

There were uncomfortable titters. This guy sometimes crossed the line and confused his cohort. Early onset sadism was not so pretty to behold.

"I highly doubt that," I said.

I felt his stomach press further against me. His groin brushing against my arm. I pulled my elbow in and his pelvis rubbed my desk instead.

He leaned over me. Sour milk on his breath.

"What?" he said, blunting the word.

I kept my eyes focused on the trees.

"I said I highly doubt that."

"What?"

Those red leaves. They shivered and considered falling. And the moon lingering there a faint white stranger, a phantom, as the sky lightened towards the blue of an autumn afternoon.

"Your dick," I said. "I highly doubt you have enough for the both of us. You're too fat. It takes some off the length."

He reached a hand to my jaw and pinched, rotating my face towards his.

"You want to say that again?"

"Though I doubt you'd notice. When's the last time you saw it? Probably in a photo you sent your dog, right?"

His peers stood silent. We'd all been here before. Violence would come next.

But the teacher came in early.

"Marius."

I felt the heat off of that immense body fade away as the boy stepped back.

"You're wanted in the office."

"Uh-oh," a chorus of foreboding.

"Enough. Marius, bring your things."

"Ooh."

I left the textbooks but took my novel. *Rendezvous with Rama*. Arthur C. Clarke. I had a thing for science fiction. A need to get off planet.

***

The principal was a skinny blonde woman named Mrs. Krucher. Her name is familiar to me now only because of the connection I have with her and what she told me. Otherwise just another shadow from my past. Mrs. Krucher.

There was sadness in her eyes. Affection. The affection wasn't feigned but I didn't know this. Affection was typically a ruse in my household.

"Marius."

I tapped the paperback against my thigh.

"Have a seat," she said.

Her office smelled of cinnamon potpourri and she had country things everywhere. Farm things. The hackneyed mythology of rural acres. A calendar and planner and pencil holder and picture frame. I sat in one of the soft chairs across from her desk and she walked around to sit next to me. Her legs pressed together and hands clasped in her lap. She leaned close. In my face with her broad, sad eyes. Perfume as potent as that potpourri.

"Marius…" a shake in her voice like the shake in the leaves. "Marius. I have some really terrible news."

I wondered if the house had burned down. We had a greenhouse out back and I'd begun the process of moving my plants into it. The first frost would come soon. I thought of the greenhouse and hoped there had not been a fire.

She sighed and lowered her head. A warm hand covered mine. Variations in color in the diamond set in her gold wedding band.

"Your parents," she said. "There was an accident."

Maybe there hadn't been a fire.

"I'm sorry to tell you, Marius, but your parents have passed away."

Her hand gripped mine firmly and I turned to see

a tear slide down her cheek, cutting a trail through thick foundation. Did she know them? Had they been friends? I didn't think so.

"Your uncle said he had to fly out to take care of—of arrangements, but that he was sending someone to get you. I'm so sorry, Marius."

An uncle? Did I have an uncle?

***

I was sitting in Mrs. Krucher's office reading my book when the delegate from my uncle arrived. I heard whispering outside the door.

"I think he's in shock. He's just been sitting there, looking at his book. Poor thing."

"Yes, well, it's a lot to take, isn't it?" This woman from my uncle had a hard voice. Dignified, though, each word clearly enunciated, clipped.

"It's good of you to come."

"I didn't have a choice."

Her name was Mrs. Moira and she was old. Old woman fragrance, a chemical isolate of earth's strongest scented flowers. I couldn't think when a smell that powerful entered the room.

I finished the page I was on and put the bookmark in, then looked up at her. She had deep lines in her face, a shelf of breasts a family could have left picture frames and souvenirs on, silver hair tied tightly back, severe brown eyes touched red around the edges.

"Marius," she said. It sounded more an order than

a greeting.

I stood up.

She shook her head at me. "How like your uncle you are. Let's go."

I followed her out. Mrs. Krucher's hand lingered for a moment on my shoulder. Then I left that life behind.

***

"Do they have a greenhouse at my uncle's?"

The driver, a tired, late middle-aged man glanced at me briefly before turning his attention back out the window of the family room of the Indianapolis house.

"Pardon?" Mrs. Moira, still seated.

"I have plants. I don't want them to die."

Her head tilted to the side. "Are we talking trees?"

I looked at her like she was stupid. "No, trees stay in the ground. Plants. Rather small."

"You saw the car."

I looked down at my bags. Stuffed with novels. More Arthur C. Clarke but also Ray Bradbury and J.K. Rowling and Neal Stephenson. My iPod and laptop and digital camera. I couldn't leave any of it. But maybe the clothes...

She saw me sizing up my belongings.

"Two plants," she said. "And they have to fit in the trunk."

***

Five hours later, with Mrs. Moira napping beside me in the backseat of the black Mercedes E-class sedan, I watched as the southern Ohio countryside passed by in low wooded hills. The power lines lonely as they paralleled the road mile after mile on poles that looked slender enough to snap in a strong wind.

Mrs. Moira stirred and cringed as she sat forward, rubbing at her lower back.

"We're near?" she said, squinting, trying to get her bearings.

"Twenty minutes or so," the driver said.

"Good. I can't take much more of this."

The driver smiled.

"Tell me about my uncle," I said.

She turned her head towards me slowly. I supposed she wasn't much used to being talked to by a child in such a direct manner. I was wrong on that account. I think this was the first hint to her that there were similarities between Emily and me.

"He's not fond of children."

"What else?" I wasn't fond of children either.

"So you won't see much of him. You wouldn't see much of him anyway. He travels, frequently."

"The principal said he's in LA. I didn't know I had an uncle."

She snorted and folded her hands on her lap and turned her gaze out the window.

"Your mother didn't want anything to do with her family."

"You knew her?" I asked. The eagerness in my voice caused Mrs. Moira to smile.

"Yes. And I was sorry to hear of what happened to her."

Through the window I saw the trees give way to open grassy meadows where sheep grazed, a river curving across the near horizon. We followed the river and the open land for a few miles with only the monotony of the power lines to break the otherwise prosaic landscape.

"It would have been better if things had not turned out as they had," Mrs. Moira continued after some moments of silence. "But what's past is past. There it is. We're home."

Chapter 3

THE FROST ESTATE was born in the mind of the patriarch of the family in the early 1920s when he had accumulated a fortune from automotive patents and had sold his nascent company in order to enjoy a life of leisure.

My mother never spoke of her family and my father's was wealthy enough that I never wondered where the money for our own sizable home came from. The Frost Estate was palatial and I stared with some wonder as the sedan turned off the two-lane road onto the wide and winding concrete drive that curled its way up through sycamores and oaks, giving only brief glimpses before the trees completely gave way and a broad green lawn rose to meet a patio and terrace and a face of impassive windows set across two stone wings.

The sedan slid through one of two porte cochère and onto a wide circular motor court where the Mercedes came to a stop in front of the main entry doors.

The driver pulled the latch for the trunk. Mrs. Moira waited for him to let her out. I hurried to the back of the car. One of the plants had fallen and soil covered the carpeting. I righted it and checked that the stems were not damaged.

"Where's the greenhouse?"

The front door of the house opened and a girl a year or two older than me came down to meet us.

Mrs. Moira turned to the driver. "If you wouldn't mind seeing to Marius's plants. They need to be taken to the greenhouse."

"And watered," I said.

"And could you water them, please," Mrs. Moira with a heavy intake of breath. She seemed tired of me already. "Flora, would you please help Marius with his bags and show him to his room. Then get down to the kitchen. I need your help with dinner."

Flora nodded and turned towards me with a smile. She was very pretty. Pale skin and a round face and brown hair tied back in a ponytail. A blue skirt that delineated lines that inspired certain thoughts in an adolescent's mind.

I took the suitcase with my books and electronics and followed her. The vestibule and entry hall were without lights at this time of day. The gray autumn sky provided illumination through high windows. A broad marble staircase that branched midway up greeted us and I followed Flora to the steps, the wheels of the suitcases clacking as they passed over the marble floor and echoed off of bare high walls and ceilings.

"Where is everyone?" I asked, feeling as if I'd stepped into a mausoleum.

"Oh, well, working, you know," she said, turning to me, smiling once again. As if smiling was a default setting for her. Or evidence of nerves. I couldn't tell.

"What about family?"

Still smiling she turned and collapsed the telescoping handle and lifted the suitcase up the stairs. I followed, annoyed that she had not answered my question. At the lower landing we took the branch off to the left, passing down hallways laid with lush red carpet, following a maze of passages, diverted by right angles, a gloomy pall from the lack of illumination, before stopping in front of a closed door in a whole row of them. She reached out and turned the brass handle.

"Well, here you are," she said. "Do you need anything?"

I pulled my suitcases inside and searched the wall for the light switch and turned it on, then closed the door on her, imagining her grin fading as I did so.

**

The room was on the second of two main stories and had high ceilings and dark green wallpaper, a queen-sized bed with an antique cherry frame and high headboard. On a dresser a TV fronted with knobs and dials looking worn out and old. A door opened onto a full bathroom and there was a sitting area with a small round table and chairs and a cushioned sofa and armchair. Everything upholstered and papered over dark. Dark wood and dark curtains and windows facing south onto a dreary dark day.

I walked over to the TV and turned it on. Static. Turned through channels. More static.

"What is this place?"

I pulled my Arthur C. Clarke book from the bag

and lay down on the sofa. Less than an hour and already I needed to escape.

Chapter 4

I WOKE IN the bed in the dark early morning. Disoriented. Only a day before I'd been in my own bed. The au pair, Katerin, turning on the light to wake me for school. What had happened to Katerin? Another of my uncle's people telling her that her services were no longer needed. Here's the severance. Thank you.

I reached for the lamp on the nightstand and climbed its metal column with my fingers until I found the switch. The room in shadows. My nose a mess from autumn allergies, the fault of farmers in their fields, plowing up wasted stalks of corn, distributing dust, mold. I sat up in bed and wondered what my first day here would bring.

I eventually got up and brushed my teeth and dressed in jeans and a sweatshirt. I opened the door to the hallway. The house was without movement, without any noise beyond the inhale and exhale of windows and shingles. My stomach grumbled. No one had bothered to talk to me of dinner. And now breakfast. And when would I begin school and what would the children there be like?

I thought better of leaving the room and instead retreated back to bed and opened Arthur C. Clarke. I liked to wander unknown places but the emptiness of the mansion, its overwhelming vacancy, was a bit chilling. Akin to the alien spacecraft Clarke's astronauts explored.

***

The sun was well up and I had the curtains at one window pulled wide when Flora came in with a covered tray. I was seated at the table and put my book down.

"Where have you been? I'm starving."

"Sorry," she said, setting the tray down. That grin again. Nervous. Definitely nervous. "It's just, well, we're not so used to having guests."

"Is that what I am?"

"No, no," she said. She moved over to the bed and began to pull at the rumpled sheets.

I thought again of my home in Indiana. It had been *my* home. No matter that my parents were rarely there. People like Katerin knew it was my home. I could go where I wanted. When I needed something, I got it. I wasn't waited on. The notion that I was a guest was an uncomfortable one.

"Then what am I?"

She didn't respond. Just worked, tucking in corners and positioning pillows.

"I hate being ignored," I said. "Don't you?"

"I'm sorry," again. Her cheeks red. She walked past me to open the rest of the curtains. She smelled of fabric softener. No perfume. I appreciated that.

I pulled the lid off the tray and found scrambled eggs and buttered toast, a glass of milk and orange juice. The eggs were already cold.

"And I'm sorry," she said, "about your parents."

I chewed on my toast. *Parents*. This word elicited no strong pull. They had simply been... What, donors of seed and egg? Being a parent required something more, didn't it?

"What's a girl your age doing working here? Why aren't you in school?"

"I am in school," she said. "Well, school's in here. We have a teacher come. Mr. Charles. My sister went to Princeton, after working here and studying with him. It's an opportunity, really. My grandmother, Mrs. Moira, she... We're very lucky."

"Strange," I said.

Flora shrugged. "You don't like eggs?"

"They're cold. And what's with the Internet here? I plugged in. Nothing happened. And the TV?"

"Mr. Frost doesn't have much use for them."

I narrowed my eyes. "My uncle's a troglodyte?"

"Hmm?"

"Never mind. So there's no Internet?"

"Sorry."

"That doesn't bother you? It seems rather isolating."

"There's plenty to read and do. You'll want to explore, then, won't you?"

"No," I said. "I'll want on the Internet. I'll want to watch television. *Discovery Channel. History*. Otherwise I'm ignorant. Like you. And I don't like that. I don't want to be ignorant."

She shrugged her shoulders again. Awkward mannerisms. I was tired of looking at her. She never seemed to want to defend herself.

"Can you go?" I said.

She did. Without a word. With hands clasped at her abdomen, tiny steps to the door, unsure, like walking on a frozen lake.

***

The next morning it was Flora telling me to go. She brought my breakfast at an earlier hour. No eggs this time, just toast and milk and juice. A small bowl of homemade strawberry jam. Sweet, and I spread it thick.

"You need to go out today," she told me as she made my bed.

"Who says?"

"My grandmother."

I grunted. I didn't appreciate being told what to do.

"It'll be good for you to explore. My grandma told me that you like plants."

I thought of my fuchsia plants and the greenhouse. It wasn't wise to leave important things in the care of others.

"There are lots of plants around here," she said.

"And what will you do all morning?" I asked.

"Work. And study."

Boring, I thought. What a life for a teenager.

***

I wore a jacket and put my iPod in a pocket.

Beethoven's Cello Sonata in G Minor. There were steps that curved down onto the grounds off of the main terrace. I followed them onto the lawn and between two pines standing sentry, stone steps set into the grass that led off in the direction of the greenhouse.

The trees were an artist's pallet blown into existence and I breathed in as I took in the riot of color. Somewhere on the grounds someone was burning leaves and other plant remnants and I was transported back to my home in Indiana. Into the backyard when our landscapers came out for the last time before spring. I would return from a walk in the woods and find a bonfire and would gather sticks to throw in. Watching the fire consume them, transform them. So easy, this transition from solid to smoke.

Through the trees I glimpsed the greenhouse. It was connected to a shallow home with sharply gabled roof and tall brick chimney. The home could not have housed more than a single person. A window pane was broken and the trim was in need of paint. Behind it ran the glasshouse, the waist-high brick wall of the home continuing for its entire length, glass rising and curving to a point like a spade on a deck of cards.

I walked around the greenhouse trying to find an area where I could peek inside, but the glass was everywhere clouded with dust and the opaque residue of hard rains. How would my plants survive if the windows were this impenetrable?

I found a door at the back of the building and tried the knob. It turned and, with a complaint in the hinges, opened and I went inside, through the outer and inner doors.

The sun had not yet climbed very high and the room was dim. The air dry and musty. Not even the hint of a scent of chlorophyll. Only plaster dust, straw, like rats had made a nest inside and no one had bothered to expel them.

Low tables stretched the length of the room. Attached to support beams at the midpoint were white cranks for opening the overhead windows and near these poles were my fuchsia plants next to an empty watering can. I plucked some of the fallen leaves and petals from the soil and dropped them on the ground, poked my finger into the soil and felt that it was dry.

"We'll get the two of you fixed up," I whispered and took the watering can to seek out a faucet.

There was an old hand pump nearby. I filled the can, studying the small gardener's house. Such an odd construction, as if it had been an afterthought.

I set the can down and walked over to a house window and blocked the glare of the morning light with my hand. I saw the hints of furniture but the gloom within hid too much.

Back in the greenhouse, I watered my plants and stared at the door to the home. Peeling white paint. Two windows set like eyes high in its face. A tarnished doorknob. My curiosity took hold and I set the watering can down on the table and walked in the direction of the door and damn near jumped out of my skin when the metal clang of the can hitting the ground behind me cut through the silence like air raid sirens.

"Shit," I whispered, heart beating hard, breath fast and shallow, staring back at where the can lay on its side surrounded by a dark, spreading pool of water. I turned and stared at the door again. Feeling that it was watching me, but feeling that it was crazy of me to think so.

I walked back and righted the can, setting it again on the table before retreating back outside.

***

I strode with no particular end in mind, following Flora's advice to explore. Gravel paths curved through various settings. An unkempt hedge maze. An oval of grass good for sport or entertaining. A brush pile near the trees where an older man, the driver, I thought, never looked in my direction as he added branches to the fire, the black smoke trailing up into the sky and carried in gusts of wind off to the east. The house visible from all of these places until I followed the path into the woods.

With my hands tucked in my pockets and my arms pulled close to my sides I shivered as I moved through the windblown trees. Feeling torn out by the roots and left here, bedraggled, untended. My parents had not been sterling exemplars of the art but they provided me a place to settle at least. Here I was among strangers and it seemed as if no one knew what to make of me or do with me. I had the sense that when my uncle returned he would make plans to move me to a boarding school somewhere. He obviously had the money to finance me, but I expected nothing in the way of familial affection from him.

I stopped walking when I saw the wall. Ivy covered, it broke the unplanned flow of nature and announced human hands had been busy here. It stood at least ten feet tall and a hundred or so yards wide before retreating back into the woods and finding greater length.

I looked around me. The house gone from view. A tendril of smoke in the sky, but the smell of it lost. I went up to the wall and pushed aside the ivy, revealing red bricks and gray mortar. I saw no passage in. Walking through fallen leaves and running my hand along the ivy I followed the wall as long as it paralleled the path, then back in the other direction. Where the path ended my hand went deeper into the ivy and I pushed it aside to reveal a heavy wooden door with black iron bands securing the thick planks, and there a metallic ring, a keyhole of the type one might find in a castle gate. I pushed on the door and, as I expected, it didn't move. I touched my finger to the keyhole, looked up at the high wall. Where was the key?

A gust of wind blew and the ivy shook and my teeth chattered. It was time to go back to my room.

Chapter 5

FLORA BROUGHT ME my dinner that evening and dusted while I ate. Roast beef, mashed potatoes, warm white bread, more milk. I disliked milk.

"Down in the woods there's a wall," I said.

"I don't know."

"You don't know?" How suddenly she'd said that.

She grinned nervously as she ran the duster over the fireplace mantle, moving the books I'd laid out there.

I shook my head and set my fork down with a clatter on the porcelain.

"There's a door, set in the wall," I said, pretending as if she'd never spoken. "It's locked. I'm wondering if you know where I might find the key. Or can someone just unlock it. I'd like to explore. I want to see what's in there."

"I don't know," she said again.

"What do you mean you don't know? How long have you lived here anyway?"

"Is there anything else—"

And then there was the scream. Far distant in the house. High. Piercing. Once and then gone.

Flora's head jerked to the door, grin gone, eyes wide.

"What was that?" I asked.

"Nothing. The wind, I'm sure."

"Bullshit, nothing," I said. "You're hiding

something. Many things. I don't know why."

She hurried to the door. "I'll be back later for your dishes, okay?"

"No, it's not okay. What…"

She left, closing the door behind her, and I thought of following. Questioning what I'd heard. Had it been a scream? Or was she right? Had it only been the wind? No, I thought, don't succumb to her delusions. She knows what's behind that wall. And she knows the wind doesn't scream. Not like that.

Chapter 6

I WENT BACK to the wall the next morning. The sky was a heavy gray and the wind blew hard, the lesser trees, the birches, bending sideways when the gales got going. I found the door again and pushed on it but it was still immovable, of course. I gripped the rustling ivy and pulled, wondering if it would support my weight, but it tore away.

I pushed the ivy aside, looking to see if any bricks had chipped, if there was any place for me to wedge in a foot or hand. Nothing, and I decided to follow the wall off the trail, to see if I could climb a tree and at the very least peek in.

The bare branches of thick brush tore at my coat. Bushes and weeds had grown up to and onto the wall. Trees lay further back. I saw nothing near enough to be of use or strong enough to support my weight and continued to look instead for handholds or footholds.

Then I found a tree that had fallen, severed at its base by lightning. The trunk was a foot or so in diameter, enough to support me. Staring at it in its nest of dead leaves, I thought that I could move it, and grabbed hold of some branches, squatted down, and using the strength in my legs, pulled. It didn't budge.

"Hey!"

I jumped back from the tree.

"Hey!"

A sharp adult voice. A man's voice.

I turned and saw the driver, the man who had been burning things the day before, standing at the end of the wall, on the trail, glaring at me from beneath his cap.

"What are you doing back there?" he shouted.

"What are you yelling for? My uncle owns this place. I'll do what I want."

"You'll get away from there." He began to follow my path, the branches snapping against his chest.

"I'll do what I want," I repeated. I reached down and grasped a branch, rolling the trunk a little in its divot, dislodging it. Encouraged and straining I got it to slide an inch or two.

His hard hand grasped my shoulder and I jumped away.

"Don't you ever touch me!"

Up close I saw his heavy brow and hard eyes and bristly whiskers on chapped, reddened cheeks. He smelled strongly of wood smoke, a little of schnapps.

"This is off limits."

"Why?"

"None of your business. Just understand. You're to have nothing to do with this place. And your uncle would back me on that, so don't test me."

"I'll ask him."

"I wouldn't, if I were you."

"Then tell me why."

"Off limits," he growled and turned to walk back towards the trail.

I spotted a rock jutting out of the dirt and picked it

up and flung it at the wall. It was absorbed into the ivy and hardly made a sound. The old man didn't turn to face me and I thought of picking the rock up again and throwing it at him. Why couldn't anyone in this godforsaken place speak?

***

I checked on my fuchsia plants in the greenhouse and stared at the door into the home. I considered approaching it again but fat raindrops began to fall and I heard the rumble of thunder in the distance and decided to go back to my room and begin another book. If no one gave me answers soon I would leave. I would walk off the property and never look back.

Chapter 7

"I'M SORRY," FLORA said. She sat with me at my table that evening while I ate. The rain continued to fall and thunder rumbled, flashes of light filtering in at the edges of the curtains.

"For what?" I said, buttering my bread and then dipping it into the hot beef stew.

"For avoiding your questions." No grin this time. A serious face. Eyes that focused on the table, darting up to me intermittently followed by an uncomfortable wringing of hands and a blush.

"It's a strange place," I said. "So many secrets."

"Yes," she said, nodding.

"But you know of the wall?"

"Yes."

"What's behind it?"

The grin again. What line would she feed me?

"A garden," she said.

"What's so important about hiding a garden? Why'd I get yelled at by some creepy old man this morning just for trying to get in the place?"

"Ben yelled at you?"

"Ben?"

"Ben Padrick. He's the groundskeeper, handyman, driver. He does a lot of things. He's been here for years. He's not bad."

"He put his hand on me."

She tilted her head in concern.

"On my shoulder." Thunder again. Followed immediately by the flash of lightning. The heart of the storm upon us.

"Oh. Well, he's just doing what Mr. Frost, what your uncle wants. I walked down there once, and, well, Ben didn't yell at me, but he told me. Your uncle doesn't want anyone in there."

"Why not?"

"I don't know."

I shook my head.

"I really don't," she said. "I'm sorry. If I did, I'd tell you. I've just been told, don't ask. Don't talk about it."

I took a bite of my stew. A soft carrot, a tender piece of meat.

"Who else lives here?" I asked, still chewing, gesturing with the silverware. "I see no pictures on the walls. No one but you and your grandmother and Ben. It's a big house."

She smiled.

"Would you stop," I said. "Enough, enough with that stupid grin."

She got up from the table, her lips quivering as if she'd cry.

"Just level with me," I said.

"You're too rude. Maybe if you had some manners—"

The lightning and the thunder came simultaneously this time and the electricity failed.

I heard Flora's footsteps move across the room,

the door open and close, and I was alone in the dark with a half-eaten dinner.

Chapter 8

THE NEXT MORNING the curtains were torn open, the metal rings scraping on the curtain rod, the harsh light of dawn awakening me.

"What's your issue?" I said, squinting and pushing myself upright.

"Your tutor is here," came the harsh response. Mrs. Moira.

"Where's Flora?"

"Do you care? The way you treat her? Hmm?" She stood with hands planted on hips, staring down at me with hard-set jaw. "If you are not kind to her you'll be dealing with me, and *I* don't have time for the complaints of young boys. Do you understand?"

"Who's kind to *me*? No one tells me anything here."

"You begin your lessons today with Mr. Charles. There, now I've told you something. You have thirty minutes, then you are expected down in the library."

"Library?"

"Thirty minutes."

***

There were two entrances into the library, from the first or second floor. I went down the grand staircase and into the wing of the house opposite my room, a place I had not been, dissuaded by the darkness and the reproving glares of Mrs. Moira, the explorer's instinct rather tempered when in the house. She always seemed to be standing in the corridor down which I planned to go.

Two oak doors gleaming under finely polished lacquer stood open and the natural light of day streamed through high windows in the circular room, bookshelves rising from floor to ceiling around the circumference, interrupted only by the columns of windows in the center and two archways ninety-degrees off center leading into smaller, more shadowy nooks. A balcony, too, touched every curve but one. A telescope stood on the upper level near the window. I stood gazing at countless volumes, marble busts, figures like Cicero and Shakespeare and Plato, inhaling the scent of bound books for a moment before noticing Mr. Charles.

An unremarkable man to inspire such passion in Flora. He had uncombed blonde hair and close-set blue eyes and a nose that hooked. He couldn't have grown a beard if he had been Robinson Crusoe, so baby-smooth was the flesh of his face.

His smile was welcoming and genuine.

"Young Marius!" he said, pushing back his chair and standing and walking over to me with hand extended. "How are you? I'm Mr. Charles. Richard Charles, actually, but we'll stand on tradition here. Come in and have a seat. How are you?"

I felt peppered as by machine gun fire, the heat of his queries.

"Fine," I said. Dour, as usual.

"Have a seat. Have a seat," gesturing, "and forget absolutely everything you ever learned in public school."

"I didn't go to a public school. My parents sent me to a private school." I pulled a chair out from the table and sat and crossed my arms, my look daring him to say more.

"Oh, God, even worse. Well, forget all of that too."

I narrowed my eyes. What a strange individual.

"To begin, a little about me." He put his elbows on the table and leaned forward conspiratorially. "You should always know who it is who teaches you, right? Make sure they're qualified and all of that. Know their agenda. It's an important job, to help guide a young mind."

"I'm sure you're qualified."

He tilted his head, squinted his eyes, rocked his head, "Anyway, if you'd humor me."

"I'm not here to humor you. I'm here to learn."

He chuckled, leaning back, slapping his knees. Usually adults would have just quit by now.

"You're funny," he said. "In an ornery sort of way."

I shook my head.

"So, let me begin by saying I attended Harvard."

"Bravo."

"And studied the classics."

"Why?"

"Oh, I've made him curious," looking around for an audience.

"I just want to know why anyone would study classics. What can you possibly do with knowledge of that?"

"The Greeks and the Romans have much to teach, Marius." He narrowed his eyes as if he'd just thought of something profound. "Marius, is it?"

"You've only said it about fifteen times now."

"Why Marius?"

"Why what?"

"No, why? Why did your parents name you Marius?"

"I don't know. Can we get on with it already?"

I did know why my mother had named me Marius. She'd told me in one of her few lucid moments. I didn't want to talk about it.

"Well, I went as far as my master's before I decided I just could not take being away from home any longer."

I hadn't asked, but I did what I'd done on countless occasions before in an academic setting when the teacher thought we cared: I retreated into my imagination and let him drone on.

A few moments later and these words brought me back: "Having grown up just down the road from here, I couldn't stand being away from the woods, the sheer expanse of them, the—"

I leaned forward. "You grew up around here?"

"Down the road, Marius."

"So you know something about this family and this estate. My mother's family. I bet you knew my mother."

"No, I did not know your mother. But, yes, I know a few things about the Frost Estate. And the family."

"That's what I'm curious about," I said.

He chuckled again and opened his arms. "What do you want to know?"

"What's behind the wall down there in the woods?"

A perplexed expression. "The wall? In the woods?"

"You said you love these woods, so what's behind the wall?"

"That must be…"

"The garden. Yes. Flora told me that much at least. But why's it closed?"

"Fascinating!"

I sighed. He never shut up. It exhausted me.

"Just, could you please tell me, what's fascinating about it? What do you know?"

Mr. Charles checked behind us.

"We seem to be alone," I said.

"Oh, the walls have ears." He dropped his voice to a whisper. "I will tell you the bit I know, and then we'll start in on your math. Deal?"

"Yes, fine."

"Peasants like my family never made it far on to the estate, if you wonder how I could claim to know this area so well and not know what you're talking about. No, Mr. Lionel Frost, the patriarch, was a bit of a robber baron, and we only heard what it was they were up to here. We didn't actually see with our own eyes. Not everything."

"What they were up to?"

"Oh, nothing sinister. Don't get that idea."

"Then why are we whispering?"

He shrugged and held up his hands like he didn't know, but continued to keep his voice low. "They had parties here, okay. Lavish. Spectacular. The oval out there, they'd set up magnificent white tents and bring in catering—this is how I know as much as I do—the people who worked here talked. You'd have the wealthiest people in America gathered round and drinking and eating," he reached at the air, searching for words, "filet mignon, caviar, escargot... I don't know, if it smacks of indulgence then they ate it."

"I'm totally enamored by this story," I said. "It really moves me."

He laughed again. My sarcasm apparently killed with him. A first.

"But," he said, leaning in again, dropping his voice even lower. "There were rumors."

"Rumors?"

"Of a garden. On par with the Garden of Eden. The Tuileries. The—"

"That's absurd."

"When the sun went down, men and women, husbands and wives and husbands and mistresses and wives and young lovers drifted to the garden. Imagine it, Marius. The soft slip of water on gentle decline, gurgling along."

"Gurgle? What an ugly word."

"Yes, a shudder vowel. But think of this. In the dark and serenaded by the overpowering perfume of roses and lilies and violets... Rich and abundant and you're sheltered away from any peering eyes. It's just you and the woman you love and what must have felt like heaven itself around you. Lavender. Roses, I'm sure. Bowers and benches tucked in near fountains. Night and the bees to bed."

"I get it," I said, disgust in my voice, but for a moment... No. Fine, yes, for just a moment, I thought of Flora. And moving in that unilluminated world. I blushed.

"Intriguing, isn't it?" he said.

"If that's what's behind the wall—"

"I'm sure it is."

"Why'd my uncle lock it up?"

Mr. Charles shrugged and grinned. "I don't know. There's a shadow that seems to lie over the place, but I don't know why he sealed it. Not for sure. Which brings us to algebra."

"That's it?"

"Always leave them wanting more," he said, sliding a math textbook across the table to me. "Pre-test. Go to page three. Time for you to show me what you know."

I studied with Mr. Charles for two and a half hours

and carried assignments with me back to my room, but I didn't stay there long. I needed to check on my plants.

Chapter 9

THE DOOR TO the little home at the end of the greenhouse again. I stepped towards it. *Nothing to be frightened of*, I told myself, but didn't half believe it.

Up close the age of the paint on the door apparent in hair-thin cracks. Such a still day, the antithesis of the day before. A sky an icy Siberian blue, no wind to push clouds and jar the trees. Just me and the door.

Even as my hand rose for the old knob I felt my heart pump blood at pressure, straining, audible. My fingertips ventured out, rested on the cool metal. Counting quietly to myself. Towards what, I don't know.

In a rush I felt the knob move beneath my palm. My hand the unafraid guarantor of my mind's intentions.

The door swung in and a decade's worth of unoiled build-up in the hinges gave way in one foul prolonged squeak and the gloom of the interior stared back at me.

"Why the hell are you scared?" I whispered. "It's just a little old home. Too small to harbor anything threatening."

It smelled of damp. Of mildew in the drywall. There was light through the windows, but like much else on the estate, the furnishings and walls were dark. I could see the outlines of water damage. A wardrobe, cobwebs drifting ghostly on unseen currents. A desk

under a window, a curtain rod half fallen-down—
ripped down—the maroon drapes spilling across the
desk. All of this at a glance, from the door.

I placed a foot inside. The wood groaned and I
retreated.

"Grow up, Marius," I told myself. My heart didn't
listen. It pounded on. But I went in, walking into the
middle of the room, arms crossed over my chest.

There was a narrow bed behind the door on a
frame that would have fit well in Bedlam. I visualized
how easy it would be to slip handcuffs through the rails.
Then told myself to give it up and tone down the
imagination. Subtract the gothic sensibility and get out.
There was nothing of use in there. Only an abandoned
domicile of a long-gone gardener, mute walls, the
leavings of a journeyman.

And then I saw the picture frame, small but ornate,
tipped over on the desk. I went to it. Pulled my hand
into my sleeve and used the sleeve to wipe dust off the
back of the frame before righting it. The face that
stared back at me stilled my breath.

"Mom?"

No. She had never grown that old. Her mother?
The resemblance was astounding. The beauty. A face,
in black and white, of perfect dimensions, the slim
jawline, the lips slightly agape, the implication of a
smile. But the eyes. Like my mother's. Lustrous and
wide. Cold and vacant. But gray, apparent even in a
photo that only existed in shades of gray.

Eager to see if there were more I pulled open the

top drawer of the desk. Plastic pens, blank sheets of stationery long since wilted, a pair of old pliers and a screwdriver, other desk detritus. I closed the drawer and pulled at the next one. Empty but I ran my hand to the back of it anyway and felt cold metal. I pulled at the object, took it out and held it up to the light from the window. A key. Large. Heavy. I turned it in my fingers, staring out the window as I let my touch tell me about it. I'd seen a lock on a door just as sturdy. Of course a gardener would have a key to the garden. I began to think of the bowers, the statues and streams Mr. Charles had described. Then I stared down again at the photograph. So like my mother.

"What are you doing in here?" the voice from the open door. I jerked back from the desk, my hand closing around the key, hiding it. "You shouldn't be in this place."

Ben's face, confused. His lips grasping for words. He'd entered so quietly, like a ghost. I sprinted past him, out of the greenhouse and into the woods.

***

I sat for some time huddled into myself against the trunk of an old oak, off the trail. I turned the key in my hands, but instead of thinking of the door it unlocked I was thinking of my mother. He'd caught me thinking of her. The last time I had seen her she and my father were getting into their silver BMW. She hadn't looked back at me where I stood with Katerin at the door. I had been forced to be there by the au pair who came from a family that preached respect for their elders. I wasn't feeling it. My father, sharing a joke with my mother as he closed the door, had laughed and then met my eyes. Hurt, that I was the source of their mirth. And even if they weren't talking about me, that I could suspect them of it. My parents.

For so many of my classmates it seemed to be a given that their parents took pride in them. Made appearances at school functions. Fussed over them before class plays or elementary school graduation. I felt akin to a cultural anthropologist with an outsider's lack of comprehension in these school lobby situations. *That boy's mother is fixing his hair and he's shrinking away. They smile even when the flash expires. They turn to each other, affection in the sarcasm, the teasing. On the periphery this boy somehow outside himself, behind a screen, invisible. Shuffling on impatient feet, waiting for the show to go on or the day to end. Not feeling envy. Or not recognizing it in himself.*

"Stop feeling sorry for yourself," I whispered. So much wasted breath. Then I said it a bit louder. Then I screamed it, as if a bellow would be more convincing. "Do not feel sorry for yourself!" Pounding my fist into the ground, I screamed it again. Until my chest heaved and my cheeks ran wet with tears and the bruised edge of my hand cried for surcease. I stood up from the cold ground, the temporary nest among the fallen leaves. Expelling that bad air. Then I whispered it once more. "No feeling sorry, Marius. Not for you. You move forward. Only."

I stared down at the key.

***

I was slight enough I could fit between the door and wall of ivy and no one could see me. I slid the key into the lock and tried to turn it. Much resistance. But with persistent pressure it gave. The key turned, and with a gentle nudge, the door swung in.

It was getting late and I didn't have the energy for any more discoveries. But I had to see. I peeked through the small opening. So this is what the earth will look like when we leave it, when nature reclaims what we consider ours. Garden of Eden? More like Garden in Need of Weeding. This is what a madman wielding a paintbrush would see in his nightmares. Brambles and tall grass and thistles. Pathless. Done in brushstrokes to approximate the hair on the scalp of a man who's forgone barbering for a decade. The chaotic signature of abandonment, the way things grow in a plot that once was tended.

I couldn't go in. Not that day. I had enough to take stock of and I was cold. I pulled the door closed and locked it, patting it, a promise to come see it again soon.

I returned to my room and took a shower and climbed into bed with Ray Bradbury. The fall sun descended quickly and when the dark came I turned off the lamp.

Chapter 10

MY DREAMS WERE a chaotic, disjointed menagerie of images.

A steel utility pole. Cracks in the pavement. My father driving fast. They're arguing. She screams for him to stop and let her out, let her out, she'll walk it. She'll get a cab. She doesn't need him. He calls her a self-centered bitch and tells her to shut the fuck up and presses down a fraction more on the accelerator and the BMW coupe surges forward. And she reaches for the steering wheel. Grabs it and pulls it hard. A steel utility pole. Cracks in the pavement. The jarring as the coupe jumps the lip of the curb. A steel utility pole just right of center. Her side. The accordion fold of metal, a pop as pressure's lost, in a tire, in a tank. The front axle rips away from the chassis and tumbles down an empty California street. The tick and drip of oil, of gasoline. Two bodies. One has flown. One is crumpled like a hated toy. Which is which?

I woke sweating. Final details like they'd been done by Vermeer through a camera obscura. Every detail down to the glistening thickness of the blood, and that's the lasting image of the dream. Maroon and pooling like the fallen drapes in the gardener's home.

What knowledge did I have to base the images of the dream on? Experience, mostly.

Chapter 11

IT WAS MRS. Moira again in the morning, pulling open curtains.

"Your uncle is back. He would like to see you today. Before your lessons. Make yourself presentable."

***

On the second floor, near the library, a short corridor ran to the south-facing wall of the house. Double-doors at the end of it, closed. I followed Mrs. Moira. She gave two curt knocks. My palms sweated and I pulled my fingers into fists.

"He probably won't speak with you long," she said. She didn't wait for a response to her knock before opening the door.

The curtains hung thick from ceiling to floor blocking out all signs of day. Somewhere off to the right a soft yellow light illuminated cluttered corners. I heard metal knock against metal and saw a dark form raise its head from the ground. I could smell it. A large Doberman. Black. Still and peering.

"Mr. Frost, your nephew is here."

Nothing.

Mrs. Moira leaned near me and whispered in my ear, "Go on. He won't bite. Just be polite. Be respectful. Go on."

She gave a gentle nudge and I walked towards the

desk. His shaded lamp radiated light down where it reflected off of white papers scattered here and there. His chair turned away from me, its back high and covering all but the top of his head where unkempt hair angled off with no evidence of recent grooming.

The dog's head turned to follow me. I heard the rattle in its collar.

A groan as the chair began its turn. I thought he might rotate all the way around, with the lamp behind him and his body hidden in shadows. But he stopped and thought better of his movement. Fluttering indecision.

"Come," a soft voice. "Come and sit. Over there. A chair." A slender hand visible and gesturing towards the side of his desk.

I reached the chair, fighting the urge to look at him. My mother's brother. Why, then, did this man who was my flesh and blood cause my chest to constrict as if a cooper were cinching metallic bands around it? Trembling, I noticed a stack of books on the chair and my brain said to move them but my hands shook and wouldn't make the effort.

"It's okay," he said. "Just set them, set them on the floor. Set them on the floor."

Thick, hardback volumes, one of them slick in my hands, my sweaty palms. I dropped it and it hit the ground with a thud.

"It's," frustration mounting in his voice, "it's fine, just, sit, yes?"

I did, with knees clutched together and hands

holding the side of the chair, my arms rigid, my legs rigid.

He sniffed.

I looked up at him for the first time. Wanting to flinch and stare away, but then my eyes went over his features as if he were a lost Rembrandt, a masterpiece, and I simply had to memorize him lest I never see him again.

Like the woman in the picture he also resembled my mother. In the cheekbones, oddly feminine, and the soft lips slightly parted, the eyes still and cool. Had my mother been that devoid of warmth? What a stupid question to ask myself. The familial resemblance was more apparent in his eyes than anywhere else, though he was also slight. Like her. Like me. Was this the manhood I had to look forward to?

"Enough?" he said.

I didn't know what he meant. That discordant moment when he was aware of the meaning of his utterance and I was at a loss, grasping at interpretations. I tilted my head. Noticed that my mouth was agape. Closed it.

"Do I look like her?"

My tongue sought words but found none.

"I saw her for the first time in years—in years—when I identified her at the m-morgue."

Her body on a cold steel table. Roman marble white except where the blood pooled in her back. Fractured. The broken toy. Goddamn these unbidden images.

"Yes," I said.

"Yes?"

"Yes, you look like her."

"What are we going to do with you?" he said. Why did I think a smile had not touched this man's face in years? "This isn't much of a place for a child, is it?"

He stared at me. Calculations taking place. Based on emotion? On the fact that family sat before him? The only child of his dead sister? I didn't think so. I didn't think it had anything to do with that and I felt the bands cinch even tighter, bearing down on my lungs. How would I breathe?

"It's not that bad," I said.

"No?"

"No," I said. Thinking of my plants in the greenhouse and what would happen to them if I had to go elsewhere. Thinking of Flora. For only a moment. Thinking that after this there truly was no family.

He nodded. Once, and then again. "Then stay. At least for a while." He craned his head towards the ceiling as if he was going to speak again then nodded a final time and picked up his pen and returned to his papers.

"Should I…"

"Yes," he said.

I stood and hurried from the room, into the corridor where Mrs. Moira waited. I ran past her. She shut the doors and followed.

***

Back in my room I dove into bed and pulled the covers over myself and hugged my knees. Katerin had once stroked my back after my mother had said things to me. I'd tapped my finger on the kitchen table too loudly, too many times, and a five minute lambast ensued, a dressing down, a targeting of my faults as she ran a hand over my cheek and then pinched the chubby child's flesh.

"Marius. Jesus Christ. Who are you? Never a phone call. Not for Marius. Never an invitation. Never goes anywhere. I'll call you Marius Never Goes Anywhere. Don't you ever wonder why? Hmm? Is it because you don't speak? You're mute? Cat's got your tongue? Or maybe you're always in la-la-fuckity-la-da land? Is that where you live most of your life, Marius? In la-la-fuckity-la-da land? Well, aren't you going to speak up? Defend yourself? Of course not. You don't know how to speak to people. That's your problem. Are you going to grow up to be alone? Isolated? Miserable? I think so. Stop the finger tapping before I snap your finger off, all right? Find a friend and go somewhere, please. Please. Get lost. Go. I can't stand to look at you right now."

Katerin had stroked my back.

And now Mrs. Moira. Outside the blanket. Witnessing this weakness in me. I didn't want her to see it. Didn't want her to see me frail and frightened and sad.

"Marius…"

"Leave me the hell alone!" I bellowed into the blanket, my hot breath thrown back in my face. "Leave me alone!" Rage as red as my cheeks and the strained tendons in my neck.

I couldn't hear her leave. Couldn't hear the retreat that I wanted. Or didn't want. I didn't know.

She pulled at the covers. Gently. Didn't rip them off of me as she might have.

"Marius," she said again. The cool air of the room on my face. "Mr. Charles is waiting for you."

"I don't—"

"Ah, ah, ah," she said, hands out. "Mr. Charles, you may find, I know Flora has found, can be a wonderful person to talk to when—"

"I don't want to talk. I want to be left alone."

"When you're ready, then."

She turned towards the door. Then stopped.

"I will say this, though. You cannot live your life hiding under covers from the likes of your uncle. Who he is, why he is… We don't know. But there are plenty more where he came from, and as harsh as it is to hear it, you can't live your life hiding from his or anyone else's moods. Can you?"

I didn't know. I just knew the red that resided in hot bands around my chest and in my mind and seemed impossible to dislodge.

She left, and moments later, the stillness, the quiet of the room, and the thought that no one else was coming moved me to get out of bed and gather my books.

Chapter 12

I LEFT THE lesson without speaking more than a few words to Mr. Charles. Deflecting his concern. Crawling back into myself when he pried.

After lunch I went outside and it felt good to be out in the open, even if the sky stood gray and the wind blew cold. I bypassed the greenhouse. I'd have to go in there later, but my body urged me to avoid it for the moment and I found the path down into the woods, the key warm in my hand.

Slipping behind the ivy. Fitting the key into the lock. Turning. An easier give this afternoon. The door swung in and I went in with it, pushing it closed behind me.

The gentle incline in front of me. Colorless ragweed bent in a gust of wind. Shrouded shapes overgrown with creeping ivy, shapes that may have been trees or may have been the bowers Mr. Charles had spoken of.

The easiest place to walk was near the wall and I moved with it, running my hand over leaves, branches, stems, coming upon rose bushes grown thick and tangled and spreading out from the wall and forcing me to divert further into the garden. I found the semblance of a path. Thistles growing from gravel on a walkway that hadn't seen human feet in a decade. How much of this estate's neglect was measured in decades?

The path curved up into the woods. I didn't know

if I wanted to follow it. I had expected at least the hint of color in this garden, but beyond the leaves and the occasional rose, everything was still and dead and gray. But I was here, and might not get another opportunity. I continued to walk.

I came upon a wooden bower no longer holding a perfect arch. A stone bench. Mr. Charles was right about some things, and I heard running water but saw no source. The romantic aura had died here. When? Why?

I pulled vines away from the bench and pushed at the collapsed ribs of the bower and sat and looked around and wondered what lovers on late night sojourns would have seen. But this was a place for breathing in and hearing, not seeing, not at night when the couples dispersed and touched each other, hot flesh and lavender-perfumed air.

I saw from where I was sitting the edge of a weathered wooden shed. Back in the trees. A trellis, to screen the functional building from sight, had collapsed. What might have been an opening of sorts, a path back, lay choked with honeysuckle. A gust of wind blew hard and the trees groaned. I felt a cold pin-prick on my hand and looked down. A snowflake melting on bare skin.

I got up, thinking I'd see what evidence of the past the shed had to offer, then go tend to my plants and go back to my room where I could be warm and open a book.

The going was not easy. I stepped through waist-high growth, pushing and ripping at unperturbed brush, thumb bit by a thorn and legs gathering cockleburs. The shed stood in a weary, half-drunken lean. It looked like a waste of my time, just an old place of storage for the gardener.

Windowless. The door slightly askew. Inside the plant growth tempered by lack of sun but still evident. A decaying wooden floor. Taking my aching thumb from my mouth, I pulled at the door, its bottom edge scratching through dirt, moving reluctantly. The smell of decay, as if something had crawled beneath the floor and died.

I was about to leave when I noticed the lines scratched into the wall in the back left corner, half hidden by a dusty old tarp. Stark on an otherwise banal set of walls. Probably an animal trapped inside and clawing to get out.

I stepped inside the shed, the wood soft beneath my feet, placing my steps carefully, not wanting to step through the floor and into the soft bloated belly of the something emitting that smell of death.

The closer I came the less the marks looked animal in origin. Something conscious, human in them. I knelt in the back corner. It was dark and hard to see there.

I pushed the tarp down, kicking up dust, sneezing. After the fit ended and the dust had settled, I ran my finger over the scarred wood. Leaned in close, barely able to make out what I was seeing.

JHH ll

Tick marks. Not the work of claws. Beneath them:

Heinrich Scherer is Peter Meyer

Beneath that:

Hannah Frost died here, December 22, 1982.

Hannah Frost. My mother. In 1982 she was fourteen years old. Was I a ghost?

1982

A SIMPLE VERTICAL line. She pinched the rusted nail between her cold-numbed fingers and ran its tip into the wood. The scratching revealed the wood's raw yellow flesh, tinted around the edges by the orange of the oxidized metal. Up and down and up and down, forming the lines, hearing the voices of her mother and father in the library.

"I fought in that war," her father said. "Against monsters like him. This can't go unsaid."

"It will go unsaid," her mother snapped.

"If you try to stop him from saying it, then I'll say it," she told her mother.

"You, you little bitch? You breathe a word of it and I'll cut out your tongue. You shouldn't even be in here."

Now a horizontal line. The nail head stuttered against the grain and cut into her finger. She dropped it.

"Ouch," breathed more than voiced.

She sucked on her bloody finger, tasting the copper-rich blood, the bitter residue of rust. She switched hands. The horizontal line.

Then I'll say it.

"Leave her alone," her father, protecting her.
"He was family. We don't do this to family."

"Family is sacrosanct only when it seems to suit you."

"Take your big words and shove them up your ass."

"I'll tell," the girl said. "I swear I will."

A glare of glistening arrow tips, an array of them, directed at the girl.

"I swear I'll tell."

A promise in those gray eyes.

Another vertical line. She was getting better at it. More than just tick marks.

Tick marks.

The sun going down again. Enough light from the gaps in the door frame for a little more work. Enough cold for another night of suffering, nothing but the tarp for a blanket. Nothing to eat. Nothing to drink, the bucket empty as of that morning. Nothing to help pass the time (the time to WHAT?). Was her father still alive? That had been, what, just prior to the first mark she made in the wood.

"Hannah!"

"Dad? Dad! I'm in here!"

"Hannah. I'm–"

That was the last word she ever heard from him. The echo of that hard stop fading into the atmosphere like a trail of smoke from a match head. Overpowered. Consumed.

A sickening crack. The impact of a hard object on skull. A body crashing to the snow-covered ground.

"Dad!"

With her head pressed to the door, gasping for air, coughing horribly, feeling faint. Long beats of silence. Soft, familiar voices. Plotting. Bashing her fist bloody onto the unyielding wood of the door, crying, screaming again but her voice was gone: "Dad..." Fading off. The last of her. Another slam of fist on door.

Then there was only wind and the familiar stress of the structure around her, sturdy in the winter weather that beat at it.

The roundness of the *a* was more challenging. She should have done a capital. She couldn't think.

Thin red pain pulsed in her esophagus with every intake of breath. She had cried some, of course, but there wasn't much of her left, and she figured she needed to finish what she'd started. The other markings that followed the *a* were not as deep. But they would be enough.

Seven days? Noted. The rest of it? In this dark night? The cold too much? Noted. Tired from the screaming. The carving. The pounding. Tired of her life.

She rubbed the soft flesh on her wrist, closed her eyes, then made one more horizontal line with the sharp end of the nail. The wrong cut, it turned out, but who could blame her, she was blind, groping. The cut not deep enough or angry enough.

She stopped then. Enough. No one would understand or even find these words, would they? Enough.

A faint breath. Her body floating in a warm, calm sea. Buoyant.

She didn't know why, but it was Jean Valjean she thought of as she faded towards unconsciousness. Jean

Valjean who'd found redemption and bested his adversary with unimpeachable honor and goodness. What a fiction. She wouldn't even have the opportunity.

Bleeding, but not bleeding out. So far from telling the whole story but she'd said all that she could, under the circumstances. She thought of what had been said in the library. Thought of nothing. Thought of Jean Valjean. And Marius. A beautiful name and man. What would his face look like on a city street? Would she recognize him? She thought she might. Then she slipped, she hoped, into a realm where nothing and no one would ever touch her again. Buoyant. Rise. Fall. Blue sky. No clouds. The beautiful black-haired girl lying prone beneath her last rites: *Hannah Frost died here, December 22, 1982.*

Descending the gentle final slip, the reed basket lowered into the calm river. Downstream. Downstream. Floating downstream into permanent unconsciousness.

II
Emily

Chapter 1

"HOW DID THAT make you feel?"

Dr. Dolnick. I'm sitting on a sofa in her office. The pages I've written, all dog-eared and marked, sit in my lap. I've shared some of it. Not all of it. I'm not comfortable with that possibility quite yet.

"How did that make me feel?"

"Yes. To see what your mother had written."

"I don't know," I say. A certain thickness has set in behind my eyes. Any time she asks me how I feel it's the same response. There have been the exercises. The times of day when I write down what I'm feeling at that moment. Trying to be in touch with it. But there's vacancy there. Who has time to pay attention to feelings? They're so often illogical. Who cares what I feel?

"How do you feel about it now?"

I shrug and raise my hands towards the ceiling in a gesture of defeat. "I don't feel anything."

She looks upon me warmly. I can always count on that. She's thinking of another way to approach this. To get a feeling out of me. The feelings are important.

"What would you tell that boy?" she asks. "He sees this writing, this scrawl in wood. His mother died before he was even born. He comes to you, confused. What would you tell him?"

"That of course she didn't die."

"'But why'd she write it, Mr. Besshaven?'"

playacting the role of the boy. Of me.

"She was confused and she was scared."

"'About what?'"

"She wasn't treated well. She didn't know… She was abandoned in there. She didn't know if she'd ever get out. She thought about giving up."

Dr. Dolnick lets my last phrase hang there in the air for a while. Giving me time to ponder before she asks her next question: "How does that little boy feel, Marius?"

"Sad. He feels sad. He wishes he could help her in some way."

She nods her head and I can see a look of sadness in her eyes as well.

Sad for my mother. How could I be sad for her after what she'd done to me?

"What are you thinking?" a kind prodding.

"Why do I feel sad for her?"

She nods with pursed lips and sympathetic eyes.

"It's okay to feel sad for her, Marius."

"After what she did to me?"

Again, a pause. "It doesn't mean that it's okay that she did those things to you. But it's okay to feel sad for her. She was obviously a deeply hurt woman."

I shake my head. I don't know what to think. I don't know what I feel. Thickening concrete behind my eyes. The accompanying whitewash of the world before me.

We read myths.

Chapter 2

WAS I A ghost? My mother had died a week ago, not twenty-two years ago, not in 1982. So who was Hannah Frost? Who had written those words?

"Marius?"

"Hmm?" *La-la-fuckity-la-da land.* "Sorry."

Mr. Charles sat back with arms crossed. Behind him, visible through the large library windows, snow continued to swirl and fall. It covered the ground like a thick white skin.

"What's on your mind this morning? I'm not averse to talking about it."

"No. Nothing."

"So you're ready to return to our little story here? To see how the House of Atreus turns out?"

The House of Horrors. Generations of murder.

"I don't get it," I said. "Orestes killed her for a reason."

"Yes, Clytemnestra killed Agamemnon, his father. It was his duty to avenge his father's death. The rub being Agamemnon's murderer also happened to be his mother."

"So he did his duty to his father, but in the balance, the Furies cursed him anyway?"

"What a glorious paradox, isn't it? The house was cursed. Murder begetting murder. Wickedness leading to more wickedness. Wife killing husband. Son killing mother. Never ending."

"But if it wasn't his mother he murdered, everything would have been okay. With the Furies, that is. The lesson here is that vengeance is fine as long as you don't kill the woman who nursed you?"

"Maybe."

Thinking of the woman who had nursed me. Without proof believing that she had been responsible for the death of my father. Were the House of Besshaven and the House of Frost equally cursed? I hadn't killed my mother. She'd killed herself. Maybe. So perhaps it ended with her.

"Let's finish the story," Mr. Charles said. And we did, taking turns reading aloud.

Putting the book down a few minutes later, I said, "I'm not satisfied with that."

"Why not?" he laughed.

"He wanders around feeling lost and dopey and just says, 'Forgive me, forgive me.' And they do. It's too easy."

"He wandered for years!" argued Mr. Charles.

"It's still too easy."

"It's a myth. Explaining what?"

"The birth of forgiveness?"

"An end to the horrors! Instead of tragedy leading to yet more tragedy Orestes becomes the first person to ask for his guilt to be cleansed and in the process he changed the minds of even the gods. How impressive is that?"

"Myths are ridiculous."

"In comparison with what, your science fiction?"

Mr. Charles, heated, leaning in, spittle flying from his lips, a mad grin. "Come on!"

"There are more things real in Arthur C. Clarke than there are in here." Tapping the mythology book in disgust.

"Are there?"

"Yes."

"You really believe that?"

"Yes."

"Oh, Marius. Well, why don't you put your thoughts down on paper? Make that claim. Support it. Bring me the finished essay tomorrow."

"I don't want homework."

"It's an exploration in thought. My challenge to you, your challenge to me. Do it."

I stared down at the book, then took up my pen and began writing in its margins.

"What are you doing?" Mr. Charles said, a look of fascination bordering on cringing disgust.

"Taking a few notes," keeping the pen moving.

"In the book?"

"It's not the Shroud of Turin. It's a piece of paper. If you don't write in it, you don't remember."

I paused when I reflected that my words were the same my mother had spoken to me when I'd caught her scribbling in a novel. Speak of ghosts.

Chapter 3

AFTER TRUDGING THROUGH snow to take care of my plants I returned to my room and settled in to write my paper. A little after six the door opened and Flora came in.

"Here's your dinner."

She didn't smile, just set the tray down and turned to go.

"Flora…"

Perhaps the tone in my voice. Not the little bastard. If Orestes could change fate by asking for forgiveness…

Fighting through the paralysis of throat and tongue, I said what I'd rarely said and less rarely meant: "I'm sorry."

Her back to me. Her hands clenched. They began to loosen. A soft voice. "Thank you."

Without turning to look at me she left the room.

Chapter 4

I STARED OFF into space as Mr. Charles looked over my essay. It was a tepid effort and I didn't want to see the disappointment I was sure would cross his face. The snow had stopped falling the night before and a white blanket of stillness sat outside. I planned, after lunch, to go back to the garden.

"What's on your mind?" he asked, the paper still in hand.

"Nothing."

Hannah Frost died here.

"Marius." He put the paper down on the table, leaned back and crossed his arms. A blonde curl hung down near his eye and he brushed it back. "Marius."

"Mr. Charles."

"I've been trying to place your name, where the inspiration for it might have come from. Gaius Marius? The Roman general, perhaps?" He waited, pushed, "Yes? No?"

"No."

"Marius Petipa, the ballet—"

"No! Definitely not."

"Nothing wrong with a man in ballet. He's considered by many to be the best there ever was, you know."

"No, and I don't care to know."

"Victor Hugo, then."

My silence and a blush gave it away.

"I knew it," he said. "How much more impressive is that? Marius Pontmercy. Your mother's idea?"

"It wasn't my father's."

He nodded, grinning. "I like that. I can see you growing up to be a fine young Romantic. Passionate, if not in love then certainly you have a fighting spirit."

"Whatever."

My mother had a strange fixation with *Les Miserables*. The book, by Victor Hugo, more so than the musical or any of the films. For the fleeting instant she thought of me after my birth she chose to name me after a fictional nineteenth-century character she had been in love with. She was always able to close the book and put it on the shelf when she was ready to move on. She found an au pair allowed her to do much the same with me.

"Though not much passion in this writing. I'm sure you'd agree. Which brings us back full circle. What's on your mind, Marius? You look like you can't wait to divest yourself of my company and go running out into the snow. Build a fort, drop down and do snow angels? No, unless I've read you wrong. We could always cut the lesson short—"

"I'd like that."

"And go for a walk."

I snorted.

"Stand-offish, are we? I'm serious, about the walk."

"You promised me you'd tell me more stories about this family," I said. "You haven't done that. You keep putting me off."

He put his elbows on the table and leaned close and I knew a deal was in the offing.

"I've got a story," he said, raising his eyebrows. "I couldn't remember all of the details the last time we spoke. So I did a little reading."

"Reading?"

"In the archives of the local newspaper."

"Okay."

"And if I'm going to share this story with you, we probably need to discuss a few things first."

"Yes, my algebra."

"Your algebra, of course, and I expect you to do that. You do so well with it. But, no, that's not what I'm getting at."

"Then get at what you're getting at."

He laughed and shook his head. Then breathed in sharply through his nose before continuing. "It's a sensitive subject."

"For who?"

"Whom. This family. Your uncle, in particular."

His eyes went around the room. We were the only two. I hadn't heard a footstep since we'd sat down.

"Again, I think we're alone," I said. "My uncle's a Luddite, in case you haven't noticed. There aren't any listening devices in the walls."

Another laugh. My sharp, unintended wit.

"Okay. Fine. Agreed. But promise me you'll keep this to yourself."

"I promise," I said, and leaned forward to hear

him, conspirators in the library under the witness of marble busts.

"Your grandfather died on this estate. In 1982," Mr. Charles began, "and the circumstances were strange, to say the least."

He paused for a moment to let me chew on the idea. The year, 1982, sent a shiver through me. *Hannah Frost died here, December 22, 1982.*

"It was a snowstorm, not too unlike this one. A little early in the season for Ohio, right? December?"

My lips clamped and my breathing grew shallow. No coincidence in these dates, surely?

"They found him—and these are the facts, the rest merely conjecture—they found him…" he put his hands out, fidgeting, and looked away from me, "naked and leaning against a tree out in the woods. Bizarre, of course."

"What happened?"

"His wife, your grandmother, claimed he went searching for your mother. That she'd run away, again. He went out in the morning and didn't come home. When he hadn't returned by evening they began the search. Two days later they found him: frozen, naked, blue, leaning against a tree, very much passed away."

"Very much dead. You don't need to spare my emotions. I didn't know him."

"'Alexander died, Alexander was buried, Alexander returneth to dust.'"

"What?"

"*Hamlet.* Never mind. Yes, dead."

"You said she claimed that's what happened."

He shrugged his shoulders and shook his head. "There's nothing definitive. Just suspicion. The medical examiner found blunt-force trauma here," and he pointed to his temple. "Or so was reported, along with the excuse. Something about a low-hanging branch. A fall."

"Somebody bashed him in the head?"

"To put it bluntly, yes, that's what I think. No pun intended. Sorry."

"So you think he was murdered?"

"I probably shouldn't have gone off on that tangent. It's a claim, without much in the way of evidence."

"What are you thinking?" I leaned in, aware, a glow in my eyes.

"I'm thinking there are other things bizarre about this family's history, rumors only, and that I don't want to say anything that might upset anyone. Not over hearsay, right?"

He slid my paper back and forth across the table, then slid it back to me.

"I think we need to discuss what needs done here," pointing at my paper, "before we open the algebra text."

"What if I told you about something I saw the other day?" I said.

"Something you think might be connected to—"

"My grandfather's death, yeah. If you want to know what's on my mind, I could tell you."

He leaned back and ran a hand over his chin. Then whispered, "I believe you, about there being no listening devices in these walls. But I'm uncomfortable all the same. Perhaps…"

"We need to take a walk."

"Exactly." He raised his voice slightly, "We shall head out, then, and go learn a thing or two about nature."

***

Our footsteps were not the first to crunch through. I assumed Ben was out and about, so I waited until we were on the grassy oval with clear sight all around before speaking for the first time of what I'd seen.

"I've been there," I said. "To the garden."

"Really?"

"Yes."

"Fascinating. And?" He had shoved his hands into his pockets and we both had to squint, the sun reflecting intensely off the snow, two figures following their shadows in slow circumnavigations.

"And… It's a mess. Overgrown. Untended. I don't think I'd call it a garden anymore. We could go see. I could show you."

He thought about it for a long time as our feet crunched through the snowy crust. "It's tempting. So tempting, Marius. But I think that might cause trouble for me." He bit his lip. "If they caught me… Damn."

It was my turn to laugh.

"What, you didn't know teachers cursed from time to time?"

"Not ones who went to Harvard."

He stopped and peered down at me. "Are you messing with me, Marius?"

Looking up at him I felt for once like I had an ally. A strange feeling and I lowered my head, smile fading.

"A little," I said. "*I'm* not going to stop going."

He nodded. "But you will be careful?"

"No, I'll put on a hot-pink ballerina's tutu like your Marius Who's-it and shout into the house as I'm leaving, 'This is Marius, dancing off to the garden! Digging up the skeletons you all have buried there!'"

"Okay, okay, Marius. I believe you. Just, watch it, you know."

We began to walk again, the cold creeping into our bones after standing still for so long.

"You're very suspicious of the Frost family," I said.

He sighed and shook his head. His turn to be reticent. He brought us back to the reason for our discretionary walk. "You said you saw something."

I felt my throat seize up. Once voiced I wouldn't be able to dismiss what I'd seen as pure fancy. It would be out there and would need to be dealt with. I felt vulnerable, then told myself it was foolish to feel that way.

"In the garden," I began, head hanging low, studying my worrying hands as we entered the shadows of some tall trees, "there was a shed that looked like it was meant to be kept out of sight. Functional, not decorative."

I kicked at the snow, watching white powder scatter.

"And this is where you saw… it?"

"Yeah. It's where I saw it."

"If you're uncomfortable—"

"I am."

"I understand."

He took a hand from his pocket and patted my shoulder.

Out with it now or you'll never say it.

Forcing the words through constricted throat and unlimber lips: "Someone had scrawled in there, below seven tick marks, a name, meaningless to me, something like Henry—or Heinrich—Sheer… is Peter Meyer. And beneath that…" I couldn't bring myself to say it. He remained quiet, listening, a disquieting dip in temperament. "Beneath that, Hannah Frost, my mother, d-died there. On December 22. 1982."

He stopped moving and stood silent and still, with none of the attendant pulsations and vibrations of the living human being he was.

"That's the same date they found her father. My grandfather. Isn't it?"

"Yes," he said, his eyes suddenly vacant. "No, I mean, that's close. Um, they found him on Christmas Eve. He went missing a few days prior. Two days, I think I said. What was the name, the name you said?"

"Heinrich…"

"No, the second one."

"Peter. Peter Meyer. Why? What does it mean?"

His mouth hung open slightly, then closed, his eyes narrowing. Not addressing me anymore. "Hmm? Yes? What does it mean?"

"Are you okay?"

"I don't know. I... I don't think there was any runaway daughter, Marius. He went looking for her. Your grandfather went looking for your mother. And someone got to him before he could find her. Didn't they? Before he could find out the truth. But what did she know? What was she trying to say?"

Chapter 5

I WENT BACK to my room after our walk and didn't leave it again, the door closed and locked. I had no understanding of why she might have written what she did. The silver lining seemed to be that I was not a ghost. The downside? That vacancy and strangeness in my uncle's eyes, my mother's estrangement from the family, all symptoms of a sociopath and the world he had fashioned around himself. To suit his needs. A world I now lived in.

The doorknob turned and there was a soft thud when the person in the hallway found the door locked.

"Marius?"

Flora.

I stood up and hurried over to let her in.

"Why did you lock the door?" she said, eyes suspicious.

"Here, come in," I said, taking the tray and closing the door behind her and redoing the lock.

"We shouldn't—"

"What do you know about my uncle?"

I set my dinner on the table but remained standing, eyes intent on her.

"What's come over you?"

"I want to know about my uncle. I met him the other day and he's strange. Scary strange."

She hadn't smiled in my presence since I'd brought her nervous habit to her attention. She looked somehow even more vulnerable, her lips a straight and impassive line and her eyes constantly flicking downward to folded hands or busy feet.

"I don't know what you want to know," she said.

"Why don't I ever see him?"

"He likes to keep to himself."

"But why?"

"I don't know," she said, cheeks bunched in disgust. "I don't know what you're getting at."

"Sorry," I said. My tone had been intense. I needed to watch it, watch how I said things. "I'm sorry. It's just been a lot to take recently."

"Of course," she said. "You moved to this…" She lowered her voice, "Your mom, your dad."

"Yes. Gone the way of Alexander."

"What?"

"Never mind."

"You don't talk to people very well. I'm sorry to say, but your words and the way you say them can be hurtful. And I don't follow what you're saying sometimes, or know what it is you want."

Criticism well-founded, of course. Flora might be another ally, like Mr. Charles, but I wasn't sure, not with her constant hesitancy. And not with the way I treated her, a source to tap, a friendship to turn on and off on a whim. And there was also that other feeling I couldn't admit to.

"I just find it strange," I said, "that I never knew I had an uncle. Did he do something to cause a rift with my mother?"

"She never talked about him?" with a sad look in her eyes.

"Not once. And I met him, finally, and maybe can see why. He was rather cold." I saw her nod and then quickly catch herself. "And his eyes…" I spread my arms out, searching for a word. "There wasn't anything in them. No excitement at seeing his nephew. No compassion. Not that I expected it. We'd never met, right?"

"But, still, you would think—"

"I don't know what to think. I just wondered what you know, what you've heard, what you've seen."

Her voice dropped to a whisper. "I can't say that I know much. But he seems tortured, somehow. You know? Like something bad happened to him."

No, he did something bad, I thought. *He wasn't tortured. He tortured.*

"What do you think that something bad might have been?"

She shrugged, but didn't have a chance to answer. There was a scream, shrill and scared. Like the one I'd heard before. And no wind to blame it on this time.

"It's time for me to go," she said, and she hurried to the door.

Chapter 6

THE NEXT AFTERNOON, after a quiet lesson with a distracted Mr. Charles, I went back to the garden. I felt self-conscious of the trail I left in the snow, but I had not seen Ben or anyone else out on the grounds. I left a crude deception, smoothed over snow along various stretches of the wall, then opened the garden door and slipped inside.

More majesty about the grounds as the ugly overgrowth and weeds lay under a white shroud.

I followed the path of my earlier visit and minutes later was in the shed again. Snow had accumulated along one wall, blown in through the open door, finding its way through the rotted roof. The back corner was dry, and I knelt there and ran my fingers over the markings. Feeling that I somehow touched the person, scared and alone, who'd put them there.

I sat with my back to the wall and closed my eyes and tried to picture the scene. My uncle brings my mother out. He… He what? I don't know. Does horrible things to her and locks her in. *I'll snap your fingers right off.* My grandfather, worried about his daughter, goes in search of her. My grandmother knows. She knows whom she's given birth to but it's her son and she can't see past his wickedness and she schemes with him to hide what he's done. No affection for my mother.

Does that explain you? I thought, speaking to her

more seriously in death than I ever had in life. *Does that explain who you were?*

It always began that way with the worst of them, the sociopaths. A firecracker in a dog's ear. A captured kitten with its eyes gouged out with a sewing needle. Then tracing up the food chain. He'd seen his younger sister as something to assert his superiority upon. *This is me. This is you. This is where you stand. Don't ever forget.*

I'll snap it right off.

Her words. His words?

Her words.

After a while, the cold from all the sitting became too much, and I stood up, brushing dust from my pants and coat, and stepped carefully back outside.

I walked further into the garden. A steep rock embankment, made by hand, cradling a stream running black under a thin layer of ice. A steeply arched wooden bridge that I tested with cautious placement of my feet, listening to the moan of boards and feeling them sink near the middle. On the other side an incline, an opening in a stand of cherry trees with stone steps leading up.

This is where I found the cemetery.

Plain headstones. Six of them. The trees had been planted in a half-circle around them. The air, cold already, seemed to be colder still there among the burial plots, the silence more complete. Perhaps under better circumstances I'd have found it peaceful. It was a retreat from 21st century noise. It was communion with those who shared my blood. I looked over my shoulder to make sure the path out of the garden was still there. Then I approached the graves of my ancestors.

I approached a tombstone and knelt by it, ignoring the cold and the wet. I brushed snow out of the inscription.

Tilda Frost. Beneath it, *1921-1942.* Nothing more.

And no sudden recognition. I didn't know what I expected. This family had been a mystery from the moment of my birth and was no clearer now.

I moved on to the other graves, cleaning the markers off.

Elizabeth Frost. 1923-1966. Tilda's sister?

Edward Frost. 1920-1982. My grandfather, certainly, fingers tracing the year of his death.

Lionel Frost. 1875-1951. His father. The inventor. The architect of this estate.

Victoria Frost. 1946-1989. A great aunt? A mistake who came along at the end of my great-grandfather's life?

Ethel Frost. 1891-1959. Lionel's wife?

Nothing familiar in these names. Nothing significant in the dates. Except for 1982. And 1989. One the year of my mother's 'death.' The other the year of my birth.

***

When I got back to the garden door and pulled it open, I wasn't thinking of anything more than a warm bed and dinner.

The thin groan of the hinges died out and I took a step towards the wall of ivy and then froze. I heard feet crunching through snow. I held my breath, thinking it was too late. But I was still hidden behind the ivy. Plodding footfalls. Near. He'd find me and know what I'd discovered.

I thought of retreating back inside the garden, but the wall of ivy was a shield. If I remained still and waited, whoever it was would pass.

Frequent pauses in his movement, moments when I no longer heard anything, and then the further crisp compression of wet snow under heavy boots, louder and closer.

My heart thudded. *Run. Run.*

Feet on snow moving with the languid rhythm of a trireme drummer's harbor speed beats. Near the garden door they stopped. I felt the weight of his heat there, outside, inches away, the ivy an impediment to sight but not to a hand daggering through. I held my breath so long my chest burned. That person knew. He knew. He knew I was there. I heard the rustle of fabric in his coat as he raised an arm.

I stepped back.

And then the footsteps resumed, a long, slow retreat, a steady diminishment of sound in the direction of the estate. Five minutes later I followed in the wake of the large footprints.

Chapter 7

"I WOULD APPRECIATE it if you'd level with me about the screams," I said.

Flora, sitting across the table from me, shook her head.

"You admit they are screams?"

She put her head down.

"More of the unknown about this place. I'll find out, you know, even if I have to go searching every room."

She didn't respond.

"He brings people back here," I said. "He imprisons them."

"No," she said, sincere concern in her eyes. "Not at all."

"He said he'd send me away from here, and fool that I am, I said, 'No, let me stay awhile.' Why? Why would I say that?"

A grin, this time empathetic, not embarrassed.

"I don't work tomorrow," she said.

"You mean they give you time off?"

"Of course."

"What do you do on your days off?"

"I walk. I read."

"But do you ever leave?" Was this estate their world? I realized that I hadn't seen a news website, a newscast, a newspaper, nothing.

"I go to see a movie sometimes, and do some

shopping."

"So there is a world outside this estate?"

"It'd be a little crazy to think otherwise, right?"

Did she just call me a little crazy? I thought, bemused. I blushed. *She's a little older than you. If she were actually interested in you, Marius, well, then that would be bizarre. For you, puberty occurred yesterday. And, besides, she speaks with affection of Mr. Charles.* A momentary stab of jealousy.

"Are you going into town tomorrow?"

"I don't know. I'm kind of uncomfortable driving when the roads are like this."

Foolish, Marius! She sees you as a little brother. Who would be interested in you?

"Why?" she asked. "Do you want to go?"

"It's a little claustrophobic here."

She laughed.

"Seriously. Why no cable or satellite? Why no Internet?"

"There were antennas, I guess. But he had them taken down."

"And now these antique televisions sit useless in every room."

"Not every room."

"I feel like I've been dropped into the 19th century."

"It's not that bad."

"Into a bad gothic horror movie. A house with secret torture chambers."

"That's terrible!"

"Screams, Flora. Locked gardens. What am I

supposed to think?"

There. She looked down again.

"What do you know, Flora?"

"Are you finished with your dinner?"

I nodded my head and crossed my arms and she gathered the dishes onto the tray.

"Enjoy your day off," I said as she made her way to the door.

She paused there. Without turning back, she said, "Maybe we could go for a walk together. In the afternoon. After your lessons."

"Maybe we could."

Chapter 8

I HAD EVERY intention of finding the source of the screams that night. After the clock struck midnight, I slipped out of bed and skulked into the unlit hallways that spread labyrinth-like over thousands of square feet of locked up rooms.

Stillness and shadows.

He's killed people here, Marius. At the very least his own father, and who knows how many more? The gods, Greek and Roman and Judeo-Christian and all others, they damn those who commit patricide. They would have to do the same to those who harm their little sisters or they wouldn't be just at all, would they?

There were no lights to guide me. The moon, of course—the clouds only flirted with masking it—its white face reflecting off the snow still spread over the grounds. The ambiance of indirect illumination, my eyes adjusting the best they could. I wound round the corners of my wing, past rooms with closed doors where Mrs. Moira and Flora may have slept. Or may not have. The enigma of this house.

I stood in the dark corridor where it came into the grand entry hall, staring across the T-shaped grand staircase at the wall of shadow mirroring the one I paused in. A dash down the stairs and up the other side? Tiptoe? Or sensibly return to my room?

No. There was someone else in this house and he or she might need help.

Unless it's your uncle himself. Screams of rage.

Bullshit.

Anything is possible here.

The ticking of the grandfather clock from below. Cloud shadows drifting across the polished marble floor. No one and nothing stirring.

I stepped out of the security of the entryway and began to descend the stairs.

Why does Flora hurry to leave when the screaming begins? Are they feeding some crying monster? Do I want to see it, this person or thing that causes her face to go white? Is it chained to the wall in its room?

On the landing leading up to the second story of the other wing I paused with my hand on the cool balustrade, waiting for the smallest hint of a sound to announce I wasn't the only one up and about. My uncle's suite of rooms lay to the left up those stairs. With the light of only a single lamp during the day, how dreary would his rooms be in the heart of night? No different at all.

A subtle sound. Movement?

His Doberman.

More than anything, that glossy black creature with its onyx eyes incited a panic attack. I looked to the entry hall's high windows and they began to spin. I closed my eyes but the vertigo only intensified. The dark. And what lurked in the dark. The dark and what lurked there. I lost my senses.

The dog would have growled by now. But turn around, Marius. Turn around.

The spinning subsided somewhat and I opened my eyes.

And then I screamed.

"Marius."

Bile rising from my stomach, tasting it in the back of my throat, eyes flung open wide, twisting away from the man who stood over me on the landing.

My uncle.

I hadn't heard a footstep or a breath. I'd simply opened my eyes and he was there. Staring down at me with his hands loose at his sides. Creature of dark. Unfazed by my screaming.

That one word. My name. Nothing more but his slim figure breathing in front of me, an anthropomorphic shadow cutting the night.

I backed away. He tilted his head, like a superior dog in a fight curious as to what its prey's next move would be. My back hit the railing of the staircase.

He shook his head, confused, "What are you doing?"

If I opened my mouth to speak it would be another scream or worse.

"You're trembling."

"What in the world is going on out here!" Mrs. Moira, appearing behind me, angry, then apologetic. "Oh, I'm sorry, Mr. Frost, I didn't know you were here."

"Marius seems to be lost. Pl-Please see he gets back to his room."

My uncle's stare lingered in Mrs. Moira's direction

(or mine?), then he turned and descended the stairs.

"Come here," she barked at me mere decibels above a whisper.

She didn't have to call me twice. I nearly flew in her direction.

"What are you doing, wandering around the house in the middle of the night? Have some sense."

Gripping my arm, she led me back to my room.

I wanted to find out who was screaming, I wanted to say. But the person screaming was me.

Chapter 9

"YOU'RE TIRED THIS morning," Mr. Charles said.

"Hmm?"

"Exactly."

"I'll be okay."

The cast iron radiators in the library kept it exceedingly warm and I felt I could put my head down and go back to sleep for a while.

"Before we begin, I wanted to tell you that I'm going to be gone for a few days. I have some things I need to take care of, to look into. I've talked to Mrs. Moira and she agrees with my determination that you'll be fine with a few assignments and no substitute instructor. Flora will help you as needed. Are you okay with that?"

"What do you need to look into?"

No answer.

"Is it related to—" I began.

"Maybe."

"I need to talk to you. About something I saw." I mouthed the words, *In the garden.*

He slid his notebook and a pen to me across the table.

I wrote the names I remembered from the headstones. Wrote, *Who are they?* Passed the notebook to him.

I saw a brief flash of recognition.

"I'm not sure that I know a lot about that,

Marius." His eyes told me otherwise and he made a show of folding the paper and putting it in his pocket, then patting it to make sure I knew he would do something about it.

Chapter 10

FLORA AWAITED ME at the door onto the veranda, bundled up in a winter coat and scarf and wearing blue jeans for the first time in my memory.

"My grandma said you went sleepwalking last night."

"That man is terrifying."

"Well, you'll be happy to know he's gone on one of his trips."

She opened the door and I followed her outside.

"Where to?"

"We never know. He just gets in his car and drives. He'll probably return in a week or two. He usually does."

"Off committing murder."

"Marius," chiding.

We walked down past the pine trees standing over the path onto the grounds, wending our way towards the greenhouse.

"You've got a green thumb, don't you?" Flora said.

"I suppose."

"That's kind of nice. When did you become so interested in gardening?"

When had I?

"Katerin was our au pair," I said. "She loved to work in the garden. I guess I learned from her. There's something satisfying about planting a seed and watching what it grows into, when given care."

"Maybe you'll have to teach me," she said. "I've never had much luck."

"There's not much to it," I said, holding the door to the greenhouse open for her.

The door into the house at the far end seemed a little less threatening with company. Flora went straight to my plants.

"What are these?" She ran her fingers lightly over the leaves.

"They're fuchsias," I said. "I'll plant them in the ground. I was going to plant them in our garden in the spring. I didn't think they were ready to be on their own, outdoors. Not yet."

She leaned back against one of the empty tables and watched as I watered them.

"I know very little about you," Flora said.

I blushed.

"And I don't want to pry. But I'm very sorry about what happened to your parents. If you need to talk…"

"They weren't very good parents." I put the watering can down and hoisted myself onto one of the tables.

"What makes you say that?"

I'd never really spoken with anyone about my parents. Katerin witnessed them and comforted me but we never said much. To speak ill of them reflected more upon me than it did them, I thought, since I was never sure whether I was the one at fault for their neglect and moods.

"My mother was very up and down. When she was

down, well, the whole house felt… heavy, I guess, is the word." *Oppressive, if you tell yourself the truth. A police state with the ability to read minds. A gesture could denounce you.*

"I'm sorry to hear that." She pushed herself up onto a table opposite me and stretched her legs out and rested her feet near my hand.

"And my father. I don't think he ever wanted children. He had his work. He had my mother. He adored her. I don't know how, sometimes. She could go days without speaking. And she'd throw things at him. Jam jars. Remote controls. Books. But then they'd be all over each other. It was gross. I don't know."

A sympathetic smile. Her hands tucked in her pockets.

"What about you?" I said.

"What about me?"

"I know you said you're here for the education. But, and I don't mean this disrespectfully, it just seems kind of strange. In the 21st century a… a person our age, working in a place like this."

"It is strange," she said, her eyes turning down and I thought that would be it, that her reticence would assert itself yet again. But she continued. "My grandma is a good woman. My mom is too, I suppose, but she's not the most responsible person."

I could commiserate.

"She and my dad, they're kind of the hippy type," she continued.

"Really? Mrs. Moira's child?"

"Daughter. Yes, hard to believe, isn't it. They

speak to each other, don't get me wrong, but I think my mother's life is something of an experiment in opposites of the way she was raised. She aspires to living a life without formalities. My grandma saw this and was concerned and asked my mother if she wouldn't mind if my sister and I spent some time here, with her."

"And your mom and dad were okay with this?"

"They were thrilled," Flora said, not looking at me. "Are you kidding me? I think it was a relief to them. They love us, but they were never quite sure of what they were doing, and seemed afraid they'd damage us in some way."

"Sounds plausible."

Flora grinned, but it didn't seem genuine. "It was okay. But there really is a contrast, between life with my parents and life here. They live in Virginia. In an old farmhouse. My dad paints—he has a studio in the barn—and my mom writes poetry and teaches at a community college. That's more or less the sole source of income. There were a lot of days when my sister and I didn't go to school. Everyone would wake up late. Breakfast at 10:30. Then do what you want."

"Sounds wonderful."

"We didn't know any better."

"But your grandma didn't like it."

"No. I think it horrified her. She didn't want us to end up like my mom. Not if she could do something about it."

"How long has your grandma been here?"

Flora shrugged. "I don't know, but she's been here a long time."

"Does she ever say anything about my mother?" I ran a finger over the leaves of my plants.

"She hadn't," Flora said. "But when we heard about the accident, she was heartbroken."

"What did she say about her?"

"That she was sad that she hadn't had a chance to see her since she'd left, and—"

"But why did she leave?"

"She didn't say."

I looked up at her. Flora's eyes warm with concern.

"Can I show you something?" I asked.

She was nervous, fidgeting, looking all around as I ducked through the ivy and opened the door.

"It's okay," I said.

"I don't know. The last time I came down here, Ben—"

"Forget him. It's an adventure."

That nervous smile. Then she followed me in.

"It's very pretty." Whispering.

"You wouldn't say that if you'd seen it without all of the snow. Come on."

We followed my footprints.

"I don't understand why he'd lock this up," she said, brushing snow off of rose bushes as we trekked along.

"Something bad happened here."

"What?"

"I don't know. But there are hints, one glaring hint.

I want to show you. I don't want to be the only one to have seen it." To continue to wonder whether my eyes had deceived me. Whether I was losing my mind.

I felt her hand touch my back and felt lighter, somehow.

You're too young for her, Marius!

Only by a year or two. Let me have this.

"Here it is," I said as we approached the caved-in bower and diversion of paths. I angled back in the direction of the shed.

"What is this place?" she asked, staring distastefully at the weathered wood, the leaning frame.

"It's an old storage shed, full of shovels and other tools, most of them rusted. Uninteresting except for what I found scratched into one of its walls."

She put her hand on my shoulder for support as we made our way over creaking floorboards to the back corner. In a moment I would know whether I was mad. I didn't want her to remove her hand. I enjoyed the sensation.

I'd covered the markings with the tarp. Afraid the weather would wear them away. Irrational. They'd have been long gone if that were possible.

"Here," I said, pulling the tarp away.

She read, a puzzled expression coming over her. "But what does it mean?"

We sat there with our backs against the wall, marginally protected from the cold, shoulder to shoulder, warmth from each other.

"I've been going over and over it," I said. "To the

point that I'm making myself a little mad. Mr. Charles told me a story. About my grandfather. Do you know what happened to him?"

"No."

I told her about how they found him frozen, dead, and her face darkened.

"Mr. Charles changed, somehow, when I told him about what I found in here."

"That's why he's been so moody?"

"I don't know what it is. He asked me to repeat the names. Peter Meyer. That's the one he fixated on. Do you think he's responsible? Did Peter Meyer do something to my mother? Did he kill my grandfather? I don't think so. I think it was my uncle."

"That's complicated. Crazy. I don't believe it."

"My mother was crazy. How'd she become so? That's what I wonder. I wonder if the answer is in here."

She pulled her arms across her chest, shivering.

"I'm so sorry, Marius."

"For what?"

"I… I don't know. I just, it seems, there hasn't been enough good for you in your life."

"You don't need to feel sorry for me."

She turned to me with her nervous grin. Why had that angered me earlier? Her lips… I'd never kissed anyone before. I'd never had the urge.

She seemed to know what I was thinking and her smile broadened but she moved no closer. She looked down, her knees pulled up close. She bumped them against mine. Once, then again.

"The scream, in the house, it's connected to all of this, isn't it?" I said.

"I can't say anything, Marius."

I was about to speak, about to say something in a tone I was much practiced in.

"But," she said, "your uncle is out of town. As I said. If you're scared of running into anyone while you're out sleepwalking, especially when you pass your uncle's rooms and continue to the farthest point on his side of the house, well, I wouldn't worry. If I were you."

Chapter 11

I WAITED UNTIL midnight again. I was less anxious than I had been the night before, but the memory of seeing him appear so suddenly wasn't far from my mind.

I stood in the darkness near the staircase and studied every shadow. Seeing nothing in motion, hearing nothing beyond the insignificant noises of a house at rest, I descended again to the middle of the grand staircase. Flora would not have hinted I should go on this quest if she knew danger waited.

I followed her implied directions and passed my uncle's rooms. That morbid corridor where the Doberman might be perched with large head rising from outstretched paws. My uncle standing there wraithlike, observing my passage. I hurried past the hall leading back to his suite and into the bowels of the other wing.

It was not quite a mirror image of the wing I resided in, but it was close. I passed the open door that led to the second floor of the library, heat from that room breathing out into the hallway. I kept going, into uncharted territory now, my feet silent on plush carpet with only the barest illumination to guide me.

I stopped at closed doors along the way, pressing my ear to them, listening but hearing nothing. Many doors. Too many to check. The hallway ended at a set of double-doors. I saw them when I rounded the final corner. I saw them because a soft yellow glow leaked out from the edges. So this was it.

Whoever was in there was still awake. I could hear low voices, song. A movie.

I tiptoed to the door and put my ear against it, careful not to rattle it against the frame.

"Audrey Hepburn is so beautiful."

It was a child's voice. A girl's.

"Look at her, Franklin. Isn't she beautiful?"

There were two of them in there?

I heard no reply to her question.

"I want to go to Tiffany's someday. And buy a necklace. It'll sit right here. Right here around my neck like this."

My hand reached for the doorknob. Then I hesitated. How could there be another child here? Who was she?

I'd had enough of not knowing anything and my hand went back down and turned the knob.

"Who's there?" a startled cry. "Who are you? Why do you keep coming? I'll scream. I'll scream again."

I put my head around the door. A frail girl. A lamp on the nightstand. An old TV and VCR combo on a table near the foot of her bed. She clutched a stuffed elephant to her chest. Her eyes wide. I was certain she'd call out for help.

But I think she recognized what I recognized. We looked very much the same.

"Who are you? Where's your mask? You're not the ghost, the one, the one…"

"I'm Marius. I'm not a ghost. Who—Who are

you?"

"So you're not the ghost? The ghost never talks. He just…" Her eyes cut to the thick tall curtains hanging majestic over the far wall. "Where's your mask?"

"What mask? What are you talking about?"

I stood there waiting for an answer as Audrey Hepburn made her way through the faded colors of a 1960s Tiffany's in New York City.

"Why are you here?" she finally said, fear hardening into a crust of imperiousness.

"I heard you screaming."

"I didn't scream."

"Not tonight. Before."

She wrinkled her nose at me.

"Why are you in my house?"

"This is my uncle's house," I said.

"It's my father's house."

"So we're cousins."

"I don't have a cousin."

"Your father and my mother were brother and sister. That makes us cousins."

Her skepticism lessened some.

"What's your name?" I asked again.

"Emily," she said quietly. "Emily Frost."

"Why haven't I seen you before?"

Her face wrinkled in disgust and she turned her attention back to the movie, stroking the worn elephant's trunk.

I came inside, closing the door behind me, walking

across the room and sitting on a chair near her bed. I watched the movie. I hadn't watched anything since I'd been in the house and I disappeared in the film for a while. I think we both did. I sat there until it ended and the credits began to roll and she reached for a remote and turned everything off.

The room had a stuffy smell about it, as if the windows hadn't been opened in a long time, as if she hadn't left the room in a long time. There were medicinal smells, too, ointments and syrups, chemical and sterile.

"What's your elephant's name?" I asked.

"Franklin," she said. "My mother bought him for me. Before I was born. That's what Mrs. Moira said."

"Where is your mother?"

Silence. A foolish question. If her mother were here I'd have known that by now. My uncle seemed to be a bachelor. Another murder, perhaps? A dead wife and a dead father.

I stood and stretched my back.

"What are you doing?" she demanded.

"Going, I think, since you don't seem to want to talk."

"You shouldn't be here. You need a mask. She'll be upset."

"I don't need a mask. Is my face that ugly?"

A grin that turned quickly serious. "Not a, a Halloween mask. A mask for, for germs. I can't be exposed to your germs."

Her teeth worried against each other, hard

breathing through flared nostrils.

"I don't have any more germs than you do," I snorted.

I saw the glint of metal in a far corner of the room, tucked between a bookcase and a desk. A wheelchair.

"It's time for me to go to bed," she said. "But... Maybe tomorrow. Maybe tomorrow we could talk. I won't tell Mrs. Moira."

I turned to look at her lying in her bed, visible from her abdomen up, the new swell of breasts, a slender and pretty face, her legs hidden beneath the sheets.

"I'd like that," I said, and walked out of the room, closing the door gently behind me.

Chapter 12

"SO?" FLORA, SETTING my tray down and sitting next to me.

"So what?" I was exhausted. I hadn't slept much and she hadn't let me sleep in.

"Did you go exploring?" Flora took the lid off the tray and stole a piece of bread. I nudged the butter and jam towards her.

"Emily," I said, feeling the syllables on my tongue. They felt like family, but cobwebbed.

Flora's voice dropped. "Was she furious?"

"She was a bit rude."

"It's in the family DNA," Flora said, biting her lower lip.

"Ha, ha."

She bit into her bread, a speck of strawberry jam red near her lip. I handed her a napkin.

"She told me to come back tonight. Said she wouldn't tell Mrs. Moira. Why is she hidden away like that? Why did she keep telling me I need to wear a mask?"

"I should have told you to take one."

"I'm not wearing a mask."

"We don't want her to get sick."

"Why is she hidden away like that?"

"I don't think I can say."

"He did it to her, didn't he?"

"I don't think so."

"Flora, Jesus. You feed me with teaspoons."

She shrugged. "I just don't want to get it wrong."

"I saw her wheelchair."

She bit off another piece of bread.

"And she'll have to tell me about that as well, won't she?"

Flora nodded. I sighed.

"Well, why does she scream?"

"She thinks she sees ghosts."

***

Flora stayed late to help with my reading homework. Mr. Charles had assigned Shakespeare. *Macbeth*. For a fourteen-year-old. Was he out of his mind?

"He thinks you're precocious," Flora said.

"And he thinks I'm interested in a family more dysfunctional than my own? First the House of Atreus. Now the House of Macbeth. Is he trying to imply something? Can't he just say it?"

"I'll ask him to go easy on you with the next book. *Bleak House*?"

"Funny. And, no."

"Your loss."

"What do you see in him, anyway?"

"He's an intelligent man. He knows a lot. He's seen a lot. He's kind of cute."

"Gah," I groaned, my face curling up in disgust. "He seems a bit... local. I don't know."

She laughed. "Local? What does that mean?"

"It seems like Harvard scared him off. Why leave the big city for this place? There's nothing here."

"And that's exactly what he wants, I think. I don't know that 'local' is quite the word to describe him, though."

"Where's he at now?"

"He didn't say. Anyway, let's get through Act I before I have to leave."

"'If it were done when 'tis done, then 'twere well it were done quickly.' I couldn't agree more."

Chapter 13

THAT AFTERNOON THE temperature was in the ascendancy, rain falling and the ground a marshland. Uninterested in slogging down the path and through a garden revealing its sad state under roiling gray skies, I decided to wander through the library collection instead.

What did Emily do all day? Did Mr. Charles tutor her as well? I thought of these things as I stood high on a ladder reading the dulled titles on leather spines. *More Shakespeare, no thank you.* Could she climb a ladder? Was she paralyzed? I wondered if she ever left her bed.

Victor Hugo. *Les Misérables.* The fattest tome I'd ever seen.

"Kill a tree," I muttered. "Or many."

I pulled at the volume that had been my mother's favorite, thinking this may have been the copy she'd first read. *This is where you were born, Marius. The idea of you, anyway.* She'd never reconciled the idea with the fact.

I'd never taken more than a passing interest in the story but decided I had nothing better to do on a day like this and took it down the ladder with me, finding a soft chair near the great window where the light shone strong and the heat wrapped me in soft comfort. A few more weeks here and it would feel like home. Flora and Mr. Charles like family. What then?

In some world of pleasant symmetry, mother and son across the decades, I would have become consumed by Hugo's masterpiece, but after twenty or so pages of the bishop's budget, the bishop's house, the bishop's sister and the bishop's housekeeper, I flipped ahead to the part that bore my name.

Marius.

Scribbled beneath it in a child's clumsy attempt at cursive: *My man.*

I found myself grinning.

"That is funny."

I sat up straight in the chair like a student rudely pulled from a daydream by a teacher's query and thirty bemused childish stares.

"Oh, no, no, don't be startled," Mrs. Moira said, holding a duster at her side. "It's just that I remember your mother sitting in that same chair with that same book. She couldn't have been any older than you, come to think of it. It's as big on your lap as it was on hers."

I ran my finger over the cursive, where the pen had made indentation in the paper, and said, "Why'd she go?"

Mrs. Moira approached, setting the duster down on a table and wringing her hands. She surprised me by sitting down in the chair adjacent to mine. She found something of interest out the window to stare at as she spoke. "She was somehow too fragile for this world, Marius. They didn't always treat her well, her family."

"What do you mean, she was too fragile?"

"Sensitive. Kind of like her son."

I blushed. Sensitive is one thing I'd never considered myself. *Think of your reactions to the sounds and the smells, Marius. A quiet garden is salve to you, isn't it? And an evening under the stars.*

"Her mother, her brother, they didn't share the same demeanor."

"What about my grandfather?"

"Well, then, your grandfather." She snorted and peered around at all of the books. "You can thank him for this collection. He loved to read. To his father this room was for display pieces. But not your grandfather, no. I'd wager he read every single one of these books."

I found that ridiculous. He'd have had to park himself in the library and not leave it. Ever. To read every word of these. The indentation of his backside a permanent record in one of these chairs. Still, I found myself thinking that perhaps he was a kindred spirit, a ghost, but another ally.

"Lord knows he spent most of his time in here. Your mother took after him. He was one of the gentlest men I ever knew. But, not everyone makes a good choice in marriage, do they?" She smiled at me. "How are you doing, Marius?"

I didn't know how to answer that. I didn't know how I was doing. My mind didn't know how to process emotion; emotions were irrational. If I felt sad, I called myself stupid for feeling sad. Ridiculous for feeling angry. No emotion was of any value, especially those that were histrionic and bound to earn me a lecture or a slap. I changed the subject.

"You didn't tell me why she left."

She shook her head. "I think she'd just had enough,

Marius. She ran away, once, for many days." Her eyes clouding up here. "Your grandfather went to look for her and…"

"He died."

She nodded grimly. "I see you've done some research."

"Why should I have to 'research'? No one here can tell me openly about where I come from. Why?"

She patted her knees and stood up. "No one has all the answers. Least of all me. Well, back to work. This house doesn't run itself. God knows there are days I wish it did."

But someone had all of the answers. I was certain of it, and I was determined to have all of them as well.

Chapter 14

THE CLOCK STRUCK midnight and I closed my bedroom door behind me and wandered into the hallway. Rain still pattered the roof and sounded soft ticks against the windows, wet shadows upon the floor as I made my way through the familiar hallways and to the doors at the end of the far wing.

Emily was sitting up in bed with a book on her lap when I walked in.

"I knew you'd come," she said.

"I said I would, didn't I?"

"No reason to be rude about it," she muttered.

I sat in the chair next to her bed. That medicinal smell. The sound of the thunder and rain muffled by the curtains. The room as still and stuffy as a burial crypt.

"What did you do today?" I asked, a premeditated question, wanting to get at the heart of this girl's existence.

"What I do every day."

"Yes?"

She stroked her elephant's tusks, pulled at his tail, seeming to commune with him, avoiding me.

"Awful weather, isn't it?" I said after waiting and hearing nothing from her.

"What's so awful about it?"

My brow furrowed. Her expression mirrored mine. Frustration for frustration. "It's rained all day. The snow melted. You couldn't take a walk outside without sinking in up to your knees. I bet there's flooding all over the place."

"I couldn't walk outside if I wanted to," she said, staring at her elephant.

"Why not?"

"Duh, I'm paralyzed."

My voice softened. "What happened?"

"A car accident. When I was a baby. That's what Mrs. Moira said. I've never been able to walk. My legs don't look like most people's legs. They're sticks. Atrophy, I think that's the word, right?"

"Yes, I think so. I'm sorry."

"Why?"

I felt a little rage rise up within my chest. Sorry should be greeted with a *thanks* or a *that's all right*. Not a question.

"Why? Because that's horrible."

"For me. Not for you."

We glared at each other for a moment, but I looked away, unable to take the judgment in her stare. I too grew frustrated when people who knew nothing of my life told me they were sorry or wanted to help. They didn't know what it was like to have a mother and father like I had. They couldn't understand why I didn't seem to care when I heard they'd died. They didn't know my parents and the way they were with me, therefore they didn't have a clue what their sorry meant. Empty words that made them feel better. Not me.

"You're right," I said. Her face softened and I

looked at the book lying next to her. "What are you reading?"

"My favorite book ever," she said, holding up the cover for me to see. It was an old paperback copy of William Goldman's *The Princess Bride*.

"Fantasy."

"Yeah?" a challenge.

"No, nothing. I like fantasy."

"Like who?" she said, eager to talk about books.

"Maybe a little more complicated than that, though don't get me wrong, I love that book. George R. R. Martin is my favorite. You might be too young."

"Too young? The pot calling the kettle black. How old are you?"

"Fourteen."

"Me too," with stress on each word.

"Do you ever get out of bed?"

"Of course. How do you think I go to the bathroom? Or eat?"

"You know, you could be a little less difficult. I think you know what I'm getting at. I've been here for over a week now and I've never seen you. Not until last night. Why not?"

She grew silent and somber and stared down at her elephant again.

"You don't like to leave your room?"

No response.

"Is it your decision, whether you stay or go?"

A finger tracing the elephant's trunk.

"Okay. It's late. I'm tired." I stood up.

"No," she said.

"No?"

"Don't go yet."

Standing with arms crossed, looking down at her.

"I don't like to leave my room," she said. "I'm comfortable here."

"That's it?"

"I think I make my father uncomfortable."

"That's crazy."

"He doesn't like to look at me."

I almost repeated my previous phrase but stopped. Crazy for a father not to want to see his daughter, but not so crazy in our family.

"Then your father, like my mother, is crazy."

She snickered. "Your mother?"

"We have strange parents, Emily."

She seemed to like this. I began to pace around the room. She had her own bookshelf. Harry Potter, *The Wizard of Oz*, *Arabian Nights*. No Shakespeare. No Hugo. No Greek myths. Good.

"What was so strange about your mother?"

"My mother," I said, "loved to spend time with complete strangers more than she loved to spend time with me. I think I'm coming to realize that I reminded her too much of herself, and therefore she didn't want to be near me."

"So she hated herself?"

"I don't know. Maybe." I pulled a book from the Narnia series off of her shelf. "Do you mind if I borrow this?"

Hesitation on her part. I understood her. These were her books. Her companions. Entire worlds. She didn't want them to go.

"You have to promise to bring it back."

"I will."

"Tomorrow."

"I will."

"Tell me more about your mother. What did she look like?"

She was beautiful. With black hair and pale skin and brown eyes, a waif of a woman, a shadow. Looking at her it seemed impossible that she could have carried me within her. Mrs. Moira had called her fragile, referring to her spirit. Her body, too, appeared fragile, with thin bones and a reservation in movement that made it seem as if the wind could do her damage.

"She looked a little like you," I said. "But with different colored eyes."

"Was she pretty?"

I nodded.

"Are you sad she's dead?"

"I don't know," I said, a rasp, a whisper, moving away from the bookshelf and going over to tug at the curtains. Near the window, hearing the rain, feeling a draft, a line of cold air as thin as a thread. Emily didn't need windows. She had books and movies.

"If my father died, I don't know if I'd feel sad either. I don't know him. I don't know if I could even tell you what he looks like."

"What a strange family we were born into, Emily.

Don't you think?"

"I try not to," she said, and yawned, and sank down under her blankets. "Please get away from the curtains. It's not safe to be there."

"What are you talking about?"

"That's where he goes."

"Who?"

"The ghost."

She spoke as if it was fact that a ghost haunted her bedroom walls.

"What is this ghost I keep hearing about? What are you talking about?"

"The face. I see his face there sometimes."

I narrowed my eyes. "How do you know it's a ghost?"

"Because he just watches. I scream and he just watches. And then he disappears."

I didn't want to believe her, but then I thought about my grandfather, and I took a step back and the chill in the air faded away.

1946

HEINRICH SCHERER WAS Peter Meyer. Heinrich
had left the concentration camp ahead of the Russians
in 1944. Wandered across Europe, west into Spain.
West and west. Ocean liners, border crossings, jungles,
deserts, fevers, snakes. Until he reached the United
States and drifted north to a community of German-
speaking Americans, some of them patriots of a
different sort of allegiance: sympathizers. With their
help he adopted a new name and became a different
man. He delivered beer for a Columbus brewery.
Drove a truck. A Ford with a temperamental stick shift
and no functioning radio or heater. The tendency to
stall in the rain. He parked it behind groceries and
carried in the cases, stacking them in cold storerooms
that smelled of lettuce and apples and cheese.

He supported his family with this income, a far cry
from what he'd made in Germany, before the war. His
wife, Ilse, was a German-American war widow. He'd
met her at a social event at the Lutheran church and
they'd married a few weeks later. Both widowed in the
war. Sharing a common language but not a common
past. No, she didn't know who he really was until later,
until he dreamed, until he woke with madness in his
eyes and she cowered in a corner with a comforter held
tight against her breast, a poor simulacrum of a shield.

His hands were cold and chapped and bloody and
his back ached when he came walking in the door of

their narrow German Village townhome. Red brick like the red bricks of the streets and sidewalks.

Ilse sat in a chair with a baby girl suckling at her breast.

"I don't smell dinner."

"Soon."

"Not soon. Now."

He didn't have to raise his voice anymore.

With daughter still anchored to breast Ilse bent forward and stood. She moved into the kitchen and busied herself at the stove with steaming pots while Peter went into the bathroom and ran hot water over his hands, which burned and itched and shook. Crate after crate after crate.

How are you, Mr. Meyer?

Oh, very good today. Would you like for me to take any of these out to the shelves?

Yes, that would be appreciated.

I'll get to it then.

He could smell the sauerkraut and hear the sausage sizzling in the pan. *Delivery man. Servant. Ache in his back. Pain in the knuckle of his index finger.* He walked out of the bathroom to see the child and its greedy mouth on his wife's breast. He'd find something else to do with that breast later.

He turned on the radio, shifting the dial from his wife's shows to something German and classical. No Wagner these days. But here was Beethoven's 7th Symphony. Peter hummed the familiar melody as he sat at the table and opened the newspaper.

Ilse, shifting the baby in her arms, reached for the tongs. The baby leaned back suddenly as if she wanted to peer up at her mother, curious eyes and smacking lips, but instead began a long tumble back towards a hot stove, into the fog rising from the pots. In Ilse's frantic grab for her daughter her elbow hit the handle of a pan and sent it tumbling to the floor. Baby embraced, she jumped back to avoid scalding metal and the hiss of boiling water splashing across the floor, crying out in shock. Ilse's cry and the clangor of the pan, the stink of burning plastic as it sank into the linoleum. The sausage rolling across the floor gathering dust. Silence in the room except for the symphony.

Ilse's eyes went to her husband.

He held the newspaper motionless. But his eyes weren't on it. They were on the sausage. His dinner. On the floor. He blinked once. And again. And was still.

She knelt down and picked the blistered red link up and put it back in the pan. Burning her fingers. "Ouch," she moaned as her fingers instinctively went to her mouth.

She heard the chair scrape back. She put her arms around her baby and stood and turned away, daughter squirming in her arms, her back to him, between him and the girl.

The second movement of the 7th Symphony was a sad dirge that couldn't drown out footsteps. Methodical. Calm. As if he appreciated the excuse.

Ilse found a spot on the wall to focus on, the head

of a nail. Peter had pounded it in and she'd hung their calendar on it, having just changed the month that morning.

It helped. To focus her attention on something minute and immobile.

She smelled him and heard him even as she felt him and the baby cried out.

III
A Breach in Nature

Chapter 1

THE COILS OF vines and clusters of weeds stared back at me like the snakes on Medusa's scalp. The garden revealed again. My feet were already soaked from the walk down, but the sky had cleared and there was enough warmth in the air that I only needed a jacket. I made sure to lock the garden door behind me.

I sought a new path, in the opposite direction from the shed and the graves, into the unseen acres, feeling like an archaeologist unearthing ancient civilizations in their ruins.

There were bowers, collapsed and soft and rotting, adorned with thistles and predatory vines in place of decorative flowers. Stone benches half-hidden, drying out from the storm. A statue stark white of a woman praying in what once upon a time had been an ornamental bed. A low fountain long silent stood choked with autumn leaves and scattered seeds and a pulpy mash of a similar brew from years past.

Up a small hill rose a great white sycamore that had shed its leaves. A solitary tree, the land around it clear. Its branches curled down like angry arms reaching out spiteful fingers to grasp and destroy any animal, any person passing near. The tree had to have been hundreds of years old. And it was injured. I could see the wound as I walked nearer to it. Where an ax had bit into it again and again and then for some reason stopped. Shame at killing something so old had halted the swings? Or sense, when faced with the futility of swinging an ax against this?

I eyed the branches warily, knowing I personified the tree, that it wouldn't really take me and hurl me or swallow me, but frightened nonetheless. Near to its broad trunk. The jagged reminder of the assault. I touched the exposed flesh, the ragged edges dulled by years of weather, cuts made long ago. The tree still appeared healthy. Stout low branches. Those goblin's arms.

A sense of foreboding here. No desire to stay. I left its circumference and continued my odyssey through the garden. Seeing things. A well with a low wall. Remnants of other paths branching off into the woods.

Chapter 2

"I NEED ANOTHER pair of shoes," I told Flora at dinner. The pair I had sat drying near the radiator. I'd rinsed them off at the pump next to the greenhouse but they were hardly wearable.

"Should we go into town tomorrow?"

"You have the day off?"

"No, but it doesn't matter. Especially if you need something."

"That would be wonderful. Can we stop at the newspaper office too?"

"The newspaper office?"

"Yeah."

"Do we have a newspaper?"

"I hope so. That's where Mr. Charles said he did his research."

"Really? Hmm."

Chapter 3

THE NEXT MORNING Flora and I walked out to the garage, a large two-story building separate from the house. The late morning sky was blue with a trace of clouds and wind but the temperature was agreeable enough for jackets. My shoes were still damp and malodorous.

"What did you and Miss Emily talk about last night?" she asked as she drove her old green Civic down the driveway. Leaving the estate for the first time felt strange, as if we passed a magical barrier when we turned onto the narrow lane and Hardivant Road.

"Books."

"She's going to like you."

"I think she does."

"That's her favorite subject."

Mine too, I didn't say.

"She writes, too," Flora said. "Though she's shy about sharing anything."

"I didn't know."

"Mr. Charles says she's good."

"I'll have to ask her about it."

"Be careful."

"I've learned that lesson. And don't tell me that tempers run in the family."

"I wasn't going to say anything."

But she bit her lip in mischief.

"We also talked about ghosts."

The look of mischief faded.

"Who is it?" I asked.

"We don't know."

"What are you talking about?"

"We've never seen anyone. She screams. We rush in. Nothing."

"So she's hallucinating. All the medicine your grandmother makes her take."

"I don't know, Marius."

"There are no ghosts."

"No."

"Only men and women. And shadows."

Chapter 4

AULIS WAS A stretch of 19th century buildings fronting a sedate Main Street a ten-mile drive from the estate. Two and three story buildings with brick facades and floors made of beams from native trees felled in the frontier spirit of the 1800s. Antique stores and restaurants and over-shop apartments; candy shops and dollar stores and a library and a bookstore. "Opera House" and "Dry Goods" carved in gray stone centerpieces mounted high on the faces of these buildings that hadn't heard opera or stored classical dry goods in nearly a century. Retouched advertisements painted large on the sides of buildings: tobacco and ice cream brand names gone on the gales of time. Behind the commercial structures magnificently preserved Victorian homes with their architectural nooks and many-gabled roofs standing serene and dignified in muted colors. The smell of horses and buggies and earthen streets somehow still there, all soaked into the skins of these structures and the random hitching posts leftover from long ago.

Flora parked in a church lot near the town center and we walked into the breeze with our hands shoved down into our pockets.

I chose a new pair of sneakers at the locally owned shoe shop, a small room crowded with displays and smelling of new leather and polish. The owner was a wizened old man with trembling hands. As I was trying on hiking boots, I asked about the newspaper.

"A newspaper? No. Not for a while now. Not for at least ten years. Not enough demand for one around here. And with the Internet, when even the *New York Times* is struggling? No way."

Then what was Mr. Charles talking about?

"Do they have a building where the archives are kept?"

The old man chuckled. "Probably. If not in the library basement, well, you can always ask Mr. Bracciolini. He owns the bookstore and was local-reporter extraordinaire when the rag still was up and running. And the son of its founder."

***

The Paper World was in a narrow building with large storefront windows where a half-hearted Christmas display of tinsel and glass ornament bulbs sat between copies of Dickens and Seuss and various comparative religion titles.

A bell tinkled above the door as we walked in and we were immediately overtaken by the smell of musty yellowed pages. Metal spinner displays and long running shelves taken from a chain bookstore liquidation sale thirty years earlier ran the length of a narrow room with a plaster archway leading further back into the building.

"Good morning," a warm welcome from a rotund man sitting behind the counter. His face was spherical like a globe and covered by a neatly trimmed white beard. Square metal glass-frames and lined bifocals magnified sharp eyes. When he stopped speaking the sound of his raspy breathing took over. A picture of health Mr. Bracciolini was not. Next to his puffy hand a half-eaten chocolate cream stick sat next to a large cup of coffee muddied with cream and sugar and a flimsy cardboard and cellophane box with the frosting and sprinkle remains of the already consumed. "Can I help you with anything?"

"I'm looking for books by Arthur C. Clarke," I said as Flora wandered off among the shelves to browse.

"The science fiction writer ambitious to get all the details right."

"Didn't he?"

The laugh that roared out of his chest startled me.

"If only!" he said. "Follow me."

He shuffled more than walked and I didn't see how he was going to squeeze through some of the narrow spaces but he managed. He had that large man smell of meat and grease, of someone who spends too much time in fast food restaurants, both dining and ordering, and I stared disconcertingly at the roll of fat all red and angry that bulged out of the neck of his shirt.

"I get a lot of these, well-loved," he said as we went deeper into the building, a wonderland of books, assorted spines shelved and catalogued and spanning every wall from floor to ceiling. "Here. Here's science fiction."

We stopped in front of a small room off of the corridor. Mr. Bracciolini's face was a combination of faint purple and pale white at this point and his chest rose and fell with all the grace of a wounded accordion.

He stepped back and I went into the room. He followed, swinging a meaty hand against the shelf to his left, his flesh landing with a soft smack.

"Here's where you'll find them. And is there anything else I can help you with?"

I saw the books I wanted. The entire Odyssey series, cracked spines, dog-eared covers. Books with personality.

"Do you know Mr. Charles?" I asked.

He nodded, his eyes making a study of me. Serious intellect there.

"He's my teacher," I said.

"Ah. So you're the boy. The one who's been asking about his family. The Frosts."

"Yes. And he came to you, didn't he? Looking for answers."

"He did. He's been doing so for years. I tell him what I know."

"I'm looking for answers too."

He stared at me for a while and I grew uncomfortable, finally breaking the connection and looking down at my hands.

"Get your books," he said. "Then come back up front. I need to sit. We can chat."

He raised his bushy gray eyebrows and turned and I heard the floor complain as he shuffled back to the front of the store.

***

With the complete series in my arms I walked up the creaking hallway to the counter. Flora was out of sight, though I could hear the groans of a 19th century floor where she squatted, the shifting of books on metal shelves.

Mr. Bracciolini took the stack and slid it towards his computer. The cream stick had disappeared. The coffee, not quite yet.

"Richard, your Mr. Charles, but Richard to me since he was a teenager getting lost among these shelves. He dropped this list off. Look familiar?"

He slid a paper across to me. It was my writing. The names from the graves.

"Yes," I said, a momentary feeling of betrayal, that all he'd done was give it away and run off to wherever it was he'd gone.

Mr. Bracciolini grunted, nodded.

"And what is it you're wanting to know?"

"Who were they?"

"That's a broad question."

"But I don't know anything about them."

"No, I don't expect you would."

And why not?

"Well, let's take these chronologically." A blunt finger tapped on Lionel Frost. "This was your great-grandfather. The man who made all the money and built the house the Frosts have called home since the 1920s. His wife, your great-grandmother, is Ethel Frost." His finger tapping again, his eyes on me. "Edward is your grandfather. His first wife was Tilda. When she died he married Elizabeth. When she died he married Victoria, who was your grandmother."

"Three wives?"

He nodded. "Widowed. Two times."

"What happened?" a bleak suspicion. Was Edward the gentle book collector? Was he a killer, a subtle monster? The floorboards creaked behind us as Flora moved along the shelves. Mr. Bracciolini paid her no attention.

"Tilda was young when she passed away. Your grandfather had gone off to fight in Europe during World War II, had married before he left because he wasn't sure he'd be coming home and wanted his sweetheart to benefit if he did not. He survived Normandy. She didn't. Pneumonia or something, I do believe. I couldn't tell you for sure. Only that it was natural."

Strange that you know so much. Pneumonia? My grandfather was not a killer. He was a gentle book collector. He was killed.

"When he came home he was heartbroken. It took him awhile, but he finally married Elizabeth, Elizabeth Bray, who came from another wealthy family. The relationship was somewhat reminiscent of aristocratic intermarrying. No children came of it. I think that was upsetting to your grandfather. I don't know that he would have remarried after Elizabeth died if they'd managed to have children."

"How do you know all of this?"

"That's a good question, isn't it?" He studied me, evaluating, weighing. I didn't know what he was looking for but I felt like he was waiting for me to speak or glance away or angrily leave his shop. "The Frost family has been a matter of some curiosity around here for a very long time, ever since Lionel decided to build his home in the hills here. My family, on the other hand, working folk, owned the newspaper, a weekly until it was a monthly and then…" he blew into his fist and then opened it to release the nothing that was there. "So it was our business to know. I can't claim knowledge of everything that happened up there. Behind the walls." He looked at me in a pregnant way after that last word. "I'm not omniscient. But there are bits and pieces and a matter of drawing conclusions, rarely speaking them, reporting the facts, thank you. I'm not a journalist anymore, as you can see, so I'm a little more comfortable in sharing what I think, what conclusions I've drawn. And will do so if you want to listen."

"I do," without hesitation.

"Elizabeth died in 1966. It was an accident. She fell into a well in the garden and broke her neck. In less than two months your grandfather married Victoria. In the same year, less than nine months after Elizabeth's death, your uncle was born. In 1968 your mother was born. What conclusions would you draw from what happened to poor Elizabeth?"

Murder. In the garden.

"You think he killed her. Because he'd had an affair? Because he wanted children?"

Mr. Bracciolini spread his arms as if to say *there you are* and leaned back in his chair, the metal in it sounding its protest.

"What did the police say?"

"An accident. Just like your grandfather's death. An accident. I suppose when you have as much money as the Frosts do it's easy to label something what you want to label it. As a reporter, I went by police reports. Interviews with officers and anyone else connected to the case willing to talk to me. We had a reputation as fair people, but the family gave no access. Not then, not now. So that's where it stands. Accidents."

His eyes beseeching me, I thought, to give him access to what I knew. I sensed some pleasure in his gaze, that someone was searching, exploring the garden, finding new information to pass along. I wondered what his motivation was. Driven by curiosity, or did he have another agenda?

"Where is Mr. Charles?" I asked.

"He brought this in and told me he was off to Columbus for a few days. I don't know what he's into. But I don't believe I've ever seen him quite so withdrawn. Something's upset him. He went down into the archives. Had me find the obituary for Peter Meyer."

I began to speak when I heard feet move across

the floor. Flora walked up to the counter and stood beside me.

"Did you find something, Flora?"

"I think so."

She put down two books. Both of them bearing Shakespeare's name. She grinned at me.

"Marius, any time you have questions, you feel free to come and see me."

"Where are the newspaper archives?"

"In the basement. On microfilm. A sad little tomb. All those pages confined to coffins no bigger round than bagels."

"I'd like to read through them sometime."

"You let me know."

Who was Peter Meyer? What was Mr. Charles looking for in the obituary? What had he found?

***

"What do you think of Mr. Bracciolini?" I asked as we walked up Main Street with the light breeze at our backs, surrounded by the friendly conversations of the town's citizens venturing out in the world after the temporary retreat of winter.

"He's always been quite friendly to me," Flora said. "But I'm a bit wary of him, honestly. Aren't you a little spooked by what he had to say?"

"He seems interested. And I don't know why."

"If there were that many strange things happening and he feels he never got a satisfactory answer…"

"Do you think he wants to use me?"

"For what?"

"To get information. He knows I've been in the garden. I'd bet Mr. Charles told him about what I found in the shed. He sees the opportunity in me to find answers he's wanted for a long time." And he didn't care about me, I thought. Not at all. Only the information that would help him to draw more conclusions.

"He might," she said. "But I'm sure he'd like to help you as well. You keep saying you want to know about your family. Your mother."

"I do."

"Then maybe it's symbiotic. Maybe not."

I nodded as I considered.

"I want to run into this drug store quickly," I said.

"Okay."

An electric chime sounded from above the door when I walked into the pharmacy and its medicinal smells, reminiscent of the scents in Emily's room.

At the counter they had what I wanted. An Earthlink connection kit—a CD, some documentation. It was time to get on the Internet.

Chapter 5

I SAT IN my room with my laptop open and a cord running from its modem to the phone jack. We'd had broadband in Indianapolis, but with basic dial-up I could at least do some web searches and catch up on the affairs of the world.

I spent the better part of the evening doing so, finding nothing on my first search attempts for the Frost family, Heinrich, and Peter. Giving up the effort, I spent more time absorbed in the news, satisfied that the world was much as I'd left it.

Chapter 6

AT MIDNIGHT I walked the familiar pathway to Emily's room.

Emily sat up in bed, dressed in a pink cotton pajama top, Franklin held close to her, a book placed spine-up on the comforter in the dim warm glow of a bedside lamp, a setting that spoke of caring hands, tucking her in. Like Katerin had done for me. I felt the temporary stab of loss but quickly buried the feeling and smiled.

"I come bearing gifts," I said.

"I like gifts."

"Arthur C. Clarke. His Odyssey series. I think you'll like these. A little something different for your collection."

I put the books on her nightstand. She smiled warmly.

"Thank you. That was nice of you."

"Sure. Flora and I went into town today."

"Oh."

"Oh?"

She turned her head away from me.

"What's wrong?"

No response. The rise and fall of her chest and eyes peering into the shadows in the far corner.

"We're just friends. You and I are family."

No reaction.

"Look, Emily—"

"I don't want the books."

"Why? You're jealous."

"I'm not jealous!'"

"Don't scream. You'll wake the whole house."

"I don't care!'"

"Fine. If you want to be a little jerk, I'll keep the books."

I grabbed them off the nightstand, my jaw clenched in anger. I flew to the door but stopped there.

"You're a brat, you know that? I brought these as a gift. I've been looking forward to speaking to you all day. And you're jealous of things that exist only in your mind. When you decide to grow up, you can come see *me*. I don't think I'll come back here. Not until you come see me first."

That set her to crying and I left. Angry and on a march back to my room but also feeling horrible at what I'd said to her. Neither one of us had been on the receiving end of much affection in our lives. We did receive a lot of hurt, though. And we knew how to deal it as well.

Chapter 7

"WHAT DID YOU say to her?" Flora, in the morning, sharing breakfast with me as had become our custom.

"She's jealous of you."

"What?"

"Yes. I told her I went into town with you and she flipped out."

"What did you lead her to believe, Marius?"

"Nothing. I led her to believe nothing. Because there is nothing." I drummed my fingers on the table. Flora looked angry. I couldn't stand it. "You too? I can't say a fucking word without the two of you losing your minds?"

"I wasn't implying—"

"You were implying. Both of you." I huffed.

"You're just like her," Flora said, standing and turning in a whirl of clothing and letting her feet speak her anger as she stomped to the door.

"I am *not* just like her!" I screamed.

Flora slammed the door.

Chapter 8

I WENT DOWN to the garden. To clear my head and to revisit the well, to get a better sense of the accident, to see how likely it was that a woman could stumble into it and break her neck. I brought my digital camera, thinking if Mr. Bracciolini wanted more information, I would give it to him. The family be damned. Damn all of them. I'd help him uncover the story. It'd be scorched earth. And then I'd go off the orphan I was. Seek out my father's family next. Dig up their skeletons. Make a thorough job of it all. Lay all the wounds bare. Rub salt in them before leaving the whole sordid mess behind, to sink into a mire of disillusionment with the sorry world that had seen fit to birth me and then leave me to fend for myself.

With the money I'd inherited perhaps I could pay Katerin to raise me.

I went in the direction of the wounded sycamore. My hiking boots were a huge improvement as the ground had not soaked up all of the snowmelt and rain, yet my feet managed to stay dry.

Standing on the rise where the tree grew, studying the landscape beneath, I stared at the ground leading up to the low stone lip of the well.

It would be easy to stumble on its wall after dusk.

I walked downhill towards it, taking pictures as I went.

The well looked as if it predated everything else in

the garden. Maybe long before Lionel had purchased this land it had been the source of water for a farmhouse. Peering into it I could see leaf-choked water about ten feet down. Who knew how deep it went. Its diameter? Enough. A woman stumbles. She's coming down the hill so she has momentum. She could spill into it. She could break her neck. It could have been an accident. But what of my grandfather's death? And Hannah Frost's metaphorical or spiritual death in the shed? Both in 1982. All of these things accidents? That seemed quite the stretch.

***

I spent time back in my room downloading the pictures to my computer, lessening the resolution, shrinking the file size, trying to pare them so I could cram them down the phone wire. I found an email address for The Paper World and sent a general inquiry to see if it belonged to Mr. Bracciolini. I didn't want to send pictures to a stranger.

With that done I climbed into bed with *Macbeth* with the intention of rereading the many parts I didn't get, but I soon fell asleep and dreamed of men and women washing blood from their shivering hands in hot tubs full of steaming water.

Chapter 9

MRS. MOIRA WOKE me in the morning. Yet again I'd chased Flora away. I didn't care. I was as angry at her as she was at me.

"Mr. Charles is here," Mrs. Moira said, yanking back the curtains. "Your lessons resume this morning. So get up. And get ready."

***

I didn't know which Mr. Charles I would see when I walked into the library. As always his hair was disheveled, but this time his head was hunched and he didn't look up when I walked in.

"Good morning, Marius." I could see the dark circles beneath his eyes when I sat down and he finally noticed me.

"You don't look well," I said.

A brief smile. "No, and I don't feel well."

"Are you sick?"

"No."

I set my books and computer on the table.

"I understand you've met Emily."

I nodded.

"I think that's good for both of you."

I nodded again. He didn't pursue it further.

"Shall we begin with *Macbeth*?"

"Or this," I said, turning the computer on.

His eyes narrowed. "What do you have there?"

"Pictures."

His eyes widened. He spent the next few minutes studying the images from the garden. He nodded his head at some of them.

"What?"

"Nothing," he said. "Or, well, it's just as if, what, you're showing me visual evidence of things that were long seen as myths. Imagine what that would be like, to see the throne of Zeus. Or the River Styx. Have you shared these with Mr. Bracciolini?"

"I will."

"He'll be thrilled." He pushed the computer back towards me. "Are we ready for *Macbeth*, then?"

"Where have you been?"

"*Macbeth* first," he said. "I intend to finish a lesson before we discuss anything else. *If* we discuss anything else."

I wanted to argue. He seemed evasive.

"What was the purpose of making me read *Macbeth*? It's a bit beyond me. I'm only fourteen, in case you've forgotten."

"I think I wanted you to understand something." His eyes dull and downcast.

I peered out the window. Gray clouds rolling in again. Dreary Ohio winters. I needed to move to a place where winter didn't exist. "What did you want me to understand?"

"Was Macbeth evil?"

To the point, then. What was he talking about? I

thought back to the play, to my dream, the blood on Macbeth's hands. "What was the body count?"

"Yes, he killed a lot of people. But was he evil?"

"Duncan, the king. His friend, Banquo. He wanted to kill Banquo's son. He killed Macduff's son and wife. Lady Macbeth's suicide. He was mad. He became a dictator." Strange to find myself passionate about the subject, though I couldn't grasp what he was getting at.

"And evil?"

"He killed children. Yes, he was evil."

"I don't like that answer."

I narrowed my eyes at him and sighed. "You obviously have an agenda. So have at it."

"Does it help us to label men like Macbeth evil? And, trust me, I've been working through this lately myself. It's not just a question for you. It's a question for me. For all of us, really, when you get down to it."

"Help us what?"

He ignored me and continued. "Macbeth is human."

"An evil human."

"But is there such a thing?"

"Yes! Macbeth. Hitler. Stalin. What, are you a fan?"

"Interesting word choice. Fan. Fanatic. Not in the least. I just don't know how saying, 'This person is evil,' helps us."

"Again, helps us what?"

"Understand."

"Who needs to understand?"

"No one will argue that murder, whether Macbeth killing Macduff's family or Hitler killing six million Jews, is wrong. Terribly wrong and horrifying. But was it a monster that did this? Or is that too convenient a label? Was it a man? And if it was a man, aren't we better off learning about the forces behind that man? The nature, the nurture, the tangible things this man dealt with in his life to lead him to his acts? Doesn't that better enable us to, I don't know, get at the heart of what's wrong and prevent it from happening again? Fix ourselves as human beings? Isn't that better than just saying, 'Ooh, evil monster'? Kind of like Macbeth and Hitler looked at others, 'Ooh, not a person. A mere insect. In my way. A trifle. An annoyance. No problem in my conscience in killing that.'"

"This is why you made me read *Macbeth*?"

"Yes and no. Maybe you're going to need some of this knowledge later on."

"For what?"

"Your mother was human."

"Of course she was human!" What the hell was he getting at?

"Your uncle is human. The world isn't black and white, it's shades of gray, and you have more in common with Macbeth than you do with an ape, don't you?"

"You don't know what she did to me." Here was the moment, wasn't it? His objective to get me to speak of things I didn't like to think about. The trauma of spending my youth with a woman who had also suffered trauma. A woman who was damaged, fractured, incoherently present. Trauma that bred trauma.

"You haven't said. You've held onto it. You're human, too, Marius."

"And nothing's excused!" Now he was looking at me. "What does that mean, to call someone man or monster? Who gives a shit? All I have is the evidence of what was done. Six million dead men, women, and children in Europe. Anne Frank. Six million. Elie Wiesel's mother and father and sister. That's the focus. What was lost. That's what matters. Not an argument in what we call a man: a man or a monster. Evidence? How about my childhood? A son who knew nothing, *nothing* of his mother but rants and rolling eyes and…" I felt the tears begin to roll down my cheeks. "And cruelty. We had a closet. Off of the kitchen. A dark closet where the brooms were kept. Full of cobwebs. Paint and wallpaper ripped up at the bottom where big brown rats had come in. She locked me in it. More than once. For doing nothing at all. Just being a kid. Playing with Legos on the floor of my room and then she's got hold of my arm and is dragging me across the house. And when I tried to get out she held the door. All the time I was in there, the whole time, she taunted me." I was finding it hard to speak. Reliving these things. I'd buried them deep, but he'd made me angry, and here they came, to shut him up, to drown him in it, to prove him wrong. I didn't know. "She made fun of me. She called me a nerd and a bookworm and a little fat ass and… Everything a kid who just wants to fit in and find his place doesn't want to hear. And I heard it. From her. From my own mother. Call her a monster or a woman or a human or whatever the hell you want to call her. Understanding her will not change the fact that she was not kind to me. Was not a mother to me."

I put my head down into my hands and tried to hide my tears, my weakness and nakedness in all these raw memories exposed to him. His warm hand touched my back. I didn't push him away. It was a connection to a sane man who wasn't seeking anything for himself, a strange thing to think, but that's where I came from.

"I'm sorry you had to go through that, Marius," Mr. Charles said. "I wouldn't want that for anyone. Least of all you. A child." I looked up and saw a mix of anger and sadness in his eyes.

"It's okay," I said after a while, stifling a sob, wanting to return to my normal stationary orbit of looking outward, of forgetting.

"It's not okay. And I'm sorry if our discussion led where it did. It wasn't my intention to upset you. I just think, when I see this family, see how they've *not* taken care of their own… I don't want the cycle to continue. I want to see you and Emily break the cycle. I want to see the House of Atreus fall, Marius. I want to see Birnam Wood come to Dunsinane. I want it all to end. And I don't think we get there with shallow understanding and labels of what lies at the heart of it. But forget the philosophical bullshit."

I wrestled in silence with what he'd said, eyes on

the stack of books, on the closed copy of *Macbeth*. Shakespeare didn't give easy answers. Monsters were men in his plays. Men were not monsters. Ambiguity ruled.

"I appreciate you sharing *Macbeth* with me," I said. "And the sentiment that you want to see me better off. If you want to see the House of Atreus—the House of Frost—fall, I think you will."

"I don't know if I will."

"What?"

"I'm taking a leave of absence. This will be our last lesson, unfortunately. For a while. For... I don't know."

"What? You, you just drop this on me and leave?"

"I understand your anger. We *need* to stay in touch. I don't intend just to leave you. I simply won't be here as your teacher. Flora said you have an Internet connection now, correct?"

He wasn't blowing me off, but it still stung, the notion that I couldn't rely on his presence here where no one else was talking to me, where no one else seemed to get the scope of the illness.

I nodded and avoided looking at him.

"I need to share something with you," he said.

"Where you've been?"

"Yes, where I've been and why the sudden change in my..." he chuckled and raised his eyebrows, "my demeanor. My appearance—disheveled to begin with and look at me now. You're not the only one with mystery in your past, Marius." A heavy sigh and a glance towards the bookshelves. "My grandmother was murdered before I was born. A gruesome, unsolved murder. All murders are gruesome, though, aren't they?" He grinned, grimaced, closed his eyes and tilted his head. "Anyway, she was Jewish, and she worked at the Ohio Theater in Columbus, and during a performance of *The Nutcracker* in 1955, someone entered her office and stabbed her. Multiple times. In..." He sighed, stared down, puffed out his cheeks. "In the chest and back and... He sawed almost completely through her *neck*. She was nearly decapitated. Someone wanted to wipe her off the face of the earth."

My jaw clenched tightly. Visualizing. Terrified. Sad for Mr. Charles. Seeing the blood.

"I don't think my family has ever quite recovered from her murder. 1955. A long time. I think, I don't know, the shockwaves with such a crime, they reverberate. They cause a Harvard man with, with limitless opportunities, to leave it all and return to the land of his youth. Damaged goods raised by damaged goods. Sad, when you think about it. Or not. I've been fairly happy, just not always sure."

He looked around the library, as if taking it in for the last time.

"They don't know who did this to her. A cold, cold case to them. An evidence box sitting on a shelf somewhere. But it's still real to me and my family. She was a lovely woman, my mother always said. Much respected. But she was, she was Jewish. And she was not the only Jewish woman or man to die like this in the 1950s in Columbus."

He was quiet for a long time and I wondered where he was going. When he finally told me, I was taken by surprise.

"'Heinrich Scherer is Peter Meyer.' That second name means something to me."

A chill ran through me. "What?"

"My grandmother's last words, written on an invoice on her desk, were, *The delivery i...* The authorities unconscionably ignored it. Said it was not what we thought it was. Not the soon to be dead woman leaving us a clue. She was writing herself a note. A reminder. They focused on bloodstains and conflicting eyewitness accounts of the men who left the theater at intermission. They claimed they looked into what she wrote, gave it due diligence, but I don't think so. It wasn't an 'i' she was writing. She was trying to write 'man,' but was interrupted. They did talk to a man named Peter Meyer. A beer delivery man. What could he have to do with it? This schmuck wasn't a theatergoer. He was just a blue-collar bum with bad English. And he had an alibi. He was home with his wife and kid and a lame back that night. He'd missed a few days of work because of his back. Doctor attested to it. 'No way this man's capable in his state of committing that kind of violence. Not with two bulging disks in his back. He couldn't do it.' His employer echoed the sentiment. The police didn't look at him hard enough, though. They didn't see that he suddenly appeared, as if out of thin air, in the year 1946. The first record of him a marriage license. That's one of the things I've found as I've done some digging. I don't know why that name, out of all the people they talked to, stuck with me. But it did. Something about the 'bad English.' That year, 1946, that's a strange time to emigrate from Germany, isn't it? And not long after the war ended, the bodies of dead Jews started to appear here?"

"How many?" I asked.

"At least four that I know of, including my grandmother."

I shivered. I don't know why, but I thought of the ghost in Emily's room. The face that appeared in her curtains. Was it him? He couldn't leave us alone?

"In 1951 they found Sara Feld's body a day after she was last seen at a nursery wheeling a cart full of annuals out to her car. They don't know what happened. An altercation with another customer? Someone there followed her out? They don't know. They found her, parts of her, in an irrigation ditch, stabbed, submerged. She'd been decapitated. They found her, her eyes dug out of her skull, her head buried face down near where they found her body. They focused on a migrant laborer but found no evidence to tie him to it and never solved it.

"Then there was David Pensak in 1952. He owned a small chain of grocery stores, worked late into the night more often than not. They found him in a dumpster in the parking lot of his office building. Stabbed multiple times. A cut across his throat but not all the way through. For some reason. His wallet was missing. Robbery attempt. Come on, let's connect the dots.

"Then there was Mary Leiber in 1961. She lived in a quiet little suburban house in Upper Arlington near the Ohio State campus. A housewife. Cooking, cleaning, taking care of the kids. Shopping for groceries. Her husband was a professor. He came home one evening and she wasn't there. They found her two years later. What was left of her. Buried in the woods in a nature preserve about a twenty-mile drive north of the city. Stabbed. Decapitated. Her head buried, eyes gone, face down.

"I don't know if there are more. I haven't found more. But it's pretty obvious, isn't it? That the same person committed all of these murders. All of them stabbed. All of them with their heads… All of them Jewish. *The delivery man.* The police put them together, finally, but no more murders like this followed Mary Leiber's and the case has just kind of died away as the interested parties have moved into old age and beyond. I think, if detectives had followed the lead my grandmother had left them, I think things would have been different. For Mary's family. And for the others, who lost loved ones and could have had answers. And for you."

"But what does this have to do with, with me? With my mother? Why would she write that? What would she know about it?"

"I have a picture of my own to share with you," he

said, reaching into his satchel.

He put a printout on the table. A black and white photo, heavily pixelated, of a young man in a soldier's uniform. The lightning bolt SS badge on his collar. Gray eyes wide and feral. The eyes of my uncle. The eyes of the woman in the picture in the gardener's home. And Emily. And me.

"This is your great-grandfather, Heinrich Scherer. This is also Peter Meyer. He was an officer at Majdanek when 18,000 Jews were killed in a single day ahead of the Red Army's approach. He disappeared after Majdanek. Through the Nazi pipeline, through Italy? Spain? Onto South America and then here? I don't know. I'm not so interested in knowing how he *got* here. I want to know about the crimes he *committed* here." He shook his head and sighed and looked towards the window with deep sadness. "A lineage of treachery, torture, murder. One family after another cast into ruin. By this man. I'm sorry."

"You don't need to be sorry." Trying to come to terms with this. That I had his blood within me. That I had his eyes. The same eyes that women, children, men had looked on with terror in the last moments of their lives. I dropped my head.

"I want the madness to end. With you. I want you and Emily to go forth clean. And I want to honor my grandmother's life by bringing this to a close. I cannot be here and be your teacher and do that all at the same time."

"I understand."

"Do you?"

"And I see what I need to do as well."

"Marius." I could see the pride in his face and I looked away. "You're a strong person, Marius. And a good human."

I smiled. Human. Human.

1955

"NO, NO, NO. Not there. Not there."

Peter Meyer. Heinrich Scherer. He was both. Both were the same man. The two cases of beer on the table with the white tablecloth in the lobby of the Ohio Theater. This woman scolding him. It was supposed to be his day off but John had called in sick and now here he was taking over that fat bastard's route.

"Who are you?" he asked. His German accent thick, fossilized.

She flinched. Recovered.

He noticed.

"I'm the one in charge."

"Where, then?"

"Back here," she said. "Come on."

He lifted the crates again. He had a persistent pain in his lower back and arthritis had begun to curl his hands. Every day a new ache in a new joint. He grimaced every time his foot touched down on the lobby floor.

He followed her into the small storage room behind the bar.

"Down on the floor there."

He squatted and felt the knife enter his back just above his waist and the crates spilled forward but only dropped an inch or two, clattering and banging against the floor but nothing broke.

"Be careful!"

Clutching at his lower back, his eyes closed tightly, seeing stars and falling forward onto his hands and then onto his belly. He lay there with his cheek pressed against the cool hard floor. Staring at the unpolished tiles through half-open eyes. The scuff marks in and out of focus.

"What are you doing?"

The pain in his back and this bitch doing nothing but scolding him.

And then she got it.

"Oh, no, do you need me to call an ambulance?"

"No," he muttered. "No, just give me…" A groan from deep within his chest.

"I'm going to call—"

"No."

The next spasm forced his eyes closed again and a barely audible moan. Heavy breathing escaping his thin pursed lips and sweat coursing down his face and back.

She stood over him. He could smell her perfume. Heavy and florid. She danced around nervously. She knew the origin of his accent and it made her uncomfortable.

Goddammit, not again.

In front of him the shadows of the hanged swaying over gymnasium floors with all the hurry of a pendulum in the belly of a grandfather clock.

"What can I do?" she said.

Bitch.

He stayed down for one minute, then two, then attempted to get back on his hands and knees, the next spasm forcing him to pause and nearly drop again but he had to fight through it before she did something foolish like call people who might ask too many questions.

"It's okay," he said, his breathing heavy. "I'm okay. If you give me a few minutes . . ."

"I think I need to call an ambulance."

"It's my back. I don't need an ambulance."

"Why on earth would you be a delivery man if you have a bad back?"

Stupid bitch! What kind of fucking question is that?

He gripped the nearby storage shelf with trembling hands and began the task of pulling himself upright, pausing frequently along the way to let his back become accustomed to the change in posture. Eventually he stood. And as long as he was upright and holding onto the shelf he could bear it.

"The papers," he said, reaching into his interior pocket and putting them on the table with a trembling hand, jerking forward from the waist up but recovering.

"Are you sure . . ."

"I'm sure. I'm sure. Just sign here. Please."

Miriam Reis. The old woman was a Jew.

***

The next day. Peter Meyer. Heinrich Scherer. Ilse cooking when he returned home from work. His back healing. The warm smells of meat and cabbage and bread. His daughter, Victoria, nine now, playing in the family room with her doll. Dancing it but without much spirit in her movements. Pausing to run her hands through its hair. Pinching its nose.

The concert was tonight and he would be going back out in his best clothing. Ilse knew this but not why. She knew better than to ask.

He turned the radio to the classical station. Tchaikovsky. *The Nutcracker.* Victoria walked in without her doll and climbed into her chair. So small for a nine-year-old, wasn't she? Oh, well, this damned Russian's music would please her, he thought. And then more of the Russian in the evening. Why not Handel instead? At least he'd been born a German.

He looked across the table at his daughter where she sat with her plate, steam rising from it. No mischief in those eyes. Or dreams of fairies. Or any other childish things as the music played. It seemed to inspire nothing in her. Hmm. Slight thing with black hair. Quiet.

***

The lobby bustling with the activity of black-suited men, wives and girlfriends on their arms in dresses with hair up and jewels glittering in their ears and around their necks and the air a pastiche of competing scents sprayed on in front of the mirror at home as they regarded themselves beautiful for an evening. Peter, or Heinrich. Yes, he was more Heinrich tonight. Heinrich stood in a corner of the lobby with arms crossed looking for the Jew woman who'd mocked him when he'd fallen to the floor in the little storeroom. She'd known who he was. She'd *known*.

The conversations around him buzzing about his ears like persistent intrusive flies.

Tchaikovsky. *The Nutcracker*. What business did a Jewish woman have with such an office? They always insinuated themselves into such lofty positions.

The elegant men and women began to make their way through the open doors into the auditorium and Heinrich saw her across the lobby. Near the bar. Dressed like the maître d' of the theater. Theater mother. Mocking bitch. She would end him. She was planning it. To report him. A rather plain blue dress and a glittering broach on her breast like she didn't seethe with thoughts of vengeance.

In the dark theater watching the ballet dancers and trying to avoid notice from the pleasant-faced people sitting near him. Heinrich found his hands clenching and unclenching with the knife tucked away in his suit jacket imagining what it would be like to get his hand around the handle but anxious at the amount of blood that would flow and would she scream meaning he'd have to make a mad dash? And then it would all be over. How happy Ilse would be.

No, if there were the chance that he'd be caught he'd not go through with it.

The ballet dancers in their tights and the moody tone of the music. The mad eyes of the nutcracker and his gaping jaw a seamless black pit threatening to swallow them all.

At intermission he stood at the top of the stairs leading down into the lobby and saw her hovering at the edge, directing bar employees and ushers, eyes that meant business and cheeks and jowls that hung neutral if not negative in disposition. Haughty. In control. The clenching in his fist. Never seeing the townhome again. He'd see it. He'd see Ilse tonight and she'd know him. The little girl best be asleep when he walked in.

As he descended the stairs he stole glimpses of her. On one of these looks he found her staring at him. Recognizing him. Recognizing what would come? Hard to tell when they made eye contact and her demeanor didn't change.

The lights flickered on and off and the audience members flowed back into the auditorium. Heinrich did not see her, but he lingered in the lobby until the doors were closed and he was alone, the bar employees packing up the bottles, some of which he'd delivered the day before, putting them away in the little storeroom, hard glass tapping against hard glass. Heinrich went in search of the Jew woman's office.

He moved with care around the corners of the corridor that led back into the depths of the theater's bureaucratic center. Listening carefully for voices or footsteps muffled on the plush carpet. A plain door open down the hallway with its yellow light spilling out. He would look in that room and if it were her he'd go in and close the door behind him. If not, he'd turn around and go home.

A wince as his foot hit the floor and its effect was felt at the base of his spine, in the muscles that winged it. He moved in the direction of the door. The sound of the orchestra shivering its way through the walls. Enough sound to bury her initial scream? Did the people in the seats next to his notice his absence? Did they remember his face? He hadn't looked at any of them. He'd kept his head down in the program, turning his face away whenever anyone moved past him.

He came to the opening and saw her sitting at a desk in a plain room counting receipts. Counting her money.

"Yes?"

She looked up from her desk and the recognition was immediate. He entered quickly and closed the door.

***

Minutes later he lay on the ground with the dagger in his back. No, the knife was still in his hand, and the blood spilled and saturated the carpet and filled the air with the scent of iron and the scent of the burial pits, those gaping hungry mouths, and the scent of the crematorium, the constant digester of flesh and bone. The spasms that had never quite left him since the day before. Hard, shallow breaths. The glassy eyes of this dead woman staring back at him. He wanted to dig those dead eyes out so he'd never have to suffer under their animal stare again.

It took time, lying there next to her, for his back to calm enough for him to push his way to his hands and knees. Lingering there as voices passed and the rise and fall of a melody played on strings filtered in down the winding corridors. Onto his feet, then, bent over like a hunchback with the added burden of a weight of bricks on his shoulders. Breathing heavily. A drop of sweat that fell onto her financial papers and scribbles. He should've read those papers but he hadn't.

Shuddering and lurching when the muscles in his back contracted, he made his way to the door and leaned against it and listened. His hands shook. The knife wrapped and secured in his pocket. His hands wiped but still maroon like a butcher's. It would take warm water and soap to wash away the defilement. The blood that had splashed onto his suit jacket hidden in its jet black fabric.

Not a sound from the corridor. With a handkerchief, he opened the door a fraction and peered out. Seeing no one he limped out and away from the lobby to where another exit onto the back alley awaited. Only once having to catch himself against the wall. Leaving her blood there. But no one would find it until he was gone. They'd ask the theater-goers about the man who had not returned to his seat after the intermission. A man who looked like any other man. They would draw him. Too general. Too vague. He'd been careful.

And he hadn't spoken.

But Miriam had begun to leave a note when she

saw him appear in her doorway. Only a cryptic scrawl.
The delivery i…

IV
Scorched Earth

Chapter 1

I KNEW THE stillness of the house at midnight and set out then with my camera and a small flashlight. When I ascended the staircase into the far wing I paused for a moment, accustomed to going to see Emily. But I had other plans this night. The doors to my uncle's suite at the end of a perfectly dark hallway. My heart pounded as I stood faced with a short walk to the man's rooms. For all I knew he'd returned. Or would return. Man and dog.

I turned the flashlight on, a thin white beam of light revealing burgundy red carpet, vases on tables that jutted out from the walls, the doors shut and looming, somehow larger in the night.

So silent when he surprised you the last time, my memories reminded me. But I'd had enough. I wouldn't wait for snippets of information to come my way. I was hunting now.

I pressed down on the door handle knowing for certain that it would be locked. But it wasn't. A man with something to hide leaves it out in plain sight as a sign of his innocence, his ego. Doesn't he?

The darkness of the hall gave way to more darkness in his rooms and I stepped inside, closing the door behind me, fighting the urge to find a light switch, not wanting anyone to catch me by the glow that would filter through door cracks.

Glass rattle of window frames. The stuffy stale air

of a room long sealed from outside air. I went towards the desk.

Shining the light of the flashlight where the Doberman had rattled its collar, a spot occupied by an empty cushion with the Doberman's large indentation.

Past it.

At the desk I pulled a cord to turn on his lamp. The green glass shade angled the light down onto the desk surface, enough for me to see by, but not enough to be caught by. I hoped. The books I'd moved from chair to floor still sat on the floor. His desk a mess of papers. Good. His recent thoughts.

I began taking pictures. Invoices for house expenditures. For travel. His destinations. West. Los Angeles. A hotel in Chicago. In Helena, Denver, and San Francisco. He traveled far. The names of those he was going to see.

The sudden crack in a beam overhead caused me to jerk my head to the side. Struck breathless by shifting shadows, accidental sounds. *He's not here.* Thinking I saw movement in a door leading deeper into the suite of rooms. Tricks of imagination.

I opened drawers. They were disorganized. Pens, paperclips, scraps of paper. I'd found a key in another drawer. Would I find a key here? I snapped more pictures. Nothing alarming. Things to be sifted through. To share with Mr. Charles and Mr. Bracciolini. To *draw conclusions* from.

I left the desk behind. What else?

Bookshelves. His private collection. *War and*

Genocide. Hitler's Willing Executioners. The Coming of the Third Reich. Night. The World Must Know. Never Again. The works of Hannah Arendt, Primo Levi. Every volume a book about Nazi Germany. The Holocaust. Totalitarianism. Genocide. Why? I took pictures of the bookshelf.

The fireplace mantel. Light white pages, tri-folded, hung half off the ledge. As if he'd stood over the fire and considered dropping the documents in and still hadn't made up his mind. I took the papers and unfolded them.

An accident report. *High rate of speed. Canyon curves.* I felt an ice dam of grief choke my veins and dropped the papers and clenched my eyes and almost fell to the floor with the pages that still hadn't hit ground.

Hannah Besshaven. Hannah *Besshaven* died in LA. In 2004. *Burned. Thermal trauma.* He'd stood there and read it. And kept it. No tears had dimpled the report. Did he feel? She hadn't died Roman statue white. She hadn't died in 1982. She'd killed herself and my father in 2004. And she'd burned. Goddammit, she'd burned.

I reached out for the wall to steady myself. Cold. Shivering in a warm room heated through by cast iron radiators.

Burned. Broken.

Broken what? Broken bones? Broken mind? Broken and bleeding inside?

I didn't need to read more to know. I knew already. She did it. She'd had enough, finally. Instinct, to reach out and end it. It was simple. Perhaps she'd even apologized as he tried to fight her off. Perhaps she'd said nothing at all.

I looked at the white papers concealed by my body's shadow. Then I took them to the desk and photographed every page with shaking hands. If I were lucky, the images would be too blurry to read.

They weren't. In my room I loaded the pictures onto my computer and I sat at the table and read every word. Neither my mother nor father had been wearing a seatbelt. Traveling at over 60 miles per hour at around 3:00 in the morning on a canyon road. The police could not know what had happened in the moments before the crash. They had simply recorded observable fact. The lack of tire marks on the pavement. The sudden jerk to the right. The pole that caught the car. The bodies and how they lay disabused of life. *Burned.* My mother and father. Burned.

I sprinted to the bathroom, making it just in time.

Chapter 2

FLORA PULLED THE curtains back the next morning.

"Emily told me what you said."

Eyes that didn't open. "I don't care."

"That you told her she'd have to walk here before you'd speak to her again."

"I didn't tell her to walk here. I told her she'd have to come here. There's a difference."

My throat was still raw and my head hurt and I was dehydrated. I turned away from the windows and pulled the covers over my head.

"What's wrong?"

It wasn't a dig. Not this morning.

I didn't answer. I trapped cold hands between my thighs and stared at the underside of the comforter.

"Marius?" tender voice.

"I had a bad night." My parents had burned. My great-grandfather was a Nazi mass-murderer. Serial killer. Maybe my uncle was too. A bad night.

I could sense her standing next to the bed. The thought warmed me but I didn't move.

"Well, the new teacher is here today. I'm sad that Mr. Charles won't be back."

"I don't have any plans to see the new teacher today. I don't feel well."

"She's nice. Mr. Charles recommended her. She's retired. She was his teacher once upon a time, when he was in high school. Hard to believe."

"Not today."

"I'll get your assignments if you'd like for me to help you with them later."

I had no desire to work on any assignments beyond the ones I'd set myself, but I also had no desire to argue, and it was an excuse to see her again.

"Thank you."

"Do you want your breakfast?"

"Maybe. Later."

"Well, I hope you feel better. And I hope you change your mind. About your cousin. You were doing her some good. You know, I talked to her. About us. She knows better, so don't worry about her being jealous."

Don't worry about her being jealous, and you don't have a chance, Marius, not with me.

She left and I went back to sleep. Into haunted dreams.

Chapter 3

I WOKE BEFORE noon and sat at the small table with my laptop open, sipping at room-temperature orange juice and water and eating cold toast, dry. Mr. Bracciolini had responded to my earlier email and I'd sent him pictures of the garden. I read his response as I ate.

Words can't quite convey what it feels like to see pictures of the garden. I've only ever heard stories. And so many things have taken place there that's it's reached the realm of myth.

"You and Mr. Charles and myth," I whispered. "It's real enough to me."

However, I would prefer you come into town again as soon as you are able. I'm not sure I'm comfortable sending smoke signals through the ether. In other words, perhaps speaking in person is best.

I walked over to the window and stared down at lawn and trees covered once again with snow, the wind-blown drifts lying like sizable white continents that would scare Flora away from driving, though the driveway was clear and tire tracks were visible. She could get out. But she wouldn't want to. *It might be a few days,* I thought. In the meantime, what?

Chapter 4

SO THERE I stood in the greenhouse, faced with the door again. Lurking behind it the inanimate ghosts of long-ago abandonment. The picture of my grandmother, the curtains that had been torn down, the single bed with the ominous frame, the water stains that had dripped down the walls. I'd been alone in there and then not. Ben was either stealthy or I lost my sense of hearing when distracted.

Before moving in the direction of the door I moved in the direction of the greenhouse windows, clearing a portal on each side, peering out, searching the grounds. He wasn't around. No trails through the snow other than mine.

The door, then.

I turned the knob but it only went so far. Ben had locked it.

"You really don't want me in there," I mumbled.

It took me a few minutes outside digging in the snow to find a rock big enough for the job. Holding it in my gloved hand, I surveyed the grounds once more. The snow still falling. The wind howling. It would cover the sound of what I was about to do.

Back at the door I brought the rock up behind my head then swung it hard towards knob and the junction of lock and frame. One hit was all it took and with a resounding and pleasant thud the door swung open. I dropped the rock and went in.

I focused my attention on the places I had not yet explored. The wardrobe, dusty and cobwebbed but empty. Kitchen cupboards of the same disposition but

with the added evidence of rodent infestation. What else?

I lifted the mattress. Yellowed. Stained. I felt along its rough fabric for cuts or bulges. Nothing.

Overhead the ceiling didn't conform to the peak of the roof. A small attic space? Where was the entrance?

The only other rooms in the abode a mudroom and a bathroom. A quick search of the mudroom revealed only a pair of old boots. Stiff, cracked leather, frayed laces, dust.

I went into the bathroom. Small and tiled, a toilet, a narrow shower stall, a sink. And an attic hatch, square and roughly framed, directly over the toilet.

Standing on the porcelain bowl and then stepping onto the tank, thinking my weight might break it (*you're slight, Marius, you'd never break it*), I pushed up on the hatch. Dust rained down with the cold and I coughed and pinched my burning eyes shut. Eyes still clenched, I pushed the hatch up and out of the way and waited for the particle shower to end.

I brushed out my hair and brushed off my coat before opening my eyes. White light invaded the space above me. At least I wouldn't be blind up there.

I grabbed hold of the lip of the opening. With momentum from a small jump I managed to pull myself up and into the frigid space.

I squatted at the hatchway, peering at the small setting. Pink insulation that lay between the joists. A space the size of the home. My white breath fogging the air. Nothing stored there. Nothing apparent to the eye. A builder's realm.

I stepped on wooden beams with the intention of going to the far wall, doing my due diligence, but then returning and leaving the attic and house behind. I'd found all that I was going to find there.

The light came through a ventilation panel. To keep my balance I put my hand up onto the ribs of the frame, careful to avoid shingle nails. Near the far wall, I jerked my hand back when, thinking I'd touched a nest or a web, an insect abattoir, I felt the soft give of paper instead of the rough texture of wood.

Near the back wall, a few pieces of paper had been tied up and concealed behind a joist, hung from a hook with a gardener's green twine. They had been cooked by summer heat and humidity and were yellow and stiff and full of waves.

I yanked on the twine and they came down easily. I unfolded them gently, just to peek. A man's blunt handwriting. Chicken scratch. Half-cursive, half-print, unflattering, but on other pages, half-mad. Written in calm and then written in rage or passion. No name, only an endearment. *Dearest.* Unsigned. The picture of my grandmother?

I tucked the letters in my coat pocket and walked back across the attic. I squatted near the hatch, listening. I'd been up less than five minutes. Plenty of time for

Ben to find the broken door. I stared down expecting to see him looking back at me, but I saw only the toilet and the brown tiles of the bathroom.

No sound but the wind and the lazy drip of water.

I lowered myself and replaced the hatch covering. I closed my eyes once more and smacked the dust off, coughing, then poked my head out of the bathroom and stared back into the empty house.

There was nothing else to find in the gardener's home.

Back in the greenhouse I pulled the door shut and did what I could to make it appear unmarred. One look and Ben would see the break. Maybe he wouldn't check, thinking his job was done. I tried to convince myself that I wasn't much concerned. Enough had been hidden from me. If they wanted to try to stop me, let them.

Scorched earth, Marius.

Chapter 5

I RUBBED AT my red nose as I closed the door to my room, foolish not to have taken notice of the fact that it had been slightly ajar. I dipped my hand into my interior coat pocket to touch the letters, ready to withdraw them and begin reading them.

The sound of the metal collar as the Doberman lifted its head startled me.

My uncle's voice, that tepid, unsure, hushed expression.

"You brought quite the library. Hmm? Or did you buy some, in—in town?"

My eyes widened and my hand went to my collarbone. A sudden shroud fell over my cognizance.

My uncle, standing at the fireplace, his fingers trailing over my books. The Doberman with the unkind eyes lying aware at his feet.

He didn't seem to notice my fear. He walked over to the table where my camera and computer sat unprotected.

"What's this?" running his finger along the phone line stretching from the modem to the wall.

I didn't respond.

"Hmm?" He tapped it.

"It's…" voice struggling to emerge. "It's for my modem."

"I see."

He stared at me. Into me. He knew what I was

doing. It was written plainly on my face. All he had to do was pick up the camera and press a button and the accident report from his mantel would appear, familiar, sparking recognition, revealing everything that was on my mind. All of my intentions.

"Mr. Charles has left, I under... understand." He closed his eyes and turned away from the windows. "A shame. I met his replacement. Ms. Gitlin. Gitlin." Distaste. "I don't think I approve of her. I think it's time..." He cleared his throat and touched a hand to his head as if it ached. "Time to talk again of a-a boarding school. Yes? Get you someplace sane, with-without the reek of a psychiatric ward about it. Yes?"

"I don't..."

Waving away my reply. Massaging his forehead, squeezing the bridge of his nose, putting his hand down on the table for support, fingertips brushing against the camera.

"Mrs. Moira said you weren't well. That you were, were in here. I... Could you close the curtains, please? The light. It..."

I looked to the windows. As if the light that came through them was protection to me. In the dark, we'd be on his terms. My feet remained in place.

"The curtains!" a roar, followed by a timid, stuttered, "Pl-Please."

I hurried to the drapes and pulled them closed and the room was left in shadows. He stood between me and the door.

"That's a bit, a bit better." His eyes stretched open,

and then he closed them before letting them open again, mere slits. He turned his attention back to me. I could see him shivering and wondered what it was that might set him off, once and for all, when I might find myself locked in a small room with him standing outside of it with the key. *Like the closet my mother put me in. Like the shed he put her in. Like the box of last repose he put his father in.*

"I know you don't want to go to a boarding school, but it has to be apparent by now that this is not a good place for you. I've already made arrangements. For winter term. After Christmas. It's a school in, in Massachusetts."

"Massachusetts," I whispered. It sounded too far away. From Flora. From Emily. From this little niche-worth of family life I'd begun to carve out.

"I consulted with Mr. Charles."

He took a deep breath. Pale and ill. His fingertips moving back and forth across the table. Up against the camera. Not paying any attention to it.

"Next week," he said, "to grow accust— accustomed." Then he walked to the door, the dog standing and following. He paused as if he would say something else. Tell me to cease what I was doing. But nothing. He opened the door and let the dog trot out first with its jangle of collar and then both of them were gone.

I turned and pulled the curtains open to let the light flood back into the room.

Next week. I didn't have much time. A few days to

do all I could to figure him out. Find the evidence. Stop him. Then I'd go. But not before. Then I'd go, after there was nothing left of this place. And maybe I'd take Emily and Flora with me. There was an inheritance, after all.

Chapter 6

I COULDN'T FOCUS after he left.

What would he find amiss in his room? Had I dropped something? Put something obviously out of place? I sat at my table putting a password on my laptop, deleting transferred pictures from my camera. My mind trapped in his suite where even now he sat at his desk puzzling over why this paper had moved there and that paper had been unfolded. He hadn't left them like that and knew it.

After finishing with the devices, I went to the door and locked it and clarity returned in increments.

The letters in my coat pocket had been my focal point before walking in to find him in my room. It was time to make a study of them and see if they held anything of value. They'd been hidden, and so they must.

The first one, to *Dearest*, hinted at an act, but defined nothing.

I want to say to you that I am uncomfortable with what you've asked me to do. I will do it because I love you but I am uncomfortable. This is my record and my feelings for you. I don't know what I will do with this paper. Hah! I'm not a monster who plotted this on my own out of jealousy. I don't share your need for having this and everything under my control. Including me. You keep me here out of some sort of power play, don't you? Ashamed to tell your family your true feelings for me. I'm angry at you, but when I think of you, and what this might mean, what you said it might mean. Days where we never get out of bed…

Followed by mentions of the bed, details that made me blush. Visualizing whom? And what? What had he done? Who was he writing to? This was the only coherent letter. He was writing to the woman in the picture. Unless that was a diversion set in place by the real subject of these letters. Had my uncle left that picture of my grandmother there to lead astray anyone who went looking?

The next page was a disaster. Spilled thoughts.

I am not comfortable with what I have done. I am not. I am not. I am not.

Handwriting bludgeoning the paper and nearly illegible.

The mother. God. The child? Like that? Because of me? Because of what you asked me to do?

The rest of the page, blank. Marred by years in the attic.

The next:

I think my father knows. Everything. I am ashamed. I am destroyed. I am nothing that he envisioned when he raised me and I am nothing I want to look at in any mirror and I am nothing and deserve the hell that I get when I finally die. You avoid me now that it's done. You avoid me because you were using me? I could tell. I could tell everyone. I am damned already and so are you but I could damn you even as I am damned in the eyes of everyone. I think my father knows. Don't you understand?

And written in small writing on the back, almost as an afterthought:

I will go, but not without leaving some sort of record. A trail. Someone will read this and know. It wasn't just me. It was me. But it wasn't just me.

What was this? What was he saying?
Draw conclusions.
A mother and a child. The child… *Like that?*
Like what?
Like Emily. My uncle had used the gardener to rid himself of a family he didn't want. He'd thrown them away, and then thrown the person he'd used for the act away as well. He'd known there would be clues pointing back to him somewhere. On the off chance it would matter, he put a picture of his mother in the gardener's shed. Point the finger at her. Because if it had been her, there would have been no picture left behind. *I'm drawing conclusions, Mr. Bracciolini. But I don't think I'm anywhere near the truth. And now he wants me gone. He knows. He knows I'm getting close.*

Chapter 7

"IT'S NOT MY fault, Marius."

Flora carried in a stack of books, turning a wary eye on me.

"What's not your fault?" He'd found out I'd been in his room. Ben had noticed the door. Everything was about to end. He wouldn't send me away now. He'd kill me. Like he'd done time and again. To keep it all a secret. My heart skipped beats.

She smiled. "*Romeo and Juliet.* I tried to tell her you just read *Macbeth* and wouldn't it be good to read someone else, someone other than Shakespeare again."

"That's it?" Another skipped beat and then a subsiding of tempo in my chest.

She laughed and the sharp edge in her glance dissolved. "What did you think I was talking about?"

I eyed the unlocked door.

"What?" she said.

"I need to lock it."

"Marius…"

I went over and turned the bolt and felt a momentary sense of security when the lock went home. Flora narrowed her eyes at me. I didn't want to alarm her, but I needed her to know, to tell me I was mad or not mad or find a way to assist me, or simply know what I had planned.

"This isn't over a play, is it?" she said, arms crossed.

I tilted my head, confused. Then she tapped *Romeo and Juliet.*

"Oh, that, no, no. That... I don't think I'm going to be reading that or doing anything else this new teacher has planned for me."

"Marius!"

"He's sending me away, you know."

"Your uncle?"

I nodded.

"Sending you away? Where? Why?"

"To a boarding school in Massachusetts. Next week. He doesn't want me here, Flora. He knows what I'm doing."

"What you're doing? Marius, what are you doing? Does this have something to do with what you were talking to Mr. Bracciolini about?"

"Yes. People have died here, Flora. My grandfather. My great-grandfather. Whose name was Peter Meyer, by the way. You saw what my mother carved into the wood. There are a lot of bad things going on here, and I think that my uncle has gotten away with murder."

"I don't believe that."

"Look at these," I said, taking the letters out from where I'd shoved them under my mattress, a hiding spot that wouldn't do for long.

It didn't take her long to read them, a blush when she read about the things that had occurred in the bed. Confusion when she read the subsequent pages.

"So? What is this supposed to prove?"

"It's another piece of the puzzle," I said.

"Saying what?"

I told her where I had gotten them. She glared at me.

"You shouldn't have done that. Ben'll know. He'll tell your uncle."

"Think about it, Flora. My uncle has an affair with the gardener because he wants to kill the woman who's about to give birth to his child. He can't stand the thought of being tied down or beholden to anyone or maybe the mother made threats against him, I don't know. My uncle or my grandmother. I'm confused. He didn't put a name in here. He should have put a name. All I know is that there was an accident that was not really an accident. Emily's mom died. Emily is paralyzed. Whoever this *Dearest* is planned it. Wanted it. If this isn't a connection, then I'm fucking blind and stupid and need to give up looking as well as studying and anything else that requires a brain."

With lips pursed she shook her head, her eyes keen on the letters. "You're not stupid. That's not what I'm saying."

"What do I need to do to convince you to help me?" I said.

She continued to shake her head, then lowered her gaze to the floor. I felt frustration. I couldn't persuade her.

"Look at my family, Flora. Look at who my mother was."

"I know she was bad to you."

"I don't need pity."

"Marius…"

"And Emily. Is she any better off? Her life. What is it? And who knows how many others this bastard has touched, has harmed. Flora, I'm not judge, jury, and executioner. But I'm the first person who's ever set foot on this property who seems to have an interest in finding out what happened here and holding someone accountable."

"What do you expect me to do?" she asked, helpless animosity.

"Share, for once," I pleaded, "instead of leaving it all up to my imagination. You have to have seen and heard things."

"I don't know."

"I don't buy that. You play dumb sometimes, which I don't get, because you're obviously intelligent, Flora."

"That's a backhanded compliment."

"It was meant as a statement of fact, not as something backhanded, not as a compliment. Have some faith in yourself. You see things. You're scared of getting things wrong. I don't get that. Where did you lose your confidence? Don't be scared. Let me be the one to err if one of us must. And Mr. Bracciolini and Mr. Charles."

"What do you know about Mr. Bracciolini?" sharply said.

"He used to be a journalist."

"And?"

"He owns a bookstore."

"Anything else?"

"He likes donuts. What do you want to hear?"

"Why isn't he still a journalist?"

"The Internet. The 21st century. You know of something else?"

"Try a lawsuit. I asked my grandma after we got back. He was sued for libel. Settled outside of court— the family didn't want any more attention than they'd already received. That's what my grandma told me, anyway. She told me to be careful about what I say to him. *If* I go into his shop again. That he might attempt to coerce me into spying. Like he's done you."

"Your grandma's why you won't talk to me, isn't she? She doesn't want to upset anyone. Lose her job."

Flora looked away, agitated.

"I... I'm not criticizing her. I'm just wondering."

Flora sighed.

"Anyway," I said, "I think Mr. Bracciolini is right."

"His newspaper was sued out of existence, Marius."

"He didn't have all of the facts."

"No, he most definitely didn't."

"I'm here to give those to him, and I need your help."

"I'll think about it, and I'm crazy to even consider it." She tapped Shakespeare again. "You're not going to work on this tonight, are you?"

Would she stay if I did?

"More Shakespeare? Really?"

"You might think *Romeo and Juliet* is romantic fluff, Marius, but it's not. It's violent and beautiful. Why not try it? You'll be an expert. A Shakespeare expert. Girls will like that."

I blushed. "I'd prefer to be an expert in other things."

"In time. Come on. We'll read it out loud."

And we did, passing the time. She was right about the passion. And the violence.

***

Before she left, gathering books, wiping dinner crumbs away, Flora had one more thing to say to me: "Go see Emily tonight."

"Her father's here."

"He usually stays in his room. Don't worry about him."

"He didn't stay in his room the last time."

"He was on his way out. He likes to travel at night. Don't ask me why."

"He's a vampire, that's why."

"Oh, he is not." Hands on hips. Head tilted to the side.

"I'll think about it," I said.

"She's over the jealousy thing. That was momentary. A girl's crush."

"Gross! We're cousins."

"And I don't know what she sees in you besides." A smile there. A tease.

I felt the heat in my face intensify. She noticed. Smiled.

"I'll think about it," I said.

"Tonight," she said again.

Chapter 8

I TOOK THE Arthur C. Clarke books with me. If stopped, I'd have an excuse, however weak.

Standing at the junction of corridor and staircase landing, I didn't want to move.

He likes to travel at night.

Hadn't I been in his room the night before? So he had returned before sunrise. What if he had walked in while I was rummaging through his things? What if he had been there all along, watching me?

Statues didn't stand as stiff as I did thinking about the prospect.

He'll find you out and he'll lock you up like he did her and like she did you. That's what they do here. They lock up people and pasts. An aversion to light. Nothing sees the light.

The clock struck twelve. The wind hammered at a loose shutter. The primordial stillness of the house where the inhabitants mostly slept.

I descended the stairs and didn't pause on the landing, ascending the other side two steps at a time and half sprinting down the carpeted hallway to the lit doorway of Emily's room, knowing I'd have to retrace my steps in an hour or two.

Closing the door softly behind me, I looked at her, sitting up in her pink pajama top with Franklin and a notebook and pen, turning her head away from me in embarrassment, shoving the notebook under her blankets.

"I thought we'd try the books again," I said, walking over to her bed.

"Thanks."

"Flora said she—"

"Yes, she did. Can we not talk about it?"

I set the books down on her nightstand, then pulled a chair over near the bed.

"What were you writing?"

"He's back, you know."

"Yes, unfortunately. I talked to him this afternoon."

"That's more than I did. Why doesn't he come see me, Marius?"

Because he tried to kill you and now he's stuck with you but he doesn't want you.

"He's a fool."

"Is he? You see, because I don't know. What's he like?" Earnest and innocent, her eyes.

"The truth?"

"Of course."

"I don't know."

"You sound like Flora."

"Yeah. I do, don't I?" *I think he tried to kill you before you were even born.* "I don't think he's a very nice man, Emily. I'm sorry."

"You don't need to apologize."

"He's rude, demanding. He hates the light. He stutters. He creeps around in the dark. I've never seen him smile, never seen any affection. He's not very tall. And I think… I think he might be a, a killer."

Alarm. "What do you mean?"

I told her of our grandfather's death. I wasn't remotely objective at this point which wasn't necessarily fair to her, but she didn't question me. She seemed to buy it all and I told myself to try to be fair because I didn't need someone to tell me *yes* and *yes* and echo my logic.

"Why would he kill our grandfather?"

"Because our grandfather was going to find out what he'd done to my mother. And that's not all. Our great-grandfather, Emily, may have taught him a thing or two. I have my suspicions. Or he may have inherited certain qualities from him. Defects. Genetics. Nature, nurture, I don't know. But our great-grandfather—he was a Nazi, Emily."

"How do you know that?"

"Mr. Charles told me. And he showed me a picture of a man who looks like our parents. A little bit like us, too, frighteningly enough. He was an officer or something in a concentration camp in Poland and fled when the war ended. Mr. Charles is doing some research because, well, he has some other ideas about what he did. When he came here. This family is full of shameful secrets and I don't intend to carry on the tradition. I hope you feel the same, since we seem to be the only ones left. And your father, of course, but…" I spread my arms.

"You need to talk to my father about this. Confront him."

"I'm going to confront him, but not directly. I'm

gathering evidence, Emily. I think there might be more he's done."

"More? Like what?"

"I don't want to say right now."

"Don't want to because you're trying to spare me, aren't you? It's about the accident, isn't it? The one that left me like this."

"I think."

"You're saying he did this to me?"

"I don't know."

"And killed my mother?"

"Again, I don't know."

"You don't know but that's what you think."

I shrugged and looked away.

"Then why don't I hate him?" she asked, a matter of fact question, a why does the sun rise in the east and set in the west query of the obvious.

I shrugged my shoulders.

"How can we hate our parents? I don't know. I don't think I hate my mother either. I don't know what I feel about her or my father. I don't think hate describes it. I don't think I have words to describe it. That's part of my problem."

"He hasn't fathered me," she said. "I mean, he fathered me, but he didn't, like, raise me or anything. If what you say is true, he's done nothing but harm to me. And now he neglects me." She shook her head, not knowing what to make of it. Staring down at her legs. Limbs she'd never been able to feel or move. What child would know what to make of such a situation?

"Tell me more about your mother, Marius. What was good about her? I need to hear something good."

What could I possibly say that was good about her?

After a moment, after scanning her room, seeing her books, I had something, something insignificant. "She loved to read. *Les Miserables* was her favorite and she named me after her favorite character, Marius Pontmercy."

"Marius Pontmercy," she said, smiling. "Tell me about him."

"He's a student, in Paris, in the early 1800s when there's a rebellion. I don't know all of the details. Rich and poor, I think, is a big part of it. And he falls in love with Cosette. A beautiful young woman with a very protective and loving father—well, not natural father, but father—named Jean Valjean. Marius ends up getting shot on the barricade, this barricade that the students built to fight against the government they felt didn't speak for them. Again, I'm not sure of all the details. To save Marius's life, Jean Valjean carries him through the sewers and to the home of his wealthy grandfather where he's nursed back to health and eventually marries Cosette. Fantasy, huh?"

"It sounds like a wonderful story."

I shrugged. "Enh."

"I can see why she'd like it. I think I'd like to read it."

"It's a monster."

"A monster?"

"Very long. Victor Hugo didn't believe in revising, apparently, and I had a hard time getting started in it. A lot about the bishop at the beginning and I don't even know that he's that important a character. Maybe. Maybe he's the one whose kindness sets the stage for everything that follows so it's important for us to know where he found the kindness to do what he did for Valjean. Sometimes one person can have a big effect, can't they? I don't know. I didn't get far enough in."

"I thought you'd read it."

I held up my index finger and thumb a few centimeters apart. "Just a little. I've seen some of the movies that have been made. My mom made me watch them, actually. Those were some of the only…" I stared off into the corner envisioning the dark family room and the blue glow of the television, my father on a business trip, my mother present for one of the few times she ever was—mentally, physically, sitting together on the sofa watching a movie.

"That's who I named you for, Marius. What do you think?"

I think he looks a hell of a lot happier than I ever have. Why can't you always be like this?

"I want to read the book."

"I'll bring it to you."

"Thank you. What else can you tell me about her? It looks like you're sad."

"No. Kind of, maybe. Sometimes, sometimes when she was there—like, present, like the shades had been lifted—she looked at me like you would think a mother should. Like she actually wanted me to be there. And she was affectionate. And the word *Mom* meant something when I said it. But there were not many of those moments. Few enough that I can remember each one distinctly. There should be so many that I couldn't pinpoint them, right?"

"I wouldn't know."

I don't know if her eyes focused or not, but she was looking down at her legs again. Had I said too much? Spoken out of turn?

"Mrs. Moira is like your mother, though, isn't she?"

"I suppose."

"She seems like she'd be a good mother. Why doesn't she get you out of here?"

"Maybe I don't want to get out of here. This is warm. And safe. It's good."

"Maybe you should try. Would you like to see the garden?"

Her eyes opened a bit wider and I thought she would say yes, but instead she said, "Maybe."

Chapter 9

PASSING THE LIBRARY on the way back to my room I noticed the tired incandescent glow of lamplight spilling out into the corridor. Thinking it was my uncle I prepared to hurry by on tiptoes, but my curiosity compelled me to peer around the corner of the open door. I was surprised to see a heavy-lidded Flora sitting in a soft chair on the upper balcony with a book open on her lap.

"What are you doing?" I whispered, walking into the dry heat of the tall room.

She raised her chin and smiled.

"I read here. Sometimes. It's quiet. I can think. How did it go?"

"Better."

"Good."

"Is that why you're really here? Checking on me?"

She shrugged and grinned.

I looked to the great window and saw the evidence of stars, the white face of the moon. The sky a winter clear, cloudless. Wide open above the old telescope.

"Well," she said, closing her book, standing and stretching her arms above her head. "I'm off to bed."

"Have you ever looked at the stars?"

She paused and seemed to think about it. "Of course... Oh. Through a telescope?" She turned and peered sleepily across the room. "No, I don't think I have."

"Come on," I said, and led the way.

I turned the telescope and pointed it towards the moon, making adjustments to bring the dark gray Mare Tranquillitatis into sharp focus.

"What are we looking at?"

"The moon first. Come here."

She stepped in front of me and I made room for her but we were near enough that I could feel her heat and smell her hair and a whirlwind of emotions, of want and longing for contact, spiraled through my body.

"Just look in?"

"Just look in. It's all set up."

She put her eye to the lens and stood still and silent for a long time.

"You're looking at the Sea of Tranquility," I said. "That's where—"

"Neil Armstrong and Buzz Aldrin landed, right?"

"Yeah. That's right."

"It's amazing."

She shifted back a little, on purpose or not, I don't know, but for a moment she pressed against me. I grew lightheaded and hot.

"We can," I began, hoarse, cleared my throat. "We can change eyepieces. Increase the magnification."

Just as she was turning, I put my arm around her to get a different eyepiece off of the tray and her breast rubbed against my arm.

The blood vessels in my face opened up bringing forth a flush of red heat. She blushed too. We stood there, near, neighbors whose orbits had intersected, had caressed. Her lips parted slightly and she didn't back away.

A slow lean forward and my lips touched hers and both of our mouths clamped shut, our lips stiffened, and I could feel her hot breath coming down on me and then we backed away. She smiled and peered down at her feet and our faces both burned as bright as ever.

"Well, now I've been kissed," she said.

"Yeah." I'd uttered a singularly unromantic word. It didn't matter. I wanted to do it again.

She stepped forward and put her arms around me. We were both stiff, but her heat was immense and her breasts again, hard against my chest. We were bad at the kissing, but I didn't know any better. We kept at it for a while.

"Your heart's beating so fast," she whispered after we parted, breathed again, her palm on my chest.

"Yours too," my glance lingering for a moment on her chest, then moving away awkwardly, eventually looking up at her face, her bashful smile, her warm eyes. Accepting.

Her features from that moment are permanently etched in my memory and I don't think there's been a moment in my life since when I've been as full of unabashed and all-consuming love.

Chapter 10

"ARE YOU OUT of your mind?" Flora, the next morning, yanking at curtains. She'd come to her senses. Last night had been a mistake. I felt my stomach churn.

"What?"

"Emily."

Emily? What about Emily?

"You told me to go see her," sitting up, rubbing at my eyes. Blood flushed through both of our cheeks when we looked at each other and we both more or less looked away at the same time.

"She said she's going to the garden today."

I smiled.

"In front of my grandma!"

"Oh, shit."

The door slammed open a moment later and Mrs. Moira, a red whirling fury, came flying into the room.

"What on earth did you tell that girl?"

"Grandma."

"Don't you Grandma me." The didactic finger punctuating each word. Gesturing at Flora. "You knew about this. You set this up, didn't you?"

"What are you talking about?" I said. Playing dumb turned out to be the incorrect approach.

She dropped her voice but it was still as full of fire as it had been when she'd walked in. "You have no business sneaking through this house like some petty thief going where you please and doing what you please.

If you wanted to meet your cousin you could have asked and we could have set it up properly, but you, both of you, went behind my back and have made me look *foolish*. And you have deluded her! And put her health in jeopardy! And this garden she speaks of, Marius, I hope, I sincerely hope that that was just another story you told her and has no bearing in reality, because—"

"It has complete bearing in reality," I said. "I've been there. I found the key. I've been all through the garden. I've seen everything."

She closed her eyes and groaned, pressing the back of her wrist against her forehead.

"No, no, no. If your uncle finds out about this it'll be the end of all of us."

"Why?"

"Because he locked the garden up." The fire gone. Her voice a frightened, raspy whisper. "He locked it up, Marius. I think he hopes it disappears, that the plants in there eat it up, turn it to ruins. Why he didn't just set fire to it I couldn't tell you."

"So what can you tell me?"

Angry again, the accusing finger gesticulating obscenely, "You are not interrogating me! You have made misstep after misstep and jeopardized everyone, not just yourself. Everyone! Your departure cannot come soon enough."

"Grandma! That's horrible. Think about why he's here, what he's gone through."

"I don't need her pity. My departure can't come

soon enough for me, either!" I threw the blankets off and marched to the dresser, grabbing out pants and socks and a sweatshirt and storming into the bathroom, slamming the door behind me.

I heard Flora's tone, scolding, the sharp retorts, the back and forth before calm took hold.

I came out of the bathroom a few minutes later, dressed.

"I'm going to take her to the garden right now," I said. "You've kept her locked up long enough."

Mrs. Moira, palm out. "Just wait, Marius."

"Why should I?"

"Marius," Flora, seconding her grandmother, supporting me as well with the look in her eyes. I paused.

"Close the door," Mrs. Moira said.

Flora and I sat at the table and so did Mrs. Moira, but only for a moment. She was too agitated and needed to pace.

"He locked the garden fourteen years ago," her eyes wide, sad, vacant. "Fourteen years ago."

"That's when I was born. And Emily." Thinking of the circumstances of her birth. "Why'd he do it?"

She shook her head. "He never said. He doesn't need to explain himself. But there's no mystery as to the timing. His mother hanged herself in that garden. And the next day, there was no more garden."

Another death. How many now? Great-grandfather. Grandfather. Grandmother. Emily's mom. Where did it end?

I was struck speechless, thinking I knew where it had been done. The ghastly sycamore with the base that had been hacked at with an ax. Why? Never ending questions. Never any definitive answers. No one escaped unscathed.

Mrs. Moira was not with us, her lips moving in and out, worried, pale, her mind focused on a moment in the past or focused on damage control, I didn't know.

"Why did she kill herself?"

It was as if I hadn't spoken. She hadn't heard me. Flora touched her arm.

"Hmm? Yes? Why'd she kill herself, you said?"

"Yes," Flora whispered.

"I don't know. Her husband was dead. Her daughter had left and didn't communicate. She and your uncle, they fought and fought, all the time. And then, then there was the accident."

"Emily?"

"Yes, Emily."

A tear ran down her cheek.

"Grandma," Flora, standing and putting her arms around her, turning to look at me, mouthing that it had been enough for one day. I wanted to argue but I could see her pain and thought I was better off leaving things alone. For now.

Flora, with her arm around her grandma's shoulders, led her to the door. Mrs. Moira stopped and turned to look at me.

"I am sorry for what you've gone through, Marius. I am sorry this family is what it is and has not been a—

a soft landing place for you. And I'm sorry I can't tell you everything you want to know. But, please, give me some time. Give Emily some time. Don't go see her today. Let me talk to her."

"I promised to take her a book," I said. Flora's eyes rebuked me, but I went on. "I'll stay away for now, but, please, could one of you give it to her. It's this one."

I took *Les Miserables* off the mantel and walked it over. Mrs. Moira put her hand out and smiled softly.

"I suppose I can do that." She patted the cover affectionately.

"Thank you," I said. Perhaps scorched earth wasn't the likeliest path towards truth, resolution, or whatever it was I sought.

Chapter 11

I LOCKED THE door after they left and reclined on the sofa with my laptop. I'd taken dozens of pictures in my uncle's study and had yet to look at them. He had or he hadn't killed people. What would the papers say?

Most of them said nothing. Receipts. Ledgers. Lists of practical matters to attend to: car maintenance, lawn treatment, roof leak. The bookshelf. The accident and autopsy reports. I thought about reading them again, the cursor hovering over the thumbnails, but the complaint in my stomach warned me away.

Then I found the names and I sat up.

He'd written the names on a white legal pad in hurried cursive. Three of them, but there could have been more on other pages I hadn't photographed. Three of them on this page. Elijah Wechsler. Neta Hirsch. Ira Berkovich. San Francisco. Chicago. Helena. What did they mean?

He traveled at night. He was gone for weeks at a time. He drove. They couldn't look at airline tickets and tie him to any of these cities. He paid for hotels with cash. There were receipts. He...

Had he killed them? And why? Why these people, in these places? How did he find them?

I'd fallen into the outer edges of a downward spiral that led straight to the sinister heart of murder. Again and again death proved central. Why should I expect these names *not* to be the names of murder victims?

I stood up and set the computer on the table and plugged it into the phone line. The search would be slow, but I'd find out if there was any mention of any of these people. But there was no dial-tone.

Chapter 12

I AVOIDED EMILY that night, though I wondered what they discussed. I sat on the sofa in my room rereading parts of *Macbeth*, trying to figure out Mr. Charles's point about the play.

Was he trying to tell me that I should feel sympathy for my uncle, my mother, my great-grandfather? That evil deeds are not done by people who think that they are evil but instead are committed by people who think they are justified in doing what it is they are doing? How did that gain me anything? Or was he trying to convince me that I, too, had it in me to do foul things, and the play served as a sort of warning, with the ghosts of my family lineage whispering in my ear like Lady Macbeth to her husband before he killed the king? *"Screw your courage to the sticking place and we'll not fail."* I had no such compulsion within me to commit any foul acts.

Your uncle might think that you digging through his past, unearthing secrets that might send him away to prison, is a foul and evil deed. Your great-grandfather thought the Jews deserved their deaths, or else he would not have killed. Your uncle thought your grandfather and grandmother—and Elijah Wechsler, Neta Hirsch, and Ira Berkovich!—deserved their deaths, or he would not have killed. Your mother thought you deserved the upbringing she gave you… Or maybe she didn't think much of how she raised you at all. Maybe that's the point. She didn't walk around lamenting her poor treatment of you, Marius. She wasn't aware of it. Were you a victim of her actions? Yes. You are bound to see what happened to you from the perspective of a victim and it's okay if you want to blame her. But in one moment, at the very least, she was unaware of what she did to you and what she did to your father. Her hand reaching for the steering wheel of that car as it sped down the winding road was just one more action that made sense to her in that moment. Dying made sense to her. There was nothing inherently evil about it. She saw no victims. A revision: she saw no victims other than herself.

Exhausted, I put the book down and fell asleep on the sofa and dreamed again of details culled from the police report—*severe bodily trauma, thermal injuries*—with gaps filled in by my imagination.

Chapter 13

THE TEMPERATURE WAS in the upper 20s when I walked outside the next morning, early, bundled up in a thick down winter coat, hat pulled low over ears and brow, scarf wrapped around my neck, gloves already allowing the cold to seep into my fingers. My boots crunched through the snow as I made my way down to the greenhouse to water my plants.

My heart sank when I got to the greenhouse. A rude metal chain had been looped round the door handle and firmly nailed into the wood of the frame. My plants, frozen, dead, lay tipped over on their sides in front of the door. My breath came up short and I stood staring at the soil spilled dark upon the snow, the soft flutter in the branches of the fuchsias, the leaves curled and dehydrated and done. Ben had found what I'd accomplished on his locked door, but why did he have to kill my plants?

**

I sat in the shed again where my mother had left her markings. I don't know why I kept returning to that spot. Maybe because it provided some protection from the cold. Maybe because that corner provided a dry place to sit. Maybe because it was one of the few places I knew with certainty she'd touched, she'd been.

I thought of my plants. Some children had pets or

siblings upon which to devote their affection, but I'd only ever had green things, things with stems and leaves that drank in sunlight and grew when you watered them and pulled the dead leaves from them and fed them with fertilizer causing them to shoot up in a magnificent way secure there in their plot of earth. In truth, I almost felt like giving up on my investigation, my prosecution. The last tangible living connection to my former life was gone. I'd be leaving in a few days. Why bother with anything anymore?

I raised my head when I heard feet crunching through the snow. Heart thudding and eyes wide, the view of me akin to seeing an animal trapped and cornered with the instinct to flee contained by the solid walls on every side of it.

"I thought I'd find you here."

The shadow that filled the doorway. The light at the back of him and his features immersed in shadows.

"You're not the only one with a key to this place, you know," Ben said. "And you shouldn't be in here. I think you know that as well."

"My mother was here." I sensed nothing malevolent in his voice, in his actions. He was my uncle's man, though. He seemed capable of looking the other way, of guarding secrets, of locking doors I needed to open.

"Your mother was here? What makes you think that?"

I sniffed. Rubbed my gloved hands together. Looked in his direction but said nothing.

"I told you to leave this place alone, or I'd tell your uncle about it. He's not going to be happy about you being in here."

"Why did you kill my plants?"

"You killed your plants."

"I didn't leave them out in the cold to die. They're in pots, not in the ground yet, and you knocked them down."

"The wind knocked them down."

"They were in pots."

"And you were in the house again. I told you to stay out. I locked the door. You broke in. Enough of that."

"Why do you care if I go into that house? It's abandoned. There's nothing there."

"Nothing there? Then why'd you keep going in? What did you find there?"

A key. And a photo. And a sheaf of never-sent letters.

"What's so offensive about that house and this garden, anyway?" I couldn't see the expression on his face. All of the light was behind him.

"Don't ask questions, just follow the rules."

"Is that what you do? Don't ask questions? When people die in here and little girls get paralyzed in car accidents before they're even born?"

Drawn-out silence and his chin sinking as the wind blew curlicues of powdered snow along behind him and the wood moaned. Then he raised his chin.

"What do you know about it?" A sudden outpour of anger and frustration and hurt. "Hmm? What do you know! You've only been here a few weeks and all of a sudden, what, you've got it all figured out? Every one of us? Don't you. Down to the feelings I've got here etched in my brain." Finger jabbing at his temple. "Don't you? Leave it alone!"

His heaving shadow swaying at the threshold. The only way out. I panicked. What if he locked the door? I went to one knee and then pushed myself up. And then it clicked. The letter. *I think my father knows. Everything. I am ashamed. I am destroyed. I am nothing that he envisioned when he raised me.*

"Your son lived in that house, didn't he?"

Silent and still in the doorway. Then I heard the deep sniff and the brief sob he tried to stifle but couldn't.

"You're wrong. I don't have it all figured out," I said. "But I want to know. And apparently, so do you."

"Leave it alone," he whispered. He turned and walked back down the path. I expected to find chains on the garden door the next time I tried to enter it.

And I was wrong, that he wanted to figure it out. He didn't need to. He already knew.

Chapter 14

"I NEED TO go into town today," I told Flora when she brought our lunch—turkey sandwiches, chips, apples—and sat down next to me at the table.

"I'm not comfortable driving when the weather's like this. I told you that."

"It hasn't snowed for two days, Flora. The roads have to be okay by this point."

She looked to the window. I could almost sense her shivering, thinking of the prospect of driving on the sheets of ice and gale thrown snow. I wanted to put my arms around her, but the sunlight dissuaded.

"Out where we live? You'd be surprised. They don't salt much and the drifts, where the fields border the roads... Look at the wind."

I'd been out in it. I didn't need to look.

"Can't we at least try?"

She seemed to think about it. Then changed the subject: "I don't trust him, Marius."

"Mr. Bracciolini? That's only because of what your grandma said to you."

"Maybe. But I *do* trust her, you know. And shouldn't I?"

"That doesn't mean she can't be wrong," I said in a harsh tone. "Sorry. Look, I understand, this is her life. This house. This estate. The people who live here. She's afraid. I am too."

"I know."

I reached my hand towards hers but didn't quite make the connection. My body stiffened and I stopped breathing and Flora took my hand and pulled it to her lap.

"We'll try. But if things look bad, I'm turning around."

"Thank you."

Chapter 15

SHE WAS RIGHT about the drifts and she almost did turn around, but turning around required driving on the snow scattered across the pavement in frozen sheets and by then it made no sense to stop and drive back over it. We'd crossed the worst, so we drove on.

In town, we walked towards The Paper World with chins low in our coats and our gloved hands shoved in pockets in a futile effort to avoid onrushing arctic gusts. My laptop bag was slung over my shoulder and the gardener's letters were in my pocket. With the sidewalks and roads abandoned, the quaint town center took on a more austere atmosphere. The buildings held their breath. The trees stood naked with a hierarchy of branches filtering down to slender gnarled fingers, thousands of them, twisting and moaning in a macabre choreography.

The bell above the door rang when we entered and the groan of wooden beams sounded from the direction of the counter where Mr. Bracciolini, with his massive face and body, shifted on his stool. The warmth, the quiet, and the smell of endless stacks of novels should have led to a state of calm. But Flora was on edge. From the drive. From being back in his shop. She was tense, so I was tense.

"You came," he said, smiling. Flora disappeared down an aisle.

"I need to talk with you," I said. He had a cup of

coffee, a nearly empty bag of french fries.

"With pleasure. Come back here and let's talk." He brushed salt from his fingers and gestured to a chair behind the counter and I set the laptop bag on his desk. We'd look at that later. I had other things I wanted to discuss first.

"My grandmother killed herself in the garden."

"No," shaking his head, confident, shooting down my first conviction.

"No?"

"No, she didn't kill herself."

"You think my uncle is responsible for that as well? That he—"

"I'm positive your uncle is responsible for that." His hands folded over his large abdomen, the sage man peering down at me with all of that intelligence, my young mind a purring four-cylinder struggling on the plains, his mind a freight train engine pulling meat wagons up a forty-five-degree incline at 200 miles per hour. Or so it felt.

"Mr. Bracciolini, I'm concerned. I know why your newspaper went out of business."

"Yes."

"I'm unsure. I don't know why you're so, I don't know, invested."

"You're not sure that you can trust me."

"Honestly, yes. I'm, I'm not sure about you."

He smiled. "That's good. And I understand. So let's back up and let me tell you about what happened to my newspaper." Shifting his bulk in his chair, reaching for his coffee cup, taking a long sip, smacking his lips before setting it down. "My father ran the paper back in the 1960s when Elizabeth Frost died by falling down a well and breaking her neck. An accident, the police said, finally, but my father found it strange then and stranger yet when Mr. Frost married the young girl a few months later. How convenient, that the barren wife, aged and not unattractive but also not twenty and stunning, should happen to die in such a peculiar way.

"But my father had no evidence. What is he going to say?" Arms outstretched, question marks in the beds of his upturned hands. "He's a journalist, not a detective, right? We have palm prints from the person who shoved her, preserved in the small of her back? No. Never. She fell into water. She broke her neck. They saw her leg poking up at an odd angle, like a limb sticking out of a mudslide, and that's how they finally found her. And the speed with which they found her was rather astounding. The body was still warm. Could have been warmer if it hadn't been half-submerged. They found her two hours after she was last seen walking towards the garden."

"My grandfather found her?"

"No. The young groundskeeper did, I believe. But he was pointed in the right direction, I'm sure. Anyway, there was no evidence of foul play. Even though Victoria was pregnant by the time Elizabeth died, if you look at when your uncle was born. From that point on, my father was suspicious of everything that family did, and so he watched, and recorded, and when I took over the paper, I watched and added to his records. I made them my own."

"What did you see?"

"Little. There's a long driveway. Trees that hide the house from sight. But the distance the Frost family kept from the rest of us was not just physical. When Victoria arrived, they went silent." He waved his fingers in the air, signifying ghosts, signifying smoke, signifying the rank fog that hung thick over my family tree. "The parties stopped. No one wanted to touch the place. It was anathema. Your uncle was born, and then your mother was born a year or two later and then it was quiet up there for a long time. A soundproof chamber. A vacuum. Until 1982."

"When my grandfather died."

"Yes. And that's when I officially made an enemy of the family by going with a story that highlighted the blunt-force trauma your grandfather, how should we say, experienced. To his head. An accident? It seemed unlikely, though I couldn't say. I presented the facts and let the readership draw their own conclusions."

"You put a spin on it, in other words, that favored your point of view."

"You say tomato, I say tomato. I presented the facts." He sipped at his coffee again. "There are many ways to present facts."

"What do you mean you made an enemy of the family then?"

"Your grandmother was vehemently outspoken in her outrage over the story and took the grieving and passionate widow's role of denouncing what I'd written as pure fantasy, as schlock, as pulp meant to sell papers and nothing more. In other words, I'd touched a nerve."

"Of course, if you made it seem like foul play."

"It was foul play. The readership agreed with me. Just not the police. Not the medical examiner."

"Which didn't help you much with the family, did it?"

"No. And when your grandmother died and I again presented the facts—"

"Which were?"

"Your uncle brought the libel suit against me. I saw where it was going. I acquiesced. Shut the paper down. And devoted myself to this little business here. But it bothers me, still, if you want to know my motivations. It's not revenge so much as it is just wanting to *know*."

"What were the facts of her death?" Leaning forward, pushing.

"The police investigated, of course. And found much bitter argument leading up to her 'suicide.' Between her and your uncle. They talked to Vera Moira and Ben Padrick and Michael Padrick and most all of them were silent on the issue—though they all mentioned arguments between mother and son."

"Michael was Ben's son?"

"Yes, yes, and he left town. They had to drive down to Portsmouth to talk to him. He damn near sprinted out of town after the car accident. I think he wanted to get as far away from that family as possible. Things must have changed for the worse after the accident."

"Meaning?"

"I think your grandmother knew, and your uncle finished tying up all the loose ends. Is it a coincidence that the accident occurred in October and she was dead in December? And take a look at this."

Mr. Bracciolini took a stack of papers from a manila folder, the photos I'd taken and sent him. He'd printed each of them out, in color. He put the picture of the tree down on the desk and tapped the lowest branch.

"How high is that?"

"It's pretty high."

"Five feet? Ten feet?"

"At least ten."

"So how'd she do it? Because that's the branch. I believe, if my memory serves." I had the feeling it did. I had the feeling his memory served him quite well. "It's the lowest one. How'd she kill herself? You think an old lady climbed this tree, tied a noose around her neck, then jumped off? You have more faith in frail bones than I do if you believe that. I'd love to see an old lady climb that big old tree with the agility of a cat. It's laughable."

"She wasn't that old, was she?"

He laughed. "Old enough. Old enough."

"Maybe she threw the rope over."

"With those weight lifter's muscles? Again, I'd like

to see that."

"So what? She brought a ladder."

"Walking down to the garden with a ladder and a rope. No one's suspicious? Come on. No, that woman either had help or was just plain murdered. There was nothing suicidal, nothing solitary about the act. And I printed as much. It was sloppy reporting. Critical of the police for not asking the questions I'm asking you. I was frustrated, and stupid. Your uncle was not happy. End of story."

"But not the end of the story for you. You're still bitter."

"Not so much bitter. Not anymore. Just convinced that I'm right. And that he did it. But why? Another timely date here, alarming coincidence, just like Elizabeth's death, this date of the death of your grandmother. This was not long after the accident that paralyzed that poor girl and killed her mother."

"What do you know about the accident?"

"That's one of the stories I've set aside on microfilm. Let's go downstairs so you can read. Let me see what new things you've brought me. And we'll talk."

***

Flora and I went down into the poorly-lit basement together, down the narrow, steep stairs bordered on one side by clammy stone foundation walls and the other by a wooden banister that bent under Mr. Bracciolini's weight as he followed us, bearing himself up on it, a step at a time. He'd put the "Be Back Soon" sign in the window as it didn't seem possible he'd make it back up the stairs without dropping dead of a heart attack if he didn't first rest for a while, and even then money could have been wagered.

"I wish I had more room," he said, his voice a high wheeze and his face a raspberry red, a shade that would have been jolly if it didn't speak of mortal illness in the weight he carried with him, a suicide vest of fat, "to keep all of this upstairs. But it's too much. And I'm the only one who finds beauty in the machine, a dinosaur, like me."

There was a long work table in the basement with the microfilm machine, yellowed plastic and a large blank screen over a tray where the film ran. Next to the machine shelves stacked with film canisters.

"This one here," he said, with blunt fingers grabbing up a case and plucking out the roll, threading it into the device, "this one here has the accident article. You read that and let me look at what you've got on the laptop. Do you know how to work one of these?"

"Not a clue."

"Hmm," he grunted. I sensed amusement.

With deft movements he flashed through ghostly images of old editions of his family paper and found the story. "It's all on one page. If you want to zoom or focus, it's these knobs."

With a pause and a hand on the table and heavy breathing, he finally turned and shuffled to a chair further down the room, leaving Flora and me alone.

She had her arms crossed across her chest. The basement was cold, musty, like a place you could imagine a murderer bringing his victims. The night we'd spent at the telescope seemed a dream as far-distant as Polaris.

"I don't like this," she whispered, barely audible over the sound of the machine's fan.

"If worst comes to worst, we'll run. Look at him, Flora. Listen to him."

She cast a weary gaze down the room.

"Let's read this. Talk a little more. Then we'll go. Okay?"

"Thirty more minutes."

"Okay. And thank you."

She shook her head and sighed.

Car Accident Claims One, Baby Saved

Karen Werstine, 22, of Chillicothe, lost her life on Hardivant Road Tuesday evening. The vehicle she was driving, a 1985 Toyota Camry, went off the pavement in the 1200 block where the road takes a sharp turn. Signs are posted warning drivers to slow to 15 miles per hour. Investigators believe speed was a factor, and are awaiting toxicology and autopsy results. Paramedics arrived on the scene shortly after receiving a call from a passing motorist. They found an unresponsive Werstine, nine months pregnant, and were able to rush her to Memorial Hospital where doctors successfully delivered the child via C-section, but were unable to save the mother. The child is in neo-natal intensive care in critical condition.

"We see too many accidents here when people disregard the signs. Alcohol is often a factor," reported Sheriff John Willingham. "In this situation we suspect there may have been a medical emergency. There's no sign she made any effort to slow down. We'll know more after the autopsy and after we go over the vehicle."

Her family has been notified, but authorities are still trying to track down the father of the child.

I thought of Emily. What a way to begin a life. Pulled from her dying mother. I turned and saw Flora crying and put my hand on her back. She nudged it away and turned from me.

"This is horrible," she said. "I don't think I want to do this anymore."

She stood up, arms around herself, and went to the stairs.

"Flora…"

"I'll meet you back at the car."

Left alone in front of the glowing box with Mr. Bracciolini staring at me from across the basement.

"It's a tragedy," he said. "I understand why she's upset. It's very upsetting."

"She was poisoned," I said in a tone that was harder than necessary. I was worried about her. "That's what you think?"

"No," Mr. Bracciolini said. He got up and moved across the room, taking Flora's seat, the groan of metal, the smell of stale coffee in his breath. He moved through the film. "There's another article. Here."

Brakes in Hardivant Road Crash Faulty, Sheriff Says

The tragic accident that took the life of a young first-time mother, Karen Werstine, was caused by brake failure, reported Sheriff John Willingham on Friday afternoon. An autopsy revealed no signs of medical emergency preceding the accident. Toxicology reports are forthcoming, but he expects those to be negative as well. The sheriff's office says they discovered a small leak in the brake lines that might have gone unnoticed by the driver.

"Typically you'll have warning signs," Sheriff Willingham stated. "She might have noticed that she had to press down further on the brake pedal because air gets in the line when the brake fluid levels are down. She might have come to the curve and gone to press the brake and found too late that a typical push was not enough or that they didn't work at all. I can't reiterate enough that if you notice any problems, any suspicious fluids pooling where you've had your car parked or anything out of the ordinary when pressing down on the pedal, it's important to get it checked out immediately. Call a tow truck. Get it taken in. Have a mechanic look at it. This was an avoidable accident."

Werstine was on her way back to Chillicothe after visiting the Frost Estate on Folger Road. No other details are available at this time.

"The brakes."

"Yes."

"Michael Padrick."

"I've wondered about that."

"Mr. Bracciolini, I found more, maybe the

evidence that... that can prove this. Or get closer to proving this."

He breathed heavily as I stuck my hand into my pocket and pulled the yellowed papers out.

"I found these, hidden away in the attic of the small house Michael lived in."

Mr. Bracciolini stared at me, the light from the microfilm machine reflecting off of his glasses and obscuring his eyes.

"Let me see."

I held onto them. "I didn't give them to you because I didn't know why you were so interested. This is the article? This is the one that upset my uncle?"

He didn't respond. A hand resting on the worktable. A loose fist.

"It's not, is it?"

After a pause of a few beats he turned back to the machine and took the film out, setting the previous roll down hard on the table, replacing it with another cassette and flashing through images until he found what he was looking for. Then he turned his attention back to me.

"After Victoria died, committed suicide—if you believe that—I published this article. This is what upset him. Read it so you know. If you find me worthy, share your papers."

He stood up.

"Flora's waiting for me."

His heavy breathing.

"Can you make copies?" I asked.

His impatience evident in his sigh.

"Yes."

"I'll bring these back," I said, holding up the letters. "I promise."

The final piece he needed within his grasp and I was being difficult. But I had to know. And I was concerned about Flora.

"How long?" he said.

"Tomorrow. If she'll drive me."

"If she won't, let me know, and I'll come pick you up. At the bottom of the driveway. He wouldn't want me on the estate."

"He has a restraining order against you?"

Mr. Bracciolini laughed and my flight response lessened. He could have held onto me if he'd wanted to. "No. No. Not at all. I suppose he figures a man like me would have a hard time camouflaging himself, huh? And he'd be right. Let me get this printed and you can go catch up with Miss Flora."

Chapter 16

I LEFT HIM in the basement, the copy of the article, "Another Death at the Frost Estate, Few Answers," folded and in my pocket next to the letters.

Flora was sitting in her car staring into space when I returned. She didn't look at me when I sat down, just started the Civic and backed out.

"I don't want anything more to do with this," she said, monotone, emotionless.

"Even if it means finding out the truth?"

"What do you expect to find?" frustration. "What, Marius? And what then? Let people move on with their lives!"

"Let Emily move on too filled with anxiety to leave that goddamn room? I see."

Her hands gripped the steering wheel, white knuckles, painful pressure.

"No one's commanded her to stay in there," I said. "Have they? There's no standing order. She's got a phobia for anyplace other than that room. She's a prisoner of all of this, Flora. She screams so her father will hear her. Or she screams when you or your grandma try to get her to leave the room. She screams because she's trapped in there with ghosts. She's a prisoner of all of this. So feel free to go on pretending it's all okay and we can leave the past alone, but I won't."

Her hands bearing down even harder on the

steering wheel as she drove out of town, the speed limit up but her foot constant on the accelerator, moving slowly, driving as an afterthought, with an SUV tailing impatiently, then swinging around in an angry pass. She didn't notice. Unblinking, straight ahead stare. Face red. Jaw clenched.

"You're not doing this for her," she whispered.

"What does that mean?" the frustration edging into my tone.

"You're doing this for you. Just you." The tilt of her head as if she knew everything. "You could care less whether this makes things better for her or not. You have a vendetta against your uncle because you think he did awful things."

"And you don't? Are you blind!"

She slammed a fist onto the steering wheel and pulled over to the side of the road, braking hard on the gravel and ice-covered shoulder, turning to face me with eyes ablaze.

"I'm not blind to what that man, that Mr. Bracciolini, is doing and doing to you!" she screamed. "He's got you turned and aimed exactly where he wants you and you're just following along, doing his bidding, without stopping to think for a moment, for one moment," pounding the steering wheel, "what it all means and whether what you believe is even anywhere near the truth."

"You think you've got a better explanation for the insanity that's occurred in that fucking house, then by all means, I'm all fucking ears!"

"Don't you swear at me."

"Fuck!" I screamed, reaching for the door handle, a blooming thundercloud of rage and confusion and helplessness within me breaking and flooding forth. With a desire to avoid drowning in the deluge, I got out of the car. I stepped out onto the road and began walking away into the teeth of the cold wind gnawing on my exposed flesh. In the direction of the house? Why not? That's where my business was. An angry, pounding march. It would take hours. Cold, windy hours. Towards a place I didn't even want to be anymore.

"Fuck!" into a wind that didn't give a shit. My mother had left that place and I understood her. I understood something about her finally.

The Civic sat motionless behind me. *I* didn't give a shit? Flora was like the rest of them. Ben and her grandmother and my uncle. Pretending that nothing was wrong when everything was wrong. Pretending that things didn't need remedied when they did, they did, they goddamn did. A child choked with agoraphobia and attended to by women in medical masks. *No one* gave a shit. Another child who hadn't even known this family existed a few weeks ago. Nothing strange about that? What the hell!

"Fuck!" with every muscle tensed and forced into the expulsion of air from my lungs.

Fingers clamping down on the laptop I'd somehow carried out with me. Fingers clamped so hard it felt like my knuckles would burst from the skin and I thought of throwing the computer into the field to my right as hard as I could like a discus with prayers it would shatter.

Leave it alone. Leave it alone? Was she out of her fucking mind? She'd read the same article I had. No sign of braking. The car goes into a tree. A mother who never laid eyes on her child dies of the injuries. The child is permanently injured. Leave it alone? *You're not doing it for Emily*, she said. What the fuck did that mean? I was doing it to find the truth and that would help Emily and it would help me. *What's the alternative, Flora? Huh?*

I stopped and stared ahead at the long, straight stretch of road, miles to go before the next turn and miles after that. Into the teeth of that iron cold gale. The warm tick and burr of the Civic's engine behind me. Filled with anger at its driver and at life and all the circumstances I'd found myself in since birth. She was staring daggers at my back, I was sure.

Standing there with feet apart thinking maybe I could just throw myself in front of the pickup truck coming down the road and be done with it. My mother had followed such an impulse. I envied her. Being through with this madness. Having it off her mind and having a pure black stillness to sink into as the minutes ticked on by for the rest of us, constant nagging reminders in the faces of every clock that this was your life and you had second upon second to go and so many of them unpleasant.

Standing facing the cold reality before me.

Breath coming through my nose in hot bursts. I closed my eyes.

The pickup truck approaching.

What was good about this world?

Tires leaving the gravel behind me. The Civic idling near.

I understood my mother reaching out for the steering wheel. She'd spent her infant, childhood, and adolescent years in the stew of maleficence of that estate. I'd only been there a few weeks. It could drive a person to do it. To do so many unnatural things.

The Civic stopped next to me. The window whirred down.

"Get in, please, Marius."

Eyes closed and breathing in and out through my nose, my breath a rhythm approximating that of my heart. Angry. Red. Angry. Red. Stresses on every beat.

The door opened a fraction and when I opened my eyes and looked down I saw a concerned face, Flora leaning across the seat. I was outside myself in that moment and she was afraid of me. Concerned, but afraid.

I dropped my head and got in. We didn't speak the rest of the drive back. Not even when we drove over the drifts and the tires lost traction and we might have gone off the road in an accident that would have been poetic, considering the day.

Another Death at the Frost Estate, Few Answers

The readers of this paper continue to pick up their papers in the morning and read about events of death connected to the Frost Estate, the palatial home and grounds a few miles south of our city center, in the rolling hills that were grazing lands and woods prior to inventor Lionel Frost's decision to move himself here in the 1920s. My father first reported the death of Elizabeth Frost in a tragic accident all the way back in 1966. Another tragic accident followed in 1982 when Edward Frost, Lionel's son and the father of the current owner, Laurence Frost, died mysteriously after 'wandering' off from his home in search of a daughter who may or may not have run away again. Now we have the news that Victoria Frost, Edward's widow, Laurence's mother, has also met an untimely and, yes, tragic, end. She hanged herself. The police found her lying on the ground under a great sycamore in the mythical garden of the estate that we can only visualize from the details of the police reports as none of us have the right to step behind its walls.

Laurence, the grief-stricken son, apparently stood over his dead mother's body. The hedge clippers he'd used to cut her down lay in the grass, covered, we are to assume, with his fingerprints. But what of his tears and intentions?

There was another accident not long before Victoria's death. It, too, tragic, a word that has become synonymous with the estate. A car accident occurred on Hardivant Road on November 26, Thanksgiving Day, where the road takes a hard turn that any reader of this paper would be much familiar with. There were no tire marks indicating braking of any kind. There was no positive result from the toxicology report or anything in the autopsy that would lead authorities to believe this was anything other than an accident. No, the pregnant mother came into the curve and found that her brakes did not work and was unable to stop and met her fate by meeting with an old oak that took her life and has left her daughter paralyzed, still in intensive care. You are asking yourself now, what does this have to do with anything else mentioned above?

How did the brakes come to malfunction after Karen Werstine, the young mother in question, left the Frost Estate? Are we to assume another unavoidable accident? A family cursed like the Kennedy family to mind-boggling, horrid ends beyond their control? Or is there pre-meditation behind any of these accidents? Not being a mind reader or a fly on the wall or privy in any other way to the conversations and actions that occur on the aforementioned estate, we are left only with observation of fact.

Fact. Laurence Frost is the father of the paralyzed child. This journalist saw him at the scene of the accident. He had trouble walking. He did not cry. The hospital employees report that on the night of the accident he did not stay to see his daughter and he has been back and seen her only once since.

Fact. Karen Werstine drove a 1985 Camry that had never previously had any brake issues per information provided by her father, the owner of the vehicle. It should be noted that he is distraught over the death of his daughter and does not believe that it was purely an accident. He provided vehicle maintenance records to this journalist. The vehicle was well maintained.

Fact. Edward Frost, he of the walk-in-the-woods death, had blunt force trauma to his head. The trauma was blamed on a tree branch he stumbled into. Doctors this journalist spoke to said he would have had to stumble into it at a run to achieve the kind of damage that the autopsy reports being done. Edward was a slightly overweight man not known to exercise.

Fact. Two months after Elizabeth Frost died by falling down a well and breaking her neck, Edward Frost married a twenty-year-old Victoria.

Fact. Victoria was present on the Frost Estate at the time of each of these accidents. Her son was present for all but Elizabeth's.

I will say no more, but allow you, the reader, to draw your own conclusions. And perhaps ask questions. And seek out further answers. Such is your right and mine as citizens of this great nation.

After reading the article I opened doors and went into rooms until I found a phone that worked. Then I made a phone call to Mr. Bracciolini that changed everything.

1966

A WARM JUNE evening. Out on the oval. After dark. A festive atmosphere: string quartet, the popping of champagne corks, conversations that floated loose on still air.

"I'm not going to leave Elizabeth. We need to end this, Victoria. It's… If you're not satisfied with the weekends, with…"

"I'm not."

"What do you want?"

"I want you to leave her. I want you to spend every minute of your time with me tonight. And after tonight."

Edward considered himself an idiot. To have fallen in love with a girl twenty-six years younger than himself. Young enough to be his daughter. Twenty years old. Oh, but she was stunning. Slender and with hair black as a river on a moonless night. White skin. Delicate bones. Small breasts that got lost in his hands. He'd seen her for the first time on a trip to Columbus. She served him dinner. Beer. At the restaurant in German Village. He flirted with her. As she came and went from his table he fantasized about undressing her and worshipping her with his lips. If only he'd kept the thoughts to himself, in the realm of fantasy. He'd opened the box on that one, though, and there was no stuffing it back inside.

He'd gone back to the restaurant the next evening

and would not take no for an answer and they spent the night in a hotel where no one knew him. And many more nights thereafter. He made excuses to go to Columbus every weekend. This night he had been foolish and daring enough to take her up on her request of bringing her down to the estate on the night of one of the soirees he had to throw to keep his society card. These events that his wife, Elizabeth, lived for. A woman he'd never really loved, his wife. A marriage of convenience, or so his father had termed it when Edward had said he wouldn't mind living out his days a widower. He'd only loved Tilda. And Victoria reminded him of Tilda. Nearly the same age, even, as when he'd married her. God help him. Did he love Victoria too? Or was he in love with a reminder of what he might have had?

"Stop flirting with the guests," Elizabeth said, walking over to him, pearl bracelet gracing her wrist, silver necklace with diamond pendant hanging near the seductive upturn of her chest, hair done up elaborately in front of the mirror in their suite by Mrs. Moira. It had taken hours as he'd sipped sherry downstairs and played billiards and wondered when Victoria would walk in the door and he'd catch her eye.

Elizabeth and her graceful smile: "Come here, there's someone I want you to speak with."

He turned and shrugged. Victoria. God, so beautiful, even angry, more so angry, her hair drab and straight and her dress filled out less than his wife's, his spouse with her Grecian curves. Victoria. Plain. Slender.

The most goddamn lovely creature he'd ever seen.

Ten minutes, he mouthed.

Looking at his watch later, trapped in inane conversation. "I may go for a walk," he whispered in his wife's ear. "I need a little air. You know how I feel about these events."

"My husband dislikes speaking to people, yes, I know." Her warm fingertips tracing his jawline.

He kissed her on the cheek and nodded and smiled his way off the oval, past the tents and the reach of the strings of lights hung for the occasion.

"I'm over here," Victoria's furious whisper from the darkness.

He found her and put his arm around her bare shoulders and she twisted away.

"She's my wife, Victoria, what do you expect me to do? End it here? At the party? In front of everyone?"

"Why not? Or do you prefer I hide in the shadows?"

A drunk guest stumbled past, grinning.

"We can't talk here," Edward said.

"I'm going to leave. And you're not going to like what happens next."

He took her hands, pleading. "Let me show you the garden. We'll have some privacy there." Running his hand down her side. Down low to her bare leg. This risqué dress she'd worn. Playing the tart?

There would be others making their way down to the garden later, but secrecy tended to win out down behind its walls.

For the moment, walking through the arched doorway, Victoria and Edward were alone. The moon rose full above them and brought the green rising lawn and the winding floral beds into a hazy sort of focus. They could see enough to navigate by, though Edward could navigate the garden in the darkest night.

"It smells wonderful here, doesn't it?" he said.

"Yes." She bit out the one syllable. He had work to do.

They walked along the gravel path. The satisfying crunch of crushed stones and sand beneath their feet, every minute coming across a new scent, all if it invigorating, intoxicating, fueling his desire to lean her up against a tree and make love to her standing under starlight while promising her anything she wanted.

But he knew how that feeling would change when he'd taken what he needed. For all of her beauty Victoria was also cold. Where his wife was warm and outgoing and maternal, Victoria was reserved and aloof and, he sensed, not necessarily the best guarantor when it came to "for better or for worse."

Then his hand inadvertently rubbed against her hip and he was out of his mind with want of her.

They walked off trail to a serenade of crickets chirring, the fading glowing light of fireflies, the motivating aroma of lavender. He pushed her up against a tree.

"Stop," she said.

"You don't mean it," his hand tracing up the

inside of her thigh. Lost in her heat.

"You use me."

"I love you," he breathed into her neck, kissing his way up to her ear.

"I can't do this anymore."

His hand pulling at the front of her dress.

"Stop," she whispered. "You'll tear it."

But he could hear that she didn't mean it and slid his hand under until he felt her, aroused.

She pushed him back.

"No," she said. "I won't do this anymore."

"Victoria…"

"You need to leave her."

"It's complicated."

"I'm pregnant."

He was confused. His mind still mired in passion. He could still feel her heat on his fingers. He felt ripped out of his skin.

"You're making that up," he said.

She took a step in his direction and slapped him.

He breathed hard, seeing only her silhouette.

"I would never make that up."

She stormed past him and he grabbed her arm.

She tried to pull free. "Let me go!"

"Stop shouting," his quiet plea. "Don't… Just, stay, we need to talk about this."

"Talk about how you know a man?"

"What?"

"Who can take care of it, right?"

"No," he said. He didn't know. He didn't know if

that's what he meant. He and Elizabeth had proven incapable of having children. He wanted children. He was getting old. But Victoria. Elizabeth was much more the mothering type. He couldn't imagine what Victoria would do with a child. Maybe he would hire a nanny. He could have Victoria. Whenever he wanted. He wanted her now. They could go away together. In the open. On the beaches of the Mediterranean. Her smile on the streets of Rome.

"No," he said again.

"Then what?"

He folded her hands in his.

"I want to be with you," he said.

"Then you know what you have to do."

"I will."

He reached his hand down for her again but she pushed it away and marched back the way they'd come.

***

The next morning he changed his mind. He sent a man to her room. Someone he trusted. He asked the man to escort her out. Drive her home. Give her money. Tell her she'd be taken care of.

A week later Elizabeth died in an accident. When they found her Edward's face turned white as a ghost and he tried to smother his weeping with his hands.

Victoria's father, his breath touched by the odor of death, paid him a visit soon thereafter. And another chapter closed on Edward's life.

V
Pursued by Furies

Chapter 1

I STOOD SHIVERING in my winter coat at the end of the driveway wondering if he'd come. The house had been silent, asleep when I'd crept out, though I wondered, I always wondered, if eyes peered out from shadows marking my progress.

Headlights appeared down the road followed shortly by the soft hum of an engine and I stepped back into the cover of trees to see who approached. A black Jeep Grand Cherokee pulled to a stop at the end of the driveway and I saw his bulk filling the front seat and darted out of hiding to the passenger door and climbed in.

"Portsmouth?" Mr. Bracciolini said, pulling away.

"You want the facts, don't you?"

"Michael Padrick? Hmm. I made some calls last night. After receiving your message. He's still there. Or still listed there. Michael Padrick?"

He drove south on winding country roads and wide state routes, through the low wooded hills of southern Ohio. I pulled the sheaf of letters from my pocket and read them aloud. Then I told him what I thought.

Mr. Bracciolini sipped at his coffee and wiped his pale lips and considered what he'd just heard.

"You're mistaken, I think, in your conclusion."

"I don't think so."

"You think the gardener had a relationship with

your uncle. I don't believe that."

"Then what's your explanation?"

"It was somebody else, Marius. Think about it. Who else could it be?"

The picture in the frame. But why would she want to kill a child?

Chapter 2

MICHAEL PADRICK LIVED in a trailer park near the railroad tracks in the small city hugging the curve of the Ohio River. We drove up the lane into the park, the sound of gravel popping underneath the tires, and stopped a few units down. Mr. Bracciolini took some time to get out of his SUV, the shocks groaning in relief as he shifted his weight from the vehicle to his own overburdened knees. He winced as we walked along.

"I'm okay," he insisted, but his breathing contradicted him.

He went up a step in front of Michael's trailer and knocked his blunt knuckles against the flimsy door. We could hear movement within and I saw the blind dip in the family room window. No one came to the door.

"He's there," I whispered.

"I know he's there." Mr. Bracciolini knocked again. "Michael? Michael Padrick?"

Stillness. The wind hitting the gap between the trailers, rattling aluminum, the creaking stress of winter tree branches.

"We're here about Victoria, Michael."

More movement from the blinds. The sound of footsteps thumping across the trailer floor. The front door opened a few inches, then more.

In some ways Michael looked like his father. In the slim eyes and the perfect width of his shoulders and the sallow cheeks and the flushed red nose from all of the drinking. The faint scent of cheap red wine on his breath. He differed from his father in other ways, though. A yellow pallor clung to him like a shroud showing signs of a liver near the end of its use. His oily hair possessed a distinguishing flatness, drabness. He wore a white undershirt covered in faint grease stains and gray sweat pants with fraying holes in the knees. I couldn't imagine his father letting himself go in such a manner.

"I know you," Michael said. His voice was not the voice of the letter. There was no passion or erudition in it. It was deep and it was worn out. It was slouching towards death.

"I'm Jerry Bracciolini."

"I said I know you. What do you want?"

Distrust in the way Michael glared at Mr. Bracciolini. But I could also see how exhausted he was. As if he'd been running. For quite a while now.

"May we come in?"

Michael stared in my direction. Snorted. Closed his eyes for a moment and shook his head.

"Yeah, yeah, yeah, come in."

The steps groaned to support Mr. Bracciolini and he and I went past Michael. He closed the door behind us. A lamp in the living room with a low-wattage bulb left shadows along the dusty edges of the room. A ragged sofa with itch-inducing upholstery. A small TV on a flimsy black particle board cart. A VCR and video boxes—John Wayne, Jimmy Stewart, Steve McQueen.

Cigarettes and cat-litter and warm beer and canned dinners.

"It's no Frost Estate," Michael said without humor.

"Nothing wrong with that," Mr. Bracciolini said, eyeing the sofa and the recliner and seeming to come to the conclusion that neither would quite hold him. Michael dragged a kitchen chair into the room.

"Have a seat."

I sat on the sofa near a calico cat curled into itself napping, one wary eye upon the visitors, its ribs rising and falling within the soft rhythms of sleep.

Michael sat in the recliner and there we were with the metal sighs of the trailer and the far off whistle of a train.

"Who's the boy? Who are you? I see a certain family resemblance."

"Hannah's son."

"Hannah had a son?" He peered more closely, then nodded. "I see. You inherited the gray eyes. She didn't. Hmm. So what do the great discredited journalist and Hannah's son want with me?"

"My name's Marius."

"Marius," an acknowledgment.

"I have something. That you wrote."

I pulled the letters from my pocket and he closed his eyes and inhaled and held his breath as the long submerged memory resurfaced.

"You said, in here," the soft rustle of papers, "that you hoped someday someone would know. I know."

He exhaled but still didn't open his eyes.

"Michael," Mr. Bracciolini said, voice warm and insistent, "can you help us?"

Eyes moving beneath his lids like a dreamer in REM sleep. "With what?"

"All evidence seems to point to Laurence being the perpetrator of great crimes. But I think you'll tell us a different story."

"Laurence is a bastard. No good. I'd fear him if I were you."

"You fixed the brakes on her car, didn't you?"

He shook his head and pinched the bridge of his nose and then his body shuddered with the onset of the tears. We let him cry. We didn't get up to comfort him. We looked at him as he gasped, occasionally, and continued to shake his head, his weathered hand, beat by soil and sun, hiding his face. Those hands had wielded a simple tool and changed Emily's life. Those hands.

After a few minutes during which I stared down at the cat and stroked its soft fur and Mr. Bracciolini kept his eyes on the defeated man, he regained some composure.

"Laurence is no good," he said, exhaling hard, "but it wasn't him who asked me to do it. Are you kidding me? He loved her. Maybe the only person he ever loved. But he was also the only person she ever loved."

"She?"

"Victoria. You said it. You said it at my door. You seem to know, Mr. Bracciolini. You seem to know everything and always have. So why don't you tell me what happened. Come on. Why don't you say it?"

Mr. Bracciolini shook his head. "No, Michael. We're here to listen to you tell it. You have a conscience."

A snort. "Yes, I have a conscience." He worried his hands for a while, his tongue darting out over his lips, his voice finally telling it, soft this time, wistful at times, but then the hurt took over. "This is my penance. But I wonder about you. I really do."

Mr. Bracciolini put his hands up in a *You've got me* gesture. Michael blew air through his lips and peered to the side and then started talking.

1989

LONELY. THAT'S HOW Victoria felt. Walking up the path from the garden to the house, trailing her hands over the pine branches and soft feathered prairie grass in the open instances of landscape where they let it grow. Lonely. How long had it been since she'd touched a man? Had her back stroked? The back of a finger trailing down her cheek? Her hips grasped, moments of mad passion with the sheets kicked off the bed and the outside world evaporating in a whirl of never-mind, and never-mind. Lonely. Her husband dead seven years. Her daughter fled the estate. Her son, Laurence, off visiting that woman he'd met and fallen in love with at college and whom he would probably want to marry. Lonely.

The door to the greenhouse was open and she saw the gardener moving around inside, tending to the plants lined up in colorful rows.

Victoria stood in the doorway, silent, watching him. His fingers with knowledge of living things. Expert plucking of leaves and distribution of soil. The residue that remained as he turned and she saw broad square shoulders and the wet sweat of exertion. The fuzz at the base of his neck and the hard flexion of muscles in his triceps.

He gasped, startled, when he turned with watering can and saw her, water sloshing out of the top and splashing his shirt and pattering down onto the floor.

"Sorry," she said.

"You're quiet."

She smiled.

"Can I help you with anything?" he asked. The respect of youth.

"No."

Mirth in her grin. She felt like she hadn't tried it on in a long time. Seven years since her husband had died and what had she done since? Driven a daughter out? Seen Laurence through college? Managed the estate? What had she done for herself since his death?

She took a step into the greenhouse, slim in her summer dress, and leaned back on one of the tables. Was she still attractive? Forty-three years old. Not the graceful, alluring twenty when she'd snagged her husband's attention in the German Village restaurant. Miles and years and the inevitable and inexorable tug of gravity on the flesh.

"Vati," *she said,* Father, "*I've met a man.*"

"*Hmm?*"

"*At the restaurant.*"

He had his Beethoven on and his newspaper out and his sausage and potatoes in front of him. Her mother, washing dishes, turned off the faucet and left the kitchen.

His hard gray eyes peering at her over the top of the paper. Holding the paper still. A warning sign.

She pressed on.

"*He's rich and he wants me to go down to see him at his home. He's going to leave his wife for me.*"

She never knew what he thought he was looking at. The stare, when he saw his wife or daughter. Did he see a human? She didn't know. Only that sometimes he woke up in the middle of the night sweating and shouting and holding his arm out before him like he was holding a gun and squeezing a trigger and being overrun.

Do not touch him then. Oh, no.

One night she'd had to pull him off of her mother as he choked her on the bed, her face gone from red to purple and her eyes rolling back in her head, Victoria screaming, "Vati! Vati! Vati!" and his eyes open and empty and she hadn't known if he was asleep or awake or in a trance or just being himself.

In the kitchen with the smell of sausage and sauerkraut and potatoes and dish soap, the steam rising from the kitchen sink, greasy pans soaking.

"He's rich?"

They'd struggled for a long time. A beer delivery man. With a bad back. And probably cancer—the cigarettes, the coughing, now coughing blood. His employer looked upon him as a liability but didn't fire him for fear. Her father felt shame, that he was seen as a liability. That had never been the case in his long life. And he would not, or could not, turn to the government for assistance.

"Very rich, Vati."

"Is he Jewish?"

She knew better. "Of course not!"

"He wants you to go down to his home? Where is this home?"

"It's an estate, he said," her eyes gleaming. "It's huge. They have butlers and maids and groundskeepers and gardeners.

Garages with gleaming luxury cars. They have parties with their wealthy friends. He told me they bring in orchestras. Outside, under the stars… And a garden a person could get lost in. Roses and streams and—"

"And he told you, this man, that he's going to leave his wife? For you?" He smiled, then, and chuckled, and the coughs tremored in prelude and then had their way with him but the humor never left his eyes even as the pain-triggered tears rolled down his rough red cheeks. His voice high and strained when the hacking had subsided back to tremors. "I don't think so."

She grabbed a glass saltshaker from the counter and threw it at his head. He batted it away and slid the chair back and stood up with that cool dead rage in his eyes, then bent hard at the waist followed by the thud of elbows on the tabletop, his knees sinking towards the floor, slumped over like someone had shoved a dagger in his back. Consumed by the pain, the companion of recent years, the ultimate retiring force, he curled over, immobile, groaning.

"He told me!*" she shouted.*

Coughing led to worsening back spasms, arms draped over the table trying to push himself upright, knocking his half-eaten dinner to the floor and crying out in anguish.

Her mother (who would be dead of a heart attack in a matter of weeks) came in and helped to get him calmed and, after much time spent immobile, into bed. When he'd had his medicine and his temper had subsided he called Victoria in to sit next to him.

"He won't leave her," he said, his eyes sage and dreamy, altered by the medicine. "But if she dies…"

"Vati!"

He chuckled again. And looked away from her.

"You take an old man too seriously. Look at me. One day, not long ago, I could have done it. I could have. That man you speak of? He'll leave you pregnant, and then leave you alone, and you'll be lucky to get a check in the mail once a month. Hmm? A little thing like you. Leave his wife for you? Hmm? Not unless she leaves in a coffin, Victoria."

Michael stood there holding the watering can in one hand, bicep and forearm stiff, the wide eyes of youth upon her. She had been about his age when her husband had wooed her, hadn't she?

Mischief in the expression with which she regarded him. The landscaper's son. The boy who'd grown up running around the estate when he wasn't walking down the hill to wait for the bus or helping his father tend to the pathways or paint the house. Now grown and employed and his chest heaving there and in those eyes, what, the glint of a fire burning deeper?

She pushed herself up onto the table and crossed her legs at the ankles, tucking her legs back, this thin layer of cotton that didn't serve as much of an impediment to what she could see he wanted.

"You don't have help with this?" she asked, gesturing her chin at the room full of plants.

"No, it's okay."

Her lower lip tucked under teeth.

"You're just going to stand there with that?"

"Oh, sorry." He looked down at the watering can and up at her, embarrassed.

"Don't mind me," she said.

He took a step in her direction and her heart flashed, wondering what it would be like to have those broad hands on her and whether they'd expertly tend to her as well as they did his plants. Whether they knew what to do with a woman.

"I…"

"Yes?"

"I need to get…"

"Here?" she said and made no effort to move.

"Yes," blushing, "I need to get to the flowers back there."

She didn't shift.

He took a step closer. She could smell the day of work on him. Dirt and sweat. The outdoors. He smelled good. Not like her husband always had, the sedentary man who did nothing but sit in the library reading books, or sit at his desk writing in his diary or writing checks. She reached out and ran her fingertips over Michael's forearm and he drew it back. She reached out and pulled it back towards her, his forearm resting on her lap.

She didn't speak. Her eyes traced up his arm to his shoulder to the pulse that beat under his neck to his face and his eyes that peered down and away from her. She put her palm on his cheek. Brought her other hand to his side, tugging at the shirt to get her hand beneath it, to touch his hot skin, the tense muscles of his abdomen.

"You're shaking," she whispered.

"Mrs. Frost…"

"Victoria."

"I…"

"You're not sure?" running her fingertips over his side, nails drawn across his lower abdomen. "It's okay."

He turned his eyes to her then and found her wanting and then it was madness with clay pots spilled and pushed off the table to shatter and soil scattered everywhere as he pushed her dress up and she slid out of her underwear and her nails in his flesh as his clothes came off and her bra in awkward, needy fumbling and heat encompassed them in the solar heated room where it, the sex, the fucking, the hedonistic abandonment to sense and desire, would occur for the first time and be over rather too quickly but there would be time later to reacquaint and further explore and know what was not yet known.

***

With gritted teeth and cheeks that still burned—whether from exertion or embarrassment, he wasn't quite sure—Michael scraped dirt back into the unbroken pots and took a broom and began to sweep up the broken glass, fumbling the shards back onto the floor the first time he tried to dump them into the garbage bag, having to squat down and pick them up with fingertips shaking and opening, at war with his wits. He let go of the bag and held the fingers of one hand with the fingers of the other and only then did he seem to regain control. Surrounded by the familiar smells of soil and fertilizer and chlorophyll but also her and their act. Confusion.

She was stunning, still, as she always had been, and maybe he had fantasized about her a time or two, though in truth Anna Moira was his first crush and a woman he still thought of, often with sadness since she'd gone and married and had children. There were the occasional flings with women from the bars in town. And he knew, at some point, he'd leave the estate and get a job nearby and find a wife—whether under the auspices of love, whether consuming passions or not—and settle in for long years of labor and holiday calm and children and all that life entailed. Never, never did he imagine anything like what had just occurred. What the hell did it mean? He could smell her on his fingertips and thought he'd go mad.

He stood up and the world went out of focus, the green and the white light around him bleeding into each other. Just a moment, tottering, with his hand out on a table for support. He went into his house and to the sink and washed away the evidence from his hands and then took off his clothes and turned on the shower, the hot water pounding against him as he took the bar of soap and scrubbed himself raw. Had it really occurred? He closed his eyes. He could see her. His head bowed under the warm, nettling downpour. It had been real. And what was this feeling? Lust or love or something other? Confused, but he'd welcome it again. God, he would welcome it again. He found himself craving that contact, craving her, her teeth biting down on his thumb in that mad push towards climax. Hips that could not have pressed any harder against him. The water washing around him. The *need* of her. Cocaine and heroin and alcohol had nothing on this, on this, on the physics in the pull of her eyes and what had been revealed when he'd pulled her dress up. God. He felt his chest constrict and it was with single-mindedness that he walked out of the steam-filled bathroom, wrapped in a towel, to find his father sitting at his desk.

"A bit early for a shower, isn't it?"

***

For Victoria, there was no confusion, only a brief amazement that she had waited so long.

"You look happy," her son said, not altogether kindly, more mocking and cutting, pulling on his leather jacket at the door.

"Riding your bike again?" she said, feigned smile.

"Going to see Karen." Watching her face for the reaction.

"Have fun."

Turning and sweeping up the stairs and not giving him the satisfaction.

***

In her room she stopped inside her door with her

arms wrapped around herself breathing heavily, her mind off the gardener and what they'd done and on her son, on his motorcycle leaning down those twisting roads to see the girl and to spend the evening with her and to stay out all night. She'd disliked that girl the first time she saw her. Knew she was up to no good. Couldn't bear the thought of Laurence with her. How she'd control him, lead him away. Take him away.

The door opened behind her and tapped her in the back, snapping her out of her thoughts.

"Oh, my goodness, I'm sorry."

Mrs. Moira.

"It's okay," Victoria said, and disappeared further into her suite of rooms, into her bedroom and then bathroom where she too stripped down and stood under a hot flow of water thinking about how the last member of her family was about to leave her. The one she loved most dearly. She began to cry and let the water consume her. How had she ended up here?

No, here. In the shower. Was it that late already? And why the soil swirling near the drain?

***

Again with Michael, this time in his bed, late at night. Again the next night. A morning, with the threat of being caught, feverish and somehow more intense. Again that night. And many more in the weeks thereafter.

In late September lying on the narrow bed in his

little home running a hand down her side he asked her for a picture because he didn't feel that he could live in the moments he was without her.

Yes, a picture, but he would have to keep it tucked away somewhere. Discreet. As they had managed to be thus far.

Absolutely.

***

"Off again, I see," Victoria said in the morning in the dining room as Laurence stood from the table, finishing with his breakfast as she walked in to have hers.

He didn't respond.

"With her?"

"Her name is not Her. It's Karen. Karen, Mom. Karen."

"Why do I need to learn her name? You'll leave her. Like you have the rest. It's a waste of my time. And yours. I don't understand you. Have your fun and leave them. It's better that way. Trust me. Look at what your father became."

He shook his head and was gone from the room.

"Karen," she said, dissecting the harsh phonetics of the name, finding fault in it. "Karen."

October

"YOU'RE NEVER HERE anymore," she said.

Standing in the doorway to his room. Laurence sat at his desk, a book open to his left, a pad of paper in front of him.

"I'm here now."

She walked over and picked up the book.

"Pablo Neruda. You're copying poetry?"

He blushed and put his hand over what he was writing.

"I'm not going to leave her, you know," he said.

"You will."

"She's pregnant."

Under heavily lidded eyes Victoria stared down at the scribbling of this young romantically inclined son of hers.

"I see."

"We're going to be married."

She nodded, but did she hear?

***

After. Propped on an elbow. Michael on his back staring up at the ceiling of his cozy little home as an early cold front stirred up leaves outside. Not for the first time wondering where this was all going, whether it was just a fling to her or whether it was something more. The fear that she someday might tell him that it was enough, that it had been pleasurable, but it was time for them both to move on, she was too old for him (and she was, in truth) and he didn't want to be taking care of an old lady when he was in his prime.

After. Propped on an elbow. Running his fingers over her breasts. Watching her react. She looked at him in all seriousness and he felt that something was going to change tonight.

"Michael," she said. A ponderous tone.

"Yes?"

"Would you," she said, patting his chest with her small warm hands, "do something for me, if I asked you, something…" a sigh and a pause and a moment of indecision in the furrowing of her brow.

"Anything, Victoria." Kissing the crown of her head. Breathing her in.

She smiled at him as if that sealed it. She ran her hands down his chest and he felt warmth within.

"Would you really?" she said.

"Anything."

And then she told him what she was thinking, and sank down the bed and awakened him with her mouth, and when she left, he sat at the edge of his bed, hunched over, his fists buried in his temple and his heart caught stuttering in this quandary. How could he do that? Her picture in his nightstand drawer. He dreamed of her. Of being with her. How could she ask him to do that?

He stood up and walked over to the desk and opened the drawer where he kept his pens and paper, putting a sheet out. Pausing. Thinking. What to write? What to say to her? Because following her request he had found his speech frozen. And she had climbed down his body and not given him the ability to speak.

***

A few days later, after the act was done. He stood in front of his sink washing away the grease, scrubbing it from under his fingernails, feeling that he could never go back.

The water running. The smell of the oil poisoning the bathroom air.

He had time, still, to run up to the house, interrupt their dinner, tell her not to go.

His heart pounding. Pounding within his chest. He pressed his head against the mirror. Tapped it. Soft. Forehead to glass. Then hard. Forehead to glass. Then harder. Then ceasing. Stopping before he broke the mirror and cut himself. Staring at his reflection.

"Who are you?"

He could have had a wife and a family and the holidays and a job as a laborer with nothing more than the mundane satisfactions of life. Humanity was never that simple. People had needs. And vices. What had he done?

He left the bathroom and went to his desk. His hands shook as he took up the paper and pen again.

***

Victoria didn't like the look of the girl. She'd invited her for Thanksgiving, yes, her son happy at the truce, that his mother appeared to be accepting of the decision he'd made.

The girl. Karen. A very round belly. Pregnant with a child kicking in there. The swollen ankles and swollen cheeks. It would be soon, wouldn't it? Or it would not.

Victoria played cordial at the dinner.

"Your parents must be very excited." Feeling the flesh in her cheeks rise and her eyes warm, showing teeth in her smile.

"They are," Karen said. Doe-eyed. Beautiful. She could see what her son saw in the girl. Fragile, though, a meager frame. Rather like her own, Victoria thought. And Hannah's. But Victoria had strength and this girl did not. Victoria had been tempered in her father's home. Not everyone could see her hardness, but it was there.

Karen looked with affection to Laurence who smiled and patted her hand. How many times now, his hands on her, since this girl had come in? Around her waist and through her hair and grabbing a handful of her ass as he'd planted a kiss on her cheek when he thought she wasn't looking.

Victoria smiled as Mrs. Moira came in with the first course, the salad and warm bread.

"It smells wonderful," Karen said.

"Yes," said Victoria. "It does, doesn't it? You'll enjoy living here very much, won't you?"

"That's just it, Mom," Laurence said. "We're going to get a place of our own, after the wedding. We want to live closer to Karen's parents."

"Oh," Victoria, forcing herself to continue to smile, thinking, *hmm, maybe not. Maybe you won't be moving.* Wondering about Michael and whether he had done like she'd asked and the complications that lay ahead in dealing with him. Put a hand on him and he'd stop thinking immediately. Put her mouth on him and he'd pluck his own eyes out with a grapefruit spoon. "Well, that's the first I've heard of that." Was her son that driven to get away from her? What would he think after tonight? She picked up her wine glass and looked at him over the top of it as she sipped and then licked the red from her upper lip.

***

When the dinner had concluded, Victoria walked with the couple to the door.

"You're sure you wouldn't want to stay the night?" Victoria asked, the gracious hostess. "It's no trouble to make up a room for you."

"No, I can't. I have a doctor's appointment in the morning. Getting close, you know."

"Oh, well, maybe another time."

"Call me, when you get home," Laurence said, holding her hands in his.

Victoria took a few steps back, sick to her stomach watching this treacle-sweet display of affection.

"I will," Karen with a hand on his chest.

"Are you sure you don't want me to drive? I worry about you. And the baby."

His hand on that pulsing bulge of flesh. Victoria felt the smile rigged to her face as if by wires. Goddamn that bulge of flesh and what it represented.

"Laurence. I'm fine. Really."

"I know you are."

A kiss. In front of her. She hated it. She stopped looking at them.

"I'll walk you out."

Karen turned to Victoria with an expression of warmth, wide open eyes, the innocent expectation of a long relationship.

"It was a pleasure to finally meet you," Karen said.

"Likewise, dear," Victoria.

Karen walked over and wrapped her arms around Victoria and Victoria froze before patting the girl on the back. That belly pressing against her. She couldn't help but envision the night this creature, this thing, had been conceived, and felt she might vomit.

Laurence, observing, must have seen the cloud cross his mother's face. Did he take pleasure in it? She thought he did. Thinking the breach would be permanent soon. Not knowing she was many moves ahead of him.

He walked Karen out to the car and should have noticed the awkwardness of the car's glide down the drive, the stubbornness of brakes that'd had no former idiosyncrasies. But he thought nothing but of Karen and their daughter and the future and the look on his mother's face when he'd told her he was moving out.

***

Victoria walked up the stairs to her room, her arms motionless at her side as she ascended and passed through the halls, her footsteps muffled and around her the serenade of ticking clocks.

***

Laurence sat near the phone in worry. 10:02. She should have been home. 10:05. 10:15. The time ticking inexorably on and the phone didn't ring. 10:17. 10:32. He picked it up and dialed and spoke to her parents. No, she wasn't home, and they, too, were beginning to worry. 10:42.

He put on his jacket and went out to his car and drove the winding roads towards town and the state route north and when he came upon the flashing lights he knew what had been done.

The police notified him. The mother had been taken to Memorial Hospital. They didn't know what had happened prior to the accident. But it didn't look good. In all likelihood she'd lost consciousness and wasn't even aware when the car made impact.

He could see that it wasn't good. The compression in the hood of the car. It had launched itself off the curve and into the staunch trunk of an old oak.

He stood swaying before regaining his senses and stumbling towards his car.

***

Jerry Bracciolini, the reporter, watched this and wondered. Had this young man's past finally caught up with him?

***

At the hospital they asked him who he was.

Who was he? The husband? No. The boyfriend? Yes. The father? What did that mean?

A commotion. A bell ringing. The rush of nurses and doctors and he knew then what would be. He turned around and walked back out of the emergency room even as the receptionist said, "Sir? Sir?"

He climbed into his car and he drove home.

***

She was sound asleep in her large bed under a pile of blankets.

He jabbed at the light switch.

"What did you do?"

"What are you talking about?" Not sitting up, her voice the tepid voice of a woman waking from sound slumber.

He knew what he would do to her. He'd planned it

before, once, but then bottled it up, telling himself it was not okay to do what he had in mind. That society frowned upon such things. That what had occurred in that earlier instance did not warrant it.

This did warrant it. This did.

***

Michael read about it the next morning in the local paper. His father knocked on the door and then walked in.

"Terrible, isn't it?" Ben said, a sad voice but hard, critical eyes.

Michael stared down at the table.

"Isn't it?" Ben said again.

Michael looked up at his dad and began to weep.

***

Victoria didn't come to see him after that. He wrote. A little more. And then he left. He disappeared south. He'd have nothing more to do with her or anyone from this place. He'd make a life out of trying to forget how he'd gotten his hands dirty and his soul damned.

***

She wandered down one day and found Michael gone. Panic set in. What if he'd left something behind?

Something that pointed to her? The police were
suspicious and had asked questions of everyone who
had been there that night, had anyone seen a person go
into the garage?

*"No, officer. It's horrible, though, isn't it? My poor son…
He's just destroyed."*

She pulled open drawers. Goddamn him if he left
any evidence, any confession. Sitting on his desk the
picture she'd given him. No longer hidden. Mocking
her. She knocked it over. She ripped at the curtains and
pulled them down on that wretched photo and she
should have taken it but there was more to do. She
pulled out the drawers and scattered their contents
across the floor. What if he spoke? What would she do
if he told? He was out of her control. She hated it. She
hadn't counted on that, this man she'd led around by
the libido for the past few months.

Ben walked in.

"He's gone," he said.

"I can see that. Leave me alone."

"He won't say anything. It's best just to leave this
all behind us, isn't it?"

He watched her as she continued to open things
and run her hand over out-of-sight surfaces. She hadn't
heard him.

"It's over, Victoria."

Pulling the mattress off the frame.

Ben left her alone.

***

"You're going to kill yourself," Laurence told his mother that night in her room.

"What are you talking about?"

"Your time is done here. You're going to kill yourself."

"Laurence…"

"I want you to write a letter."

"I'm not writing anything. Get out of my room. You're insane."

He left.

***

The next evening she walked down to the garden as she often did after dinner when nothing but the mums still bloomed and the roses shrank and curled in on themselves. He stayed behind, watching as she stopped to touch the plants, the uncertainty of November weather, cold and snow a week or two ago and now thunderheads and flashes of lightning in the west.

He didn't know what it was she thought of on her walks. She had murdered and now stepped lightly through a wealth of natural riches without the slightest seeming guilt. She had done murder. He thought of Karen and he thought of his daughter and he saw this woman who moved about on two legs with a gleam in her eyes touching these growing things with the scent and electricity of rain and storm foreshadowed on the wind. The child, Emily... The name Karen had chosen when the ultrasounds had shown they were having a girl. After her beloved maternal grandmother. Laurence saw Karen in the girl. The life they could have had. The instances when he could have predicted what his mother would do and stop her. He couldn't look at Emily without all of the guilt and longing and sadness hurling itself into his gut and knocking him to the floor.

The nurse in intensive care asking him if he'd like to hold her.

"No. I don't think that'd be a good idea."

The nurse's expression of discomfort in his presence.

Could he do it? She was slender enough. He'd considered it for years. How to do it without being caught, that was the rub. And did he care anymore if they discovered he killed her? No, he didn't think he did. *So don't worry about it.*

He followed her towards the sycamore. She ascended the hill and paused on the slight rise with her back to him. Lightning flashed and thunder let loose its ponderous roar.

He covered the last few yards at a sprint and lowered the noose over her head even as she turned in astonishment to see who had come upon her so swiftly.

Eyes wide in acknowledgment and terror and a hard need to still breathe. She reacted by attempting to slip her fingers between the twine and the fine skin of her neck. Sensual fingers fond of touching flowers and dabbling in streams and manipulating others into getting their own hands dirty. He cinched the noose further. It had little give in it. She couldn't pry it away. One hand tried. The other grasped for him but he stepped away.

He had a few moments to toss the rope over a branch of the sycamore and lift her. Or leave her alone to disentangle herself and live knowing it could come at any time and it could have come on this night.

God. She was his *mother*.

The lunacy.

The meandering lectures. Sober-eyed threats to his sister: *I'll blind you with this meat thermometer, Hannah. We'll see the temperature of your eye when all the fluid drools out.* A smile. A wink. A joke. But the pointed end still held out in front of her.

His father harangued and beat. The day she threw her bowl of soup in his face and caused him to scream in pain as the hot liquid dribbled down and stained his shirt a faint red, pieces of potatoes and carrots clinging to him. He had drifted away like smoke from a fire that burned violently and then suddenly ceased: wispy, faint, and then gone. In the library. Reading and writing. And the final argument.

Hannah. Had this woman ever even loved the girl? The baby just home from the hospital and she'd probed the soft spot on her skull with her thumb. *It'd be like punching through a rotten tomato, wouldn't it?* The girl who couldn't even focus her eyes at that point never had a chance. Nor when she began to lock her in the hall closet. Starting at age one. And when Hannah outgrew that, the shed in the garden. Once and again till it became rote and Laurence even tasked with leading her there.

Had it all been a compendium of horrors? No. But she knew how to suck the atmosphere out of the entire estate for weeks at a time.

These thoughts that flashed in an instant as he looked at the sturdy branch eight feet up and nearly thick around as his waist.

Locking Hannah in the shed for days the last time when the threat had been made. The girl had nearly died. His father *had* died. Karen had died. His daughter was paralyzed. His sister was gone.

His mother.

The branch.

"Laurence! Laurence!" those rasping shrieks slightly muffled by the pressure cinching her neck. The first drops of rain falling and lightning that flashed so near his vision all around was white and the boom of the thunder nearly knocked him to the ground.

It was time. In her frantic pulls at the rope she hadn't yet seen where he had been looking. But now she did.

It was a race. He sprinted for the branch and threw the rope over as the heavens above opened up and she tried to run in the opposite direction but she tripped and fell and it was too late. The rope over his shoulder as her fingers continued to work the thinnest gap between rope and neck and he cinched it even further by continuing to pull.

"Laurence! What are you doing…" Sheer cornered

terror in her eyes.

The last word drowned out as her feet left the ground and then she was incapable of speaking. Ever again. He felt the burden of her weight but he kept her a foot off the ground, then more, lifting her pirouetting into the air. The friction of rain on the branch making it easier for the rope to slide over it and slide down, slipping down, wrapping the rope around his forearms and pulling back on it. Her mad swinging struggles to release herself, kicking, causing his hold to stutter, Laurence looking to the heavens and thinking it would be okay if lightning struck him now because he could be done with this and never have to think about this moment and what he was doing and what had led here and what would come after, God help him, what would fill his moments hereafter.

Her body moved in sick orbits, thin fingers still trying to insinuate themselves between cutting twine and her faintly breathing neck, those gargling, horrid gasps, the rope fighting him as he tried to hold it in place, to keep her aloft until it was finished and he could do the rest of what it was he needed to do.

She held onto her life for a long time. A hard woman and from what? What in her own past? Only hints. Confusion in her eyes quickly gave way to sadness and then pain and then vacancy. She had a hard time letting go.

In the end her eyes half-lidded and her face asphyxiated, blue, her mouth distorted and agape, her tongue half chewed through, the tip of it poking through pale lips. He thought he saw the flicker of a stare loaded with intelligence. But her chest didn't rise and fall and he let go of the rope. Her slender body hit the ground with a soft inhuman thud. A sack of potatoes. A sack of grain. An object.

He left her there and in his bathroom with sopping wet clothes and hair plastered across his forehead he looked at the rope burns on his arms. The wounds ached. They wouldn't disappear before the police came to investigate. He hadn't counted on that. There could be no prison, he knew that much. He'd find another way out if he had to.

***

Later that night, when the storm had moved east, he came back to the garden with a ladder.

Clammy, pale, his stomach empty and unsettled, he laid the ladder against the branch. How was he going to get her aloft again and tie this off? To make it look the suicide? How was it possible?

"You need help."

He startled at the voice.

Ben walked into the clearing with a flashlight.

"And you'll want to make it look like you did something about it. Like you were trying to save her. Don't bother putting her back up there, right? Let's get the noose off, tie the rope up, then cut it with these shears. We'll need to make you look irrational first, because a son, coming across his beloved mother in such a state? You wouldn't be thinking straight. What would you do?"

"I'd light a fire beneath her."

Ben didn't smile or otherwise make note of what had been said.

"You'd probably try to lift her. She was dead already, but that might make sense to you."

"Pull down on her. Speed the job."

"Never mind."

Ben reached down with the hedge clippers and after a few whacks cut through the rope.

"They won't believe she did this to herself," Laurence said.

"We'll make them believe."

At least they seemed to. He had her buried in the family plot, in the garden. Consecrated ground, but he needed to keep up appearances. The grieving son. He would have been happier to put her next to her father. Where she could be more easily forgotten.

***

Six weeks later Laurence stood under the tree with an ax. Her screams still echoed through his sleep. The flashes of lightning from that night scalded his eyes whenever he tried to close them, illuminating the final accusatory and pleading stares, hearing her thoughts: *You are supposed to take care of your mother, Laurence. You wanted to leave me. I had no other choice.*

Her hands grasping at the rope loop he'd tied and

put around her. The final movements of her life telephoned through the rope. The vision of her. Thin shadow. Guttural hacking, straining. Stillness but for the pendulous swinging that ensued when she struggled no more.

He woke in the night sweating with her distended eyes and bitten-through tongue and still sentient face breathing down the stench of rot and grave upon him.

After too many nights of this he walked out to the garden with an ax.

"Like eating an elephant," swing, "a bite," swing, "at," hard swing, "a time." He brought the ax down again but his back cried out in pain and he dropped the tool and lay on the ground helpless looking up at the white, reaching branches.

Seeing her swinging there.

"Why can't you leave me alone!" Grabbing at his aching back. Tears coursing down his face. He hated her. "Leave me alone." A pathetic whimper. "Leave me in peace. Let me forget you. Please."

***

The next day, medicated and in bed, he told Ben to lock the garden up. Let it consume itself. A fitting end. He didn't want to see it or think of it again.

Chapter 3

"DID YOU GET it all?" Michael said. "Because I'm done, I think. I don't want to talk about it anymore. Ever. So I hope you got it."

I stared down at my hands, not knowing what to make of what I'd just heard. Feeling a void between sternum and spine, a hollow skull. Emily. Sad. What could she have been? *She's not dead, Marius. She will live as much as she wants to live. So will you. If you can both get distance from all of this.*

But where would it go now? Mr. Bracciolini was recording this. He'd publish. The police would be involved. Things would get ugly. I was already leaving the estate, but now there'd be plenty of conflict and controversy and everything had become immensely uncertain.

"I've got it all," said Mr. Bracciolini. He stood and winced as his knees took responsibility for his weight. "Thank you."

"You might think Laurence was the victim. Maybe he was, in a way. But he's not innocent. He's got blood on his hands too. Besides hers. You'd do best to be careful around him."

"I think I'll be okay."

"Do you?"

They locked gazes for a few tense moments.

"You'll excuse me if I don't see you to the door." He stared down at his hands, his left hand running back and forth over the right.

***

Driving north in the afternoon I sat in silence while Mr. Bracciolini recorded notes for his story. His eyes were as giddy as a child's at a toy sale. I felt sick to my stomach.

"I don't understand anything," I said as we left the houses and fields near the river behind and entered the forested hills that would see us most of the way home.

"Speak."

"My uncle's innocent."

"Innocent? No, Marius."

"He killed his mother. But look. Look at the circumstances. Isn't there an excuse? Wouldn't the Furies leave him alone?"

"You heard Michael. That's not the only blood on your uncle's hands."

"But he loved her. Emily's mom."

"So?" Mr. Bracciolini said, staring at me over his glasses.

"How can a man capable of love do wicked things?"

"You're thinking he must be a sociopath, and that sociopaths don't love?"

"Don't give me a Mr. Charles lecture on evil, please. I don't think I can handle it right now."

He laughed and set himself into a sputtering cough. When he cleared it he continued to laugh.

"I don't think it's funny," I said.

"No, no. I just… Ah, Mr. Charles, ever analytical. A good quality. Your uncle is not a sociopath. Your grandmother was not a sociopath. Your great-grandfather was not a sociopath. Sociopaths kill with all the emotion of a plumber fixing pipes. There was emotion in what these people did, Marius. Fear. Think about it. Your great-grandfather had been brainwashed by Nazi ideology to fear the Jews, the Soviets. Others. Your grandmother feared losing her son. Your uncle was capable of love, but that doesn't exclude him from murder. He feared what? What he might become? Having to look at her every day and be reminded of what she'd done? I don't know. I don't think the decision he made to kill his mother was an easy one. I don't imagine it was that at all." He sniffed and shook his head as if befuddled. "And isn't it obvious why your mother ran away? She feared the madness. She wanted to get away from the madness."

"You're assuming she wasn't also mad."

"You're right. Sorry."

I didn't say another word and he continued to record his ideas. In the late afternoon he left me off at the end of the driveway and I began the long climb home.

***

Flora was dusting in the entry hall when I walked in. I paused. I wanted to invite her upstairs, to share what I'd learned, but at a glance she knew where I'd been. Her face flushed with anger and she crossed her arms and turned and walked away with clenched jaw.

A couple of hours south Michael Padrick put the hard cold end of a pistol into his mouth and pulled the trigger.

Chapter 4

I SAW EMILY during the day now. Everyone else was against me at this point. She's the only one who seemed to care as much about the truth as I did.

When I walked into Emily's room, she had *Les Miserables* on the bed next to her and she was nearly finished with it.

While Mrs. Moira hovered around the room, dusting, arranging, and otherwise keeping an unhappy eye on us, Emily talked to me of the plot and her excitement at reading the book. The sorrow at the way the Thenardiers treated Cossette. The incredible transformation and goodness of Jean Valjean. The romantic garden meetings of Marius and Cossette on the Rue de L'Homme. When Mrs. Moira lingered, beginning to pull all of Emily's books off the shelves to dust beneath them, Emily had finally had enough.

"I don't know what you're worried will happen, Mrs. Moira, but please give us some time to ourselves."

Mrs. Moira formed her empty hand into a fist and set the duster down on the bookshelf with an emphatic smack.

"Very well," she said, tension writ large on her countenance, in her bearing. "But not for too long. You have your therapy in an hour."

"Then give us an hour of peace."

I saw the hurt that crossed Mrs. Moira's face as she left.

Once the door had closed, I was about to tell Emily of everything I'd learned, knowing it would be upsetting, trying to prepare myself for that. But she spoke first.

"Your mother has written all over this book," she whispered.

"What?"

"Tiny little clues written in the margins and between the lines."

"Clues?"

"Yes!"

She eagerly opened the book to a page number she'd memorized. How had I missed the notes? I'd read part of the book. Flipped through it, skimmed it. Perhaps its massiveness had worked against me. All I'd seen was the phrase *my man* and hadn't thought to search for anything else.

"Look here," she said, her finger underlining the following words, black ink camouflaged between lines on the page. *Father did this too.*

I tilted my head in confusion and Emily flipped to another page.

She hates the color of my eyes. Father knew. Father knew everything.

The soft slap of paper as she turned the page again.

My man, in a more childish script than the other notes.

Again.

I know.

Again.

Nazi.

Again.

They murdered him. Hide the past. I can't stay. She hates me. She's always hated me. She's cruel to me. He is too. He can't disappoint her.

A final time.

Father left his own clues. If you're reading this, find them. And know. I promised.

Emily's eyes were alive with excitement. "It's a real mystery, Marius."

It had been a real mystery for me for some time.

"Where do you think he left his clues?" she asked.

Where? Where did he spend his time? Every waking moment of it in the library, according to Mrs. Moira. But that's not what stood out the most. The rest made sense to a degree. But one line stood out. *She hates the color of my eyes.*

I looked at Emily and saw those gray wolf's eyes peering back at me. The same eyes my uncle had. And my grandmother had had. And my great-grandfather and I. My mother's eyes were brown. She was an *other*, wasn't she? That was part of it.

"Marius?"

"Hmm?"

"Where do you think he left the clues?"

"The clues… The library, probably." I thought of all those volumes. The impossibility of searching them for small markings, the hidden notations of a man a prisoner in his own home. To lust and guilt and fear of what she might do to the children. To him.

"I want to go, Marius. To the library."

I could see the fear in her eyes at the thought of leaving her room and I came back to myself.

"Do you want me to get your wheelchair?"

"Tomorrow, I think. I have therapy."

"Emily?"

Looking away from me.

"When's the last time you left your room?"

"Hmm?"

"Emily?"

"Tomorrow, Marius. I think I want to rest a little right now."

"Not tomorrow, Emily. Now."

She began to shake her head, a look of mortification like she was staring into the gaping maw of hell.

I walked to the corner and got her chair.

"I don't want you to see my legs."

I could see the fear, the embarrassment, the hard red blush.

"You think that's going to bother me?" I said. "After all you and I have been through in our lives, that I would possibly judge you or think less of you?"

I stared into her eyes as I said it and she met my gaze.

"You and I are all that's left of this wretched family, Emily. I'm with you. I hope you understand that."

A faint smile and a nod.

"Thank you," she said. She hesitated and then

pulled the blankets back and her legs were there, exposed. Limbs meant to move her around that had never supported her weight, had never developed adequate muscle. I tried to keep my reaction hidden, a mix of pity, anger, and, yes, the slightest hint of disgust—wasted flesh so atypical of a person would cause such a reaction in most unaccustomed to seeing it.

"Are you ready?" I said.

Her lips were pursed, monotone emotions, unsure whether to cry or yell at me or just get on with it.

"Yes," she said in the tiniest of whispers.

I reached for her legs, to swing them to the edge of the bed.

"Don't," she snapped. "I can do it. I do it all the time."

She bent forward at the waist and put her hands under her calves and swung herself around.

"You have to bring the chair over here, parallel to the bed, not facing it. I'm not going to do a somersault into it."

"You sure?" I said, not able to stifle a smirk.

"My Olympic dreams were officially dashed long ago. Yes, that's it. Thank you." She smiled, too. Perhaps we had cut through the awkwardness.

She moved to the chair and settled and then wheeled herself within a few feet of the door. She stopped, trembling. Her face had gone white. If we lingered, if she thought about it too long, it would never happen. She would never leave. I needed to open the door and we needed to go through it without any hesitation and she needed to see that everything would be okay, that the hallway she had long looked at from her bed was no mirage, that no abyss would open up and swallow her if she moved beyond the boundary.

I took a step in the door's direction.

"Wait, Marius," she said, hand up, horizontal vertigo in those out-of-focus eyes. "Wait."

I opened the door.

"I think I'm going to faint. I'm feeling dizzy."

I went behind her wheelchair and took the handles and began to push forward, her hands stretched out over the wheels, flexing, jerking, not touching them, ready, though, to reach down and put a stop to our progress.

"No, Marius. I'm not ready."

"We have to, Emily. I know you're scared, but you'll see. It'll be okay."

Inches to go.

"No, Marius."

I didn't slow, and her hands shot down and grabbed the wheels, putting a firm stop to our momentum, her feet through that mythical barrier, the front of the wheels touching the hall carpet.

"Let go of my chair, Marius."

"Emily…"

"Let go of my *chair!*" The scream. The piercing scream that Flora had blamed on the wind.

"Emily…"

"No!" wheeling herself back into me, her face

enflamed, her heart pounding, her eyes as wide as if she were perched precariously on a ledge and staring down a thousand feet to the city street below.

I saw Mrs. Moira marching down the hall.

"What are you doing?" she snapped.

I let go of the chair, stepped aside, and Emily turned herself back towards her bed.

"What on God's green earth are you doing?" Mrs. Moira shouted as she stormed nearer.

"He's trying to help me," Emily said, out of breath, hoarse. "It was my idea."

"Your idea? Your idea to do what?"

"To go to the library."

"The library? Well... Not today, you're not."

"Baby steps," I said. "Before I take her to the garden."

Mrs. Moira scowled at me.

"It's almost time for your therapy. If you want to go to the library then we'll talk about it. After. But you won't leave this room without me. Do you understand?"

"Yes," said Emily, cutting out the rebuttal I was about to voice, the one where I told Mrs. Moira that she had enabled this condition and that in truth she probably should not be around. But what did I know?

"You," said Mrs. Moira, "you should go so she can get ready. She's not even dressed properly, is she, to be leaving her room?"

She still wore her nightgown. Thin. Cold. Revealing. I hadn't wanted to leave the room to let her change and give her a chance to stall.

"What time should I come back?"

"Not today," said Mrs. Moira, stressing each syllable. "She can't be screaming like that, can she, or she'll bring the roof beams down upon us. She'll upset her father."

"Who cares," said Emily.

"I care," said Mrs. Moira. "For your sake and his. Now, go, Marius."

Chapter 5

I WENT TO the library on my own to begin searching. I came in on the second floor and heard voices and peered down over the railing to see Flora and an older lady with shoulder-length gray hair: Miss Gitlin, the replacement teacher.

"I feel bad for him," Flora said and I took a step back. "They didn't even have a funeral for his mother. My grandma said Mr. Frost brought the ashes back in an urn and has them in his study."

What?

"It would be nice if he'd reach out to Marius, wouldn't it?" Miss Gitlin said.

"I don't think that's going to happen. Unfortunately."

"Mr. Charles said as much. He's worried. About all of you."

"How's he doing? Have you heard from him?"

"A few days ago. He asked how Marius was. I told him he didn't want to see me. I think that upset him. But then he asked how you were doing."

Silence but for the sound of the radiator going through its fits of swelling and contracting.

"Aren't you a bit young for him, Flora?"

"Oh my goodness. No, don't get that idea."

I envisioned her with flushed cheeks, avoiding eye contact. The sharp stab of jealousy.

"I think he has a crush on my sister, anyway. He's

always asking how *she's* doing."

"She's more his age, isn't she?"

"Can we change the subject?"

They laughed.

"Relax, Flora. It's okay if you have a crush on him. He's a good man. And sensible. He would kindly turn you down."

"They're right, you know," a raspy whisper from behind me.

Jolted out of my trance, I turned to stare into his narrowed eyes. The tall, broad windows of the library open wide to the late afternoon sun threw naked light on him. The Doberman pacing, sniffing around the edges of the wall.

His attention withdrew to a spot of flooring nearby, but he continued speaking to me, hushed.

"I have her ashes. In my room. I—I should have shown them to you, let you say goodbye. Or…"

"But you don't think about anyone other than yourself, do you?" I said, not bothering to control the volume of my voice. The discussion below had stopped. Now they were listening to us, I knew, but didn't care. "What about your daughter?"

"W—We're not talking about my daughter."

I heard anger.

"You never do. She asked me what you looked like. Did you know that?"

He turned away. I thought he would leave, but he didn't.

"Why don't you see her?" I asked.

"L—Leave it alone."

"No. What will you let her believe about you? It wasn't you. I know that."

"W—What?" he whirled and I could see rage in his eyes and my heart flared up in fear, breath stuck in my throat. The Doberman stopped pacing and turned its head towards me. "What? You don't know anything. What are you talking about?"

"I—I know," I said.

"Nothing!" he shouted. "You know *nothing!*"

He retreated from the room in agony, followed by the metal clangor of dog chains, fleeing down the hallway and to his room or to the stairs and out of the house, I didn't know. I didn't know.

When I turned around Flora was moving towards me across the balcony.

"Marius…"

"I'm okay," I told her. I wasn't okay, though. I was scared. And she knew it.

Chapter 6

FLORA PUSHED FOR me to follow her and Miss Gitlin to the kitchen for tea and I sensed a slight thaw in her anger at my time spent with Mr. Bracciolini. I think she was worried I would run to my room or go back out onto the grounds and isolate myself yet again. My habitual nature had urged me to do what she feared I would, but just as I'd asked Emily to fight her inner demons, I felt that I needed to continue to fight mine as well.

I had never set foot in the kitchen. The food had always magically appeared on trays borne to my room by Flora or Mrs. Moira. It was a poorly lit room on the lower level in the wing in which I resided. It smelled good, like gingerbread. Flora turned on the fluorescent lights as we walked in to reveal a large steel french-door refrigerator and a steel island, industrial-sized sinks, an eight-burner gas stove and multiple ovens, with innumerable pots and pans gleaming and hanging from hooks along the ceiling.

Miss Gitlin put her purse and bag down on the island and walked over to the pantry. She and Flora had done this before.

"How long were you spying on us?" Flora asked.

I shrugged. "Long enough to hear you talk about my mother's ashes. That's what he said to me. That... that he'd show them to me. Scared me half to death."

She reached out and squeezed my arm as Miss

Gitlin walked out with a sampling of tea bags.

"What'll it be?" she asked.

***

Flora brought out stools as the water boiled, putting out teacups and saucers and a few cookies.

"Are we British now?" I asked.

"Not quite, but I love England," said Miss Gitlin. "Have you ever been, Marius?"

"No," I said. "But I'm familiar with her writers. Overly familiar. With Shakespeare, at least."

"Mr. Charles warned me about your sarcasm. I was sorry I didn't get the chance to meet you earlier. He's rather impressed with you. Precocious, he said. He was too, so maybe he knows."

I dipped my head.

"How goes *Romeo and Juliet*?"

"Enh," I grunted.

"We've read through Act 2," said Flora, looking at me over the teakettle, steam beginning to rise from its spout, her hand ready to pluck it off the gas flame. An inch worth of forgiveness in her glance.

"Exciting, isn't it," said Miss Gitlin. "To be young and in love and have everything in front of you."

"They kill themselves at the end," I said. "I know that much."

The tea kettle whistled and Flora poured hot water into our cups and then sat.

"It is a tragedy," Miss Gitlin said. She dunked her

tea bag up and down a few times in the hot water.

"Things get worse and worse and then they die," I muttered, thinking of my own sad youth to date. She and Flora seemed to sense this.

"Flora told me about what you're going through. I'm sorry to hear you're having a rough time."

"Yeah, well, there are others who have it worse, aren't there?"

"And others who have it better. But it's okay not to worry about them right now. Tell me about you and Mr. Bracciolini."

"I don't know that it's any of your business," I said. Flora avoided my glare.

"I've been around a long time, Marius, in case you couldn't tell. You might be surprised to hear that I knew your mother."

Flora stared down into her tea. She tugged at the string and pulled the bag out, setting it on her saucer, not picking the cup up to drink.

"How?"

"Her last year in this house she came to the public school. I'm sure it was some sort of battle here that led to it. I was her English teacher. She stayed after school sometimes and talked to me."

"That's why my uncle doesn't like you."

"I didn't know he didn't like me."

"He said so."

"Hmm. Well, it's funny I'm here, then, isn't it?"

"What did the two of you talk about?"

"Your mother was a lovely person with an

unlovely childhood."

"And she made my childhood equally unlovely. So what does that mean?"

She picked up her teacup between her palms and sipped. "We were speaking of tragedy."

"And what happened to her—"

"And you. What happened to both of you. She never seemed to move on from it and… It's so sad, what happened. But you're young."

"What does that mean?"

"I see a lot of her in you. The good things. The intelligence. But also the vulnerability."

"You don't know me."

"I've heard a lot. And what I see now? I see her."

"Maybe that's not the best thing to say to me."

"She was delicate."

"I've heard that before."

"Sensitive. A talented writer."

"I have no interest in writing."

"And I think under different circumstances, with her intelligence, her talent, she would have been something. Someone extraordinary. You still have time, you know."

"Can we move on from the empty praise, maybe, a moment? Can you tell me something concrete?"

She snorted, perhaps realizing what a blessing it was not to have to put up with me five mornings a week.

"She hated your grandmother. Only one time did she tell me anything specific about what she'd done. It was in her journal, actually. She dressed it up as fiction but it was obvious it was the truth of her life."

"What was the story?"

"A young girl falls and scrapes her knee and goes to her mother, standing nearby, for comfort. The mother has her sit down on the grass, puts a tender hand on her back, the other hand reaching behind her. The other hand comes forward with a fistful of gravel and pushes it down into the wound. The child screams and cries and the mother looks on and tells her, 'You're not one of us.'"

"Jesus," Flora said.

Miss Gitlin stared at me as if to say, *Is that concrete enough?*

"What about my uncle? What did she say about him?"

"Nothing. Which I think speaks volumes, doesn't it?"

Chapter 7

I STAYED TO help Flora clean after Miss Gitlin left.

"I'm sorry about the way I treated you yesterday," Flora said. "It wasn't my intention to make you feel bad for doing what you're doing. I know you're not being voyeuristic about what happened to Emily, but it's just, she's flesh and blood to me, right? Not just words on a page, and it hurts, to read those things, and see that man with nothing but calculation in his eyes. Mr. Bracciolini's using you, Marius. And I know—"

I began to speak and she raised her hand to shush me.

"I know that you say you're aware of that and that you're getting what you want out of him as well. But it bothers me. That doesn't mean I should have handled it by… by being angry at you. I'm sorry."

"I'm sorry too," I said. "For my behavior, on the road. And for not confiding in you about my plans."

"It's okay."

I thought for a moment of stepping out in front of the oncoming truck, I wanted to say, but I bit down on that thought, and drying a cup that she handed me, said instead, "So you have a crush on Mr. Charles?"

"You," she said, her finger pointing at me like her grandmother's had, "should not eavesdrop on others."

There was playfulness in her expression, though. "He *is* too old for you."

She blushed.

"Never mind," I said.

"Never mind? I'll never mind you," and she threw a cup of water on me and laughed hysterically as I toweled myself off and then slapped her across the back with the towel, leading to a full-on water war and a mess we had to get down on hands and knees to clean. Which inevitably led to another kiss and I was back in her good graces and more deeply in love than ever.

Chapter 8

I WENT TO Emily's room after dinner and a change of clothes. Mrs. Moira was just leaving, closing the door gently behind her.

"She's napping," she said. "Poor thing. Therapy wears her out."

"That's convenient."

She stood with arms folded over her breasts. "What are you looking for in the library, anyway?"

"I'm looking to get her out of that room."

"And? I'm not stupid, Marius. I've seen enough people creep around this house to know when their motives are innocent and when they are not. Tell me what the two of you are looking for."

"What do the names Heinrich Scherer and Peter Meyer mean to you?"

"Oh…" with a dip in her chin. "Well, I haven't heard that name, not in a very long time."

"Which name?"

"Peter. Peter Meyer. Your great-grandfather. Victoria's father." A grin or a grimace, a shaking of her head. "No, he wasn't with us for very long."

"He died here. In this house. Right?"

"Yes, in the room right there." She gestured with a finger towards a door two down from Emily's.

"Can I see it?"

"Why? There's nothing to see."

Probably not. No Nazi keepsakes, no flag with the

rich red and the white circle and the bastardized black swastika. No brown shirt or leather boots with soles worn from the marching. No Luger with worked in handle. No, all of that lay across an ocean and sixty years in the past.

"Oh, come on then. It's rather a morbid curiosity you have about him if you ask me, but it's as good a place as any to talk, if that's what you want to do. We don't want to wake your cousin."

I did want to wake her. And would.

***

The room was furnished similarly to mine and I imagined a series of these rooms with the dark wallpaper and queen-sized beds with small tables and sofas and bathrooms opening off of them. This one lacked a TV, though, and all the furniture stood covered in dusty white drop cloths.

The faint click of a light switch being turned on, a lamp and warm incandescence spilling over the surfaces. Mrs. Moira closed the door behind us.

"Where are you going with this, Marius?"

He had died in this bed, hadn't he? And the covers shrouding all the furniture, thrown on the day they buried him? What legacy had this one man been responsible for? One great-grandfather, Lionel Frost, builds the estate on the earnings from an invention, the work of his fertile imagination and technical skills, and the other arrives a fugitive and within years of his death the rot has set in, the foundation has been compromised. Bodies in the ground turned to dust. Or burned in the crematorium fires. My mother and father.

"Wherever it leads me," I said. Seeing where his cancer-ravaged body would have lain, the cadaverous sink of the flesh on his face, pale, lacking purity, perhaps speaking a final confession. Here.

"Even if it means dragging your family through the tabloids?"

"What family?"

"Oh, Marius. Marius, Marius." She closed her eyes and shook her head. What else could she do?

"How many people has my uncle killed?"

She didn't respond. A faraway look in her eyes.

"You see, because I know about his mother," I said, and she looked at me with narrowed eyes. "And his father. Two parents."

"No."

"No? You mean yes. What I'm unsure about is the names. The names he's written down on a legal pad in his room. They're all Jewish. And with this family's history…"

"Your uncle is not a killer."

"I just want the facts. I'll draw my own conclusions. He killed his mother. He killed his father. That makes him a killer, doesn't it?"

"He's not a murderer."

"He hanged his mother. He hit his father in the head, stripped him naked, and left him to die in the woods."

"No."

"And he locked my mother up."

She shook her head. "No, you don't have the facts. You don't have the facts at all."

"You know what happened, don't you? You know exactly what happened."

"It was an ugly night." She relived it, eyes glassing over. She saw ghosts. She heard them speak. "They argued. Edward and Victoria. They argued a lot. But it was different this time."

"What was different?"

"I was with your mother. Trying to stop her from going in there."

"In—"

"The library. Where... Oh, Marius, your mother wanted to do a brave thing. She wanted to come to the defense of her father. She sensed it too. That this wasn't going to end like the other arguments. This one was different."

"What were they arguing about?"

"Her father. Peter. He'd been dead for at least ten years. Edward thought that was enough. He thought enough time had passed. He couldn't handle keeping quiet any longer."

"What was he going to say?"

"He knew things about her father."

"The truth."

"I don't know how he knew, but he did. About his past. His... his escape, from Germany, during the war. But... I think there was more. I don't know what it was.

I really don't. But she wanted none of it. She wanted her father to rest in peace. She didn't want what it would mean for her and her son."

"She was protective of him."

"I think she was scared, too. That revealing her father's past would reveal her."

"What do you mean?"

"She was cruel to your mother."

"Why?"

"Victoria wasn't right, Marius. Never was. There was something off about her, always. Even when your mother was a little baby she treated her terribly. I kept your mother away. As much as possible. I kept your mother away from Victoria. But who am I to… to… I couldn't keep her away always."

"Why didn't she love my mother?"

"Your mother had brown eyes."

"Brown eyes? How dare she."

"Your uncle has gray eyes. Like Peter Meyer. Like Victoria."

"Yes?"

"So your mother was… Other."

"Other?"

"Not one of them."

"That's ludicrous."

She shrugged. Of course it was ludicrous. Who said it had to make sense? "I don't think it was just the eyes, though."

"Then what?"

"She was more like your grandfather, Edward, in

temperament."

"So? What would that matter?"

"They were both… Other."

"You keep saying that."

"I was Other too."

"What are you talking about?"

"I never got the sense that when your grandmother looked at your mother that she saw a child. Her child. I remember… I remember a time, in the nursery, when she was holding your mother, and your mother threw up. Babies do that. Babies throw up sometimes. Their little… their little digestive systems are not all developed, and… and your grandmother, in that situation, dropped the baby. Dropped your mother into her crib and began to scream at her about the germs. How dare she get her filthy germs on *her*. This was her child. And I've no doubt your uncle, as a baby, made much the same messes. All babies do. But I don't ever recall her doing that to him. Dropping him. Screaming at him. She could have killed your mother."

"You were there?"

She peered at me.

"And you let her?"

"I was scared. I should have done more. You can't beat me up any worse than I've already done to myself, Marius."

"What happened the night my grandfather died?"

"I couldn't stop your mother from going in. She hated Victoria and loved Edward and she was going to defend her father. She told her mother that if she stopped Edward from... from sharing what he knew, that she would share it herself. And your grandmother lost her senses. She said... Called her awful, awful things. Threatened her. She threatened her and called for your uncle to come and take her away."

"Take her away?"

Mrs. Moira had tears running down her cheeks at this point.

"I should have stopped it."

"What did my uncle do?"

"He did what she told him to do. He took her away."

"Where?"

She shrugged helplessly.

"Yet you don't think he's bad?"

"She was a frightening woman, Marius."

"She was a small woman. What could she do?"

"Your grandfather died. I don't know how. But he died. And your mother was gone."

"Does seven days sound right?"

She peered down at her hands. They trembled like weak limbs in a strong storm.

"I had my own daughter to worry about, Marius."

"And my mother was 'Other' to you as well. I see."

"No."

"Then help me out here. I'm lost. Why didn't you help her? You could have taken her away from here."

"Because I left. I left, Marius. I didn't think... I didn't think your grandfather would die, that your mother… I thought Laurence would take care of your mother. I wanted to get my daughter and leave until things calmed down. I couldn't stand to be around the bitterness, and didn't want her to see. So we left. We went to stay with my mother. Until I heard… Until I heard what happened."

"That my grandfather was dead."

She nodded.

I shook my head in bewilderment. "Yet you stayed here. After all of that."

"Someone had to look after your mother and your uncle."

"The authorities could have done that."

"I should have called the police."

"Yes, you should have."

"But I was scared. And my own daughter. I had to protect her."

"Why did she let Flora come here?"

"What do you mean?"

"Why did she let Flora and her sister come here? If she knows what happened?"

"She didn't let them come, Marius."

"What are you talking about?"

She tilted her head, bewildered that I didn't know. "They took them away from her." Her cheeks began to shake. "They put them into foster care. I—"

She turned and left the room.

Chapter 9

LATE. OUR MIDNIGHT hour. Emily closed her eyes and communed with whatever demons held her hostage. A steady and deep breathing with her lips pinched tightly together. Eyes still clenched, she pulled the sheet back. She wore a sweatshirt and sweatpants, a sign that this time was going to be different.

"Bring my chair."

When I brought it to the bed, parallel to it this time, she was already sitting at the edge of the mattress. She put a hand up and let me help her. A warm body. A trembling heart.

"You're not going to scream this time?" I said in an attempt to make light of our earlier expedition.

She shook her head but didn't speak, settling down into the chair and staring across the floor, an expanse that looked to her like miles laid with landmines.

She hesitated, then wheeled herself towards the door and I opened it. Utter blackness in the hallway. I envisioned our path. Halfway back to her father's suite and then out onto the upper level of the library where there were more tables and lamps and I could go searching through the stacks and bring volumes back to her at the little table on the balcony.

"Maybe it's a little easier. At night," she said. "It's comforting somehow. Everything's not so stark."

"Should I?" I said.

"No. I need to do this." She put her hands back

on the wheels and inched herself forward. Until she arrived once again at the threshold where she'd panicked and screamed. Her arms quivered visibly and I moved around behind her.

"No," she said, her voice shaking as violently as her arms. "No. Just… I'll do it, Marius. Just give me a moment."

With the light behind us spreading out into the hallway I expected to see the figure of my uncle's dog or my uncle himself, the fellow nocturnal traveler, stepping out of the shadows to greet us. But what kind of greeting? Mrs. Moira claimed he was benign. I didn't see it that way.

Emily shook her head. Lifted her hands. Put them back. Gripped with a thousand pounds of pressure. Raised her head and said, "Okay."

The metal in her chair sounded its unfamiliarity with her rate of movement as she entered the hall in one swift movement and then stopped and peered around at an unfamiliar corridor. Sweat dampened the curls of her hair at the base of her neck.

"You can push now," she said, her voice shaking, her arms crossed over her chest and her hand worrying her neck. I did. We didn't speak. Not until we were in the library and I had turned on a few lamps.

Her wide-eyed fear softened into wonder. "It's beautiful."

"Where do we begin?"

She stared around at all of the volumes. Hardback. Leatherbound. A lifetime's worth of reading material.

The collected memories of over a thousand men and women sacrificing for their art. Sacrificing families and pleasures and lives in order to put down on paper and into the world something that had never been there. The essence of what it meant to be a human, this shared experience.

I struck out aimlessly at first, gathering stacks of books from nearby shelves and bringing them back to the table where we both flipped through pages mostly unmarred by pen. Great stacks of poetry and philosophy. Shelley and Keats, Plato and Aristotle. Dante. Virgil. Dickens. Shakespeare. Cicero. Homer. Excitement upon seeing a note, only to face disappointment when we saw that these notes highlighted key ideas of the texts or the reader's impassioned response. Fingers weary of fanning the pages, eyes that could barely focus in the dim surroundings of that large, warm room.

"It's going to take us weeks," I said, slapping closed a volume of Emerson's collected works.

Emily closed her current volume with gentle hands. "We need to stop and think."

"Read a dead man's mind?"

"What book did your mother write in?"

"*Les Miserables*. Why are you—"

"Where did you find it?"

"Up rather high. I was up on a ladder. Stupid…"

"Go check."

I descended the stairs, found the ladder, and slid it down its squeaky track towards Victor Hugo. Peering up at the shelf I knew this was it. The shelf was out of sight. *Les Miserables* was significant. It was her clue. Why hadn't I started here?

I climbed the creaking wooden steps and perched there near the top. A brief glance at the few works on the uppermost shelf, next to the gap where *Les Miserables* had resided for years, unread, brought me quickly to another book eerily appropriate: Victor Hugo's *History of a Crime*.

I grabbed the volume and hurried down the ladder and up the stairs to the upper balcony where Emily sat in her chair staring towards the window and the outdoors, the clear sky, the spread of stars a ceiling on the world.

"I think I've got it," I said. She didn't respond.

"How much have I missed, Marius?"

"What?"

"Hiding in my room. How much have I missed?"

"Emily—"

"No. Never mind. You think you've got it?"

I held up the book and she read the title and smiled. "I think you do."

Hugo had written of Napoleon III's crimes. Our grandfather had provided the X on a map.

Near his grave stand four white birch trees. Look there. For what? For his final confession. For the truth. Dig for it.

"Marius." The color was gone from Emily's face.

"I have to find it."

"It's real."

"He confessed."

"Tomorrow?"

"First thing."

"I'm scared, Marius. What will it mean? For us?"

"I don't know."

But I felt a chill too.

Chapter 10

I SET MY alarm for six and on a few hours of sleep I shuffled across the mist-covered yard and down into the woods. I expected to find the garden door locked, but it was not. It was open a fraction of an inch, beckoning me in like an elongated finger curling come-hither. I should have paid attention to this fact but my mind was firmly focused on the task.

The clouds moved in lines, stacked like mountains, spitting rain and threatening more. Fine dew covered the stalks of the weeds and the wild-growing branches of shrubs and the hibernating grass bent down by my various expeditions.

I knew I was looking for another grave, another spot of land open enough for a body to be buried in. And for a stand of birch trees with their white paper skin peeling off in patches. Beyond that I didn't know anything.

I passed the rose bushes and angled away from the garden wall.

What would I find when I dug, anyway? *His final confession.* I envisioned shaky German handwriting. Simple words admitting to crimes against humanity. Yes, we knew that already. We knew. What in the confession was worth my grandfather's life?

I came to the collapsed bower and angled past the ruined trellis. Nearer and nearer.

His final confession. Would the words in the

confession illuminate my mother and uncle in some way? My uncle had killed once for it. What would stop him from killing again? From killing me?

The shed a horizontal face with its askew door a laid-out madman's grin, toothless, foul.

Get the shovel. Get the shovel and there's the hint of a trail, just a little beyond the shed, where the stalks are bent down. I'd never noticed. I'd never even considered there'd be anything beyond it. What was within the shed had been too arresting.

I stepped inside and the floor creaked beneath my feet. Careful plodding into the damp and musty darkness of a building no more than the final afterthought of these acres of landscaped earth. The shovel leaned against the wall in the corner, cobwebbed and rusted.

I was reaching for it when the door creaked.

I spun around to see the light disappear, the rectangular plain of smoky gray turning to black, turning to complete darkness, turning to sound, and the sound from the whine of hinges turning to the small clatter of a metal padlock.

"What are you doing?" my voice an ineffective weapon.

I ran for the door but tripped where the floor had rotted through and I fell even as I heard the lock snap into place, a high-fidelity echo in that miserable space. My left ankle bent and sent white light flashing through me and my heart thudded as I lay there gasping and afraid, bruised and cold.

"I know where all the keys are." A man's voice, sounding somehow mournful. "So…"

Then I was alone.

Chapter 11

SO THIS IS you, I thought, curled up in the corner with my mother's words. *This explains you.*

The blackness around me and the sound of steady rain ticking on the roof, the distant complaint of thunder. Pushing on the walls and doors gained me nothing. Enclosed. Entombed. Or call it what you would.

Nothing here on this property has aged since 1982, has it? It all stopped with this moment. When your father died and you, Mom, claimed you did. Here on the floor you spilled your blood. Didn't you?

Like a shipwreck, the estate was frozen in the moment of that accident. The tube TVs broadcasting static. The antique vehicles under tarps in the garage. The empty halls and furniture wrapped like the drowned in their dining clothes floating pale and white and engorged at the bottom of the sea. Did anyone survive, or were we all fooling ourselves into believing we would ever surface and taste the air again?

My mother had lost her mind, her will to live, her ability to show affection to her son on this goddamn sinking ship. Hers was a mind on fire until it hit the inescapable reality of the water and then hit the air as little more than a sigh of steam, drifting away into the fog. Invisible.

Her ashes lay in a room up in the house. She came home. She never wanted to come home.

I ran my fingers over her words in the corner with the tarp pulled over me for warmth as the intensity of rain increased and the thunder roared near.

Emily knew where I was. Someone would come eventually, right? But could they get into the garden? Would he let them get in? Or was he simply waiting? Was he going to make this his final stand? His own version of scorched earth?

Running the tips of my fingers over her words.

"Your son's going to die here too."

Because even upon rescue, even upon leaving this place, would I ever be the same?

Chapter 12

THE LIGHT THROUGH the crevices faded out as the day drew towards evening. Still the hammering of rain on the roof, the sudden bright lights, a subtle distant boom as the storm moved east.

Was it obtuse to consider I could have a family and know affection in the 21st century?

My mother wrestled with the same problem. No one who ever roamed the halls of that house knew any different. Our tribe, it seemed to damn us.

The rain finally faded away and then stopped and my thoughts were accompanied by gusts and moans and the tiny clawed footsteps of rodents navigating the cavity beneath the floor. For seven days she'd listened to the same sounds. The rats would grow braver the darker it became. I closed my eyes.

Chapter 13

I THOUGHT IT was a hallucination when I heard movement at the door. It might have been midnight by now. Who knew how to keep track of the hours?

No, that wasn't movement at the door. That was the hand of the wind pushing in on the wood.

No. That wasn't the wind.

It was a staccato rhythm. A thump, thump, thump of force exerted.

Someone was there.

I reached my hand out for the wooden handle of the shovel. Then I crawled across the boards to the door. My heart pounded and my mind schemed and panicked, imploring me to go back to the corner and make myself small.

No. The door would open and I would beat the person who walked in out of the night.

Thump. Thump. Thump.

A perfect rhythm in the banging on the lock. The rats grew quiet. The wind disappeared.

Thump.

And then the door swung out with all the speed of a weak dying man lowering his jaw to suck in a final breath.

A silhouette filled the space, backlit by moonlight.

"Marius?"

I lifted the shovel.

He took a step forward, framed by the opening.

"Marius? Are you there?"

"Stop."

He exhaled. It sounded like relief. The tension in my chest and arms ebbed slightly.

"Come. Come out from there."

"Why did you lock me in here?" I had to find my voice and the first words came out brittle.

Silence for many beats before he answered. "I didn't."

"You're lying. You're here to kill me!"

"I'm here to take you home."

"I don't have a home."

"No."

"Because of you. None of you should have had children. You've cursed Emily and me with life. Why?"

"I'm sorry."

"You're sorry?"

"Come out of there, p-please. I... I have bad memories here." He reached his hand to his head.

"So did my mother."

"Yes."

"Because of you!"

"Yes."

Yes.

"Why?" I asked.

"C-Come out. Please."

I wanted him to answer my question. I wanted to know without having to draw conclusions from scraps of paper and margin scribbles and the suppositions of other parties. I wanted to know from him. But I couldn't let down my guard, as sincere as he seemed in his intention of rescue.

"Back up first." I'd give myself a chance to run. *Plan, Marius. You're not clear yet.*

He stepped back a half-dozen paces and I limped out, groaning when I put my full weight on my wounded ankle for the first time. The light at night had never been so overwhelming or so welcoming. The foul rotted air of the shed swapped for the damp earthy smell of a cool December evening among the soaked remnants of the garden.

I hobbled in the direction of the path to the bower and trellis, the path to the garden door and beyond. Then I heard the clangor of a dog's collar and saw the movement of a wraith, his Doberman patrolling the perimeter of the clearing, agitated, its nose busy gathering input from the shriveled stems of the weeds.

"Why did you torture her?" I asked, leaning my hand against the wet trunk of a maple tree.

"You're hurt."

"Why?"

"It… It all went wrong, that night. I…"

"You killed your father, too."

"No."

"No?"

"My m-mother killed my father. And my sister, she… she was going to tell. Tell it all."

So he told me.

"My f-father, he… he knew something about my grandfather, my mother's father. He knew something and that night, he said… he said he couldn't leave it anymore. He couldn't *not* say something."

"What did he know?"

"I don't know," my uncle said, shaking his head. "I don't. He… he said, and they argued… He said that he knew that my grandfather was a Nazi. That he would have hanged for what he'd done. And my mother, she denied it. She told him he didn't know anything. He didn't know what it was like for him. The… the nightmares he suffered."

Even with the storm in the east there was a glow in the far distance as lightning flashed.

"But my father said… he said that man was not the victim. My grandfather was not the victim. And he couldn't be quiet anymore. They argued."

He sniffed and stood with his arms crossed over his chest and his eyes peering towards ground and feet that twisted back and forth in the mud. His Doberman still circled us, reconnoitering.

"My father said he had evidence. Evidence of more than just that. The Nazi past."

"What evidence?"

"I don't know. He wasn't able to say."

"Because she killed him?"

"Yes."

I took my hand from the trunk of the tree and tested my weight on my ankle. The sharp pain had lessened slightly, though not enough for me to run.

"What happened to my mother that night?"

His head turned towards the shed. He exhaled a

long sigh and I thought he might be crying but then he spoke and there were no tears there. Regret. But no tears.

"Your mother, my… Hannah loved our father. She heard the argument. In the library. She was on the upper balcony. Like you were the other day. She called out to our mother that she would tell. That if she tried to stop our father, she would tell. My mother never liked Hannah."

"Why not?"

"I wish I could say. She was innocent and… Even when she was a baby, and I was a child and didn't know better. She called me over one day, my mother. Hannah was in her crib. Crying. She–she had a pained expression on her face. She'd been in there for hours. She needed fed, a diaper change. Our mother was testing her, she said, to see how long Hannah could go without being touched. Hours. Torture. Who says that? Who does that?"

I could envision it. I closed my eyes and saw it. From birth no comfort for my mother. From birth.

"She was never that way with me," he said. "She spoiled me. And she used me."

"How did she use you?"

"That night, in the library, when Hannah spoke up, made her threat, my mother called for me. I was there, of course, with Hannah. My mother called and told me to… to take Hannah, and put her in the shed."

"Had you done it before?"

"She'd done it before. I knew about it."

"Why? Why would she do that to a little girl?"

"Does there have to be a reason? She wasn't right." He shook his head and shrugged his shoulders.

This explains you, I thought. *And why you were not kind to me. But did it hurt you, Mom, to mother me like she mothered you? Did it cause you any pain? Realizing you had become her, is that why you reached out for the steering wheel on that canyon road?*

"Why did you do it?"

"There's no excuse."

"No."

"I was young. I was afraid of her. So I did it. I didn't know what would happen next."

"What? What—"

"I took her. She went with me. She didn't argue. She trusted me. When we stepped outside she asked why we didn't run away and go to the police. I should have listened. We should have run. But I told her let's just go, let's just do what she says. I didn't want to see our mother erupt. It was horrible when she did. The whole house. Everyone held their breath and kept their eyes down when she grew angry. My father. Mrs. Moira. Everyone."

"Why didn't he divorce her? She was abusive."

"She wouldn't have allowed that."

"You make it sound as if she were some sort of god, as if she had unlimited power."

"She did."

Only because you let her. Only because no one stood up to her. Or left her.

"I locked Hannah in, but I stayed with her. Near her. She didn't know. Our father came later that night to let her out. But my mother followed him. I was walking out to meet him. Thinking that this time would be like every other time. That it would blow over. That she'd calm down. I was coming out of… of that place, over there." A finger raised in the direction of a low boxelder. "And we both heard a noise. The… the snap of a branch breaking. Unnatural. We both turned. She held a branch the size of a baseball bat. A limb. You wouldn't think a woman her size could do much with it, but she swung. He turned right into it. It hit him here," he said, pointing to his temple. His voice faded, "Right here."

The Doberman had stopped its search and sat at my uncle's side, sensing a shift in the tone of the conversation. I thought that I could see her, the woman from the photograph, coming up the path with madness in her eyes.

"Did he die right away?"

"No. He was still breathing. But he was unconscious and… I don't know, I think it was a mortal hit. I don't think he would have survived. He was older. Older than she was. My sister screamed. She heard it."

I exhaled into the night, shaking my head, looking again at a sky that glowed intermittently with the fury of lightning.

"My mother was very calm, and she came up with a story. That Hannah had run away again, and he'd gone looking. But he hit his head on a low-hanging branch and became confused. That's why…" He shook his head again and the Doberman whined. He put his hand down on its head and its ears relaxed for a moment. "I helped her to strip him, and then we dragged him further into the woods and left him under an oak. If he ever regained consciousness, I don't know. But it was cold and there was snow on the ground and the hypothermia eventually would have claimed him."

"Killed him. She did. You helped."

"Yes."

"What happened to my mother?"

"We left her. My mother told me to wait. And wait. It was her intention to leave her to… to die. I almost let it happen. But then I couldn't. I couldn't stand the idea. *What am I doing? What am I doing?*' I think that's when I started to change. To come out, from under her spell."

"So you came back for her."

"Yes."

"After seven days."

"Yes. She wasn't well. She'd cut her wrists. She was already… It was horrible."

"How could you get away with it? You took her to a hospital, right?"

"No. We nursed her here. I had to convince my mother she wouldn't talk."

"She never did, did she?"

"No. She left. The second she had the chance, she left. I never saw her again. Not until…" Here he did shake, from his shoulders down, and the tears entered his voice. "Not until I had to identify her…" He couldn't speak. He couldn't speak for a long time. His Doberman stared up at him, lapped at his hand. I looked away.

After a while he exhaled but the quaver remained in his voice. "I didn't see her again until I had to identify her body. And I told her I was sorry. I said I was so sorry. But it didn't matter. It didn't matter anymore."

I could see her on the table, burned and prostrate like one of the dead in Pompeii but without the aesthetic advantage of a few thousand years disintegration, without the white sculpted purity of a plaster cast that didn't quite speak the horror of inferno. A room that reeked of charred flesh. I could see my uncle standing over her apologetically and I was angry at him. He was responsible for her being on that table. He was responsible for her lack of kindness. What did it buy him to apologize? She was dead. He should have acted when she was a child and needed his protection. He should have been a father to her, but apparently he didn't have it in him.

I tried to block him out. I'd come to the garden for a reason.

She promised her father she'd tell the secret and she left clues. In books. She named me Marius. She shared her love of that story. She must have known I would seek it out. That I would find her. The loved daughter. That I would find her clues. That they would lead me to the next book on the shelf. And then to the birch trees.

"She said she would tell the secret that your father was going to tell."

"Yes."

"It's time for that secret to come out."

"Yes."

"Where is your grandfather buried?"

"Is that where it is?"

"Near a stand of birch trees."

"I know where those are." He nodded. "I know where those are. Can you walk?"

"I'll manage. But… It was Ben, wasn't it, who locked me in?"

"Yes."

"Where is he?"

"I don't know. He…" He gestured back the way we'd come. Had my uncle already killed him? "I saw him leave. He doesn't know I'm here. But maybe we should get what you came for. Hmm?"

I nodded. "Let's go."

Chapter 14

HE LED DOWN the path past the shed with a flashlight illuminating a narrow path. Honeysuckle. Thistle. My uncle pushed branches aside with caution, not allowing any to strike me. Every aching step through the strangling growth I felt that we were coming to the end of the deceptions and the cruelty. But a fear still lingered that he would do something to me, once he got me further in. Or that Ben would come back.

I kept my hand wrapped round the shovel's handle, using it as a crutch, but also ready to swing it.

And then he stopped.

"We're here."

Tall trees encircled a small plot that when well-tended must have been beautiful. Under a canopy of oak branches with the white trunks of the birch trees clustered at one end, the sun would have come through the high branches and cast light like a meeting of auras on the grassy ground.

"Not appropriate for him." My uncle crossed his arms at his chest, his jaw clenched, his head shaking in a subtle back and forth disapproval. "Not when he put them in pits and covered them with lye."

"I don't see a grave."

He raised a hand and extended a finger towards an area near the base of a great oak. I walked in that direction. Feeling the chill in the air. Evil buried there.

Don't give it such an easy label. Not evil. Human.

Fine. A man who murdered buried here. Far from the graves of his victims, both in miles and kind.

I saw the stone outline, the rectangular monument set into the ground.

Peter Meyer.

Not Heinrich Scherer. And nothing else. Nothing but a name, and the wrong one at that.

"The birch trees are there."

I tensed to know he stood behind me. I hadn't been thinking, to let him be there. But he was right. It was time to dig and get the journal and leave the garden. It held nothing more and perhaps it was best to let it continue its return to wilderness.

Arms still encompassing his chest he walked softly in the direction of a clear stand of four birch trees on the far edge of this one-person cemetery.

I followed at a hobble and listened to the rattle of dog chains as the Doberman trotted around its new perimeter.

The four trunks grew out of the same space as if they were a single entity. Around them grew long hunched clumps of grass and willowy stalks of thistles and there was no wild X marking any spot.

My uncle stared up. Imagining his mother swinging from the white branches of a sycamore? The white branches of a birch resembled that other tree only in pallor.

I chose a spot and pushed the head of the shovel down into the dirt. It did not go far before meeting the hard resistance of roots.

"Try here," my uncle said, ending his self-embrace long enough to point at a spot where the roots branched off in a V.

I put my foot on the shovel but the pain was severe and I groaned.

"Here," he said, taking the shovel, handing me the flashlight. He drove the point down into the soil, tearing the cohesive thatch of years of wild growing grass. Depositing the damp soil and positioning the shovel for another bite into the earth.

Behind us the Doberman quickened its pace and growled. Some nocturnal animal wandering the trees.

Pressing down with his foot, the tip didn't sink far before it met a hard resistance that resounded with the sound of metal on metal.

"We seem to have found it."

I gave him the flashlight and knelt and began to dig with my hands. I cleared the edges of the box. A metal lock-box, it was wrapped round and round with thick plastic.

I turned to peer up at my uncle, the flashlight shining down on the folds of the opaque plastic, his face neatly hidden in shadows.

"Sh-Shall we go?"

"No," a deep voice a mix of sorrow and anger from behind us met initially by the furious barking of the Doberman dancing back and forth in anger and fear. "I thought we were done here."

"G-Go back to the house, Marius."

"No," said Ben, glancing towards the Doberman.

My uncle's hand tensed on the shovel with the promise of violence.

"Go, Marius."

Ben stood still in the open area of the grave, a flashlight in his hand, his other hand hanging heavy at his side. He tilted the beam towards us, trying to read our intentions, trying to blind us.

"He's got something in his other hand," I whispered.

"Don't worry."

"We were done with this," Ben said again.

"We are done," my uncle.

I began to edge back towards the path, gritting my teeth against the pain in my ankle. Ben stepped to the side to intercept me. That's when my uncle and the Doberman ran at him and I hobbled towards the path with tears of intense pain in my eyes.

Chapter 15

WITH NO LIGHT but starlight and moonlight I limped through the brush with the metal box under my arm, trying to hear the fight that occurred behind me. Shouts or screams or blows. Near the shed, breathing hard, soaked through with sweat, I didn't rest as I moved past it and the collapsed trellis and the collapsed bower and the hard gurgle of the stream fed by rain and snowmelt and the spongy ground beneath my feet on a well-trod path, a veritable highway in the preceding weeks, down parallel to the wall and towards the door, taking slight detours around rosebushes, thinking I couldn't take another step but then finding the strength to go on through the wet stalks of goldenrod and finally to the garden door. Closed. And locked. And the lock jammed and ruined with a railroad spike hammered through its heart.

Ben didn't intend for any of us to get out of here alive.

I shook my head and fought back tears of desperation. The night would not end. The horror of this estate would not end.

"Keep moving, Marius," I whispered.

Move where?

Hide.

Chapter 16

THE SUN ROSE and no one came. I found myself nodding off, sitting in the damp embrace of prairie grass, out of sight, waiting to see who walked back along the path. Days ago I had tried to get into the garden without going through the door. It hadn't worked. I did not see how I would have any better luck getting over the wall this time.

My exhausted mind played tricks on me and I heard what I thought were footsteps along the path. Peeking through slender stalks parting and gathering in the wind I saw Ben or his ghost stumble forward with blood staining the front of his coat, glistening and heavy. And then he fell. I held my breath and listened, seeking out evidence that this was not a hallucination. If he was dead then I could move. If he was not dead, then he might still be stalking about with a sledgehammer.

I was cold and wet and exhausted and the shivering was severe. I could feel fever burning through my head and knew I couldn't stay hidden any longer. I might sleep and never wake. I stood and closed my eyes on the pain. The blood stayed low and the world spun and I reached out to catch myself but nothing was there and I stumbled back to my knees and hit my head hard on the ground. The world ceased to be and then came back fainter, more tenuous. Pushing to my hands and knees I dry-heaved and stared down at the trampled grass.

He would have seen me stand or heard me fall if he was near and able, but he did not come.

I stood in a more deliberate fashion the second time and managed to keep my legs beneath me. I saw the shoulder of a man down the path. He had folded to the ground. A brown winter coat. One arm outstretched, another beneath him at an awkward angle. The back of his neck ivory white. The only movement the wind blowing through his coat and his hair. It was the first time I had ever seen a dead body, a man gone the way of Alexander, and I peered at the wall and dissolved into tears. Bricklayer hands laying the sinister scales of a boa constrictor. Inanimate, yet stifling my ability to breathe, its circumference infinite and inescapable.

I'd tear my hair out, or my heart out, if I couldn't get out soon.

I hobbled up the path following the blood. The world spun on me numerous times as I placed my feet. Sharp sounds as birds erupted in black fanning clouds from the capillary fingers of winter trees.

And then I saw him. He sat on the bench at the collapsed bower. Beyond him the shed's gray lumber a reminder of what the dead man had intended.

"Uncle Laurence?"

My voice was weak and he didn't look in my direction. His eyes were glassed over. He didn't see any of what surrounded him. His Doberman lay at his feet, its eyes alert and following me.

I cleared my throat. "Uncle Laurence?"

He sniffed and tapped his bare raw fingers against the concrete bench and turned his head towards me but he didn't look above my feet.

"Hmm?"

"What... What happened?"

"Hmm?"

He came back to the world and made eye contact and I saw a softness in his eyes I had never seen before. Regret. Exhaustion. Maybe he cared.

"Marius."

"Ben's dead."

He closed his eyes and nodded. "I thought he would be. No threat anymore, at least."

"What happened?"

"We're two tired old men, Marius. It couldn't have gone on."

I saw the glint of a blade near his feet. A knife with blood on it. Still wet.

He followed my gaze down then turned his attention back to me. His Doberman whined.

"We're trapped in here."

"You're never trapped, Marius."

"There's no way to climb these walls. I've tried before."

He grinned and stared down at his hands, flexing them.

"There's a way. Here," he said, rising unsteadily to his feet and coming towards me. He placed his arm around me. "Let me help you."

I could smell the exertion of the fight, the dirt and the mud on his clothing, the odor of blood. He was warm and strong and I let him help me though I recoiled inwardly to be touching him.

We walked back towards the garden door with his dog scouting ahead. I think he still believed we'd be able to exit the way we'd come in, despite what I'd already told him. I didn't have the strength to traverse the garden seeking another way out. I wouldn't make it. Neither would he, it seemed. He grew more winded the further we walked and eventually I didn't know whether I was supporting him or he was supporting me.

"Who are all those people?" I asked.

"Hmm?"

"The names on the legal pad on your desk." Why pretend I hadn't spied?

Not far ahead lay Ben's body, the Doberman sniffing at it.

"The names?"

"The Jews. You're not like him, I don't think."

"Like my grandfather? No. No, I'm not like him."

"But I saw. I saw all the names. Why?"

He closed his eyes and pinched the bridge of his nose.

"I won't say."

"Why?"

"Please."

He didn't pause at Ben's body and didn't look down at him and soon he was behind us and the Doberman had run ahead again. As we approached the door I was about to remind him, not kindly, what I had already said about the lock. But he angled us back into the garden.

"Where are we going?"

"There's always a way out," he said again. "Always."

As the sycamore came into view I understood.

"We carried it a ways in. Left it. I didn't think I'd see it again," he said, skirting the edges of the rise the sycamore stood upon. "It'll be corroded at this point, I think, but it should work. Let's stop for a minute."

He took his arm from around me and collapsed, grimacing. His face had grown paler.

"How badly are you bleeding?" I asked.

He closed his eyes. His Doberman sat next to him and licked his cheek. He patted it affectionately.

"I won't tell you about the names," he said. "It's not because I don't want to. I don't want to be difficult." He stopped and his chest rose and fell heavily. I looked down at him and saw the maroon signature of blood spreading its way down a pants leg. He followed my gaze. "Don't worry about me."

"Shouldn't we tie a tourniquet around it?"

He shook his head. "I'll be okay."

I sat down near him on the damp ground.

"I can't deal with this world, Marius."

"What does that mean?"

"I... Maybe I read too much. I know too much. But during the war, the Nazis... There was a woman, a German woman. A woman. She went up to Jewish children at the ghetto walls and told them she had candy. Told them to open their mouths and she'd give them candy. I'm sure their parents were nearby, watching, ready to yell out to them to stay away. Stay away. Instead they saw them open their mouths. She didn't have candy. She had a pistol. What is it like to watch a child, innocent, trusting, opening his mouth while a grinning woman promising candy blows his brains out?"

He stared away, at the tree, and I could see a tear fall from his eyes, could hear it in his voice when he spoke again.

"This world's too painful, Marius. Why would someone do that? To a child? To anyone?"

He shook his head and pursed his lips.

"You've hurt Emily," I whispered. "She's a child."

He nodded his head and then the sobs began to wrack his body and for a while we sat in silence as the sky grew lighter and lighter and the clouds drifted away and it seemed it would be a clear and beautiful day.

"I know," he said, breathing out hard on the last syllable. "I know I've hurt her. I'm not meant for this world. I shouldn't be here."

"She's needed a father."

He nodded. "Yes. Yes, she does. She needs a family. But not me. I'm afraid I'm not good for her. But I love her. I go to see her sometimes. She's beautiful."

The ghost.

"But she's… she's permanently," he began.

"She's permanently nothing," I said.

"Because of me, she's that way."

"Because of your mother, not you."

"But it's all the same, Marius. It's all the same."

"It doesn't have to be."

"It's too late to change anything. The names… I can't live with who we are. Not just my family—our family—though that's part of it. I carry our guilt. But more than that. We. We as people." His eyes narrowed. "As humanity. The cruelty. Offering candy and firing a bullet. These children. God, Marius, they were innocent. They believed her. They believed in her. And she wasn't the only one. The camps. God. I'm afraid, with those names… It's not enough. It could never be enough. But I tried. Maybe for you and Emily it will be enough. I hope so. Can you be her family, Marius?"

"Of course. And you, too—"

"No. No, no, no. It's too late for me. I've said that already."

"So what are you going to do?"

"There's enough money. And my will. It'll be enough."

"You're not going to—"

"I'm going to fade away, Marius. I'm going to fade away."

"You'll leave?"

"I'm good at leaving. And it's time for you to leave this garden. Come. I know we're both in rather a sorry state right now, but it's time to find the ladder."

We both stood on shaky legs and I followed him

towards the side of the hill. A few times he cringed and nearly fell back to earth. His wound wept.

I found the ladder, a white, pitted surface overgrown and sunk into the earth. It was no easy extraction, but together we took hold of the rungs and pulled and the ladder ripped away from the undergrowth. We both sat back, gasping.

My uncle stared at the tree. At the branch where it had been done. The color of his skin so near to the color of its bark. Then he closed his eyes and communed with his ghosts.

"You tried to cut it down," I said.

He nodded.

"To forget what you did to her. Didn't you?"

"I tried. But there's no forgetting. Here I am, right?" Heavy breathing. "You need to go. Can you manage… the ladder?"

"What about you?"

"You go. Bring back help. Bring them here."

"Hang on."

With the plastic wrapped box under my arm, I dragged the ladder behind me, stopping frequently to catch my breath. The sun was nearing the apex of a winter afternoon when I got to the garden door. Only a hint of gray in the sky. With more strength than I thought I had, I propped the ladder against the wall and looked up at a distance that could have been miles.

I fought one rung after the other. My ankle glowed the hue of molten metal. I thought I would fall, the closer I got to the top of the ladder. That would have been the end. I couldn't have gotten up again. But I got there. I got to the top.

Getting over the wall was another matter. It was slick and the ivy was not anchored enough to serve as a handhold, only smooth enough to discourage confidence. I teetered there at the edge, reaching out, drawing my hand back, then reaching out again before finally gripping the lip of the wall as hard as I could. I lifted my bad leg and slid it over, then hugging the top of the wall, pushed with my good leg, lost my grip, went tumbling down. I thought I would impale myself on a fallen limb or metal stake or worse, but the growth near the wall was dense and softened the hard blow and I had to lie there and wait for my breath to come back.

I was beyond the wall. I was out of the garden.

"There he is," I heard a voice. Flora. Then she was running in my direction.

Lying on the ground, looking towards the sky…

"Is that smoke?"

She smelled like smoke. I saw plumes of it rising above the trees. And were those ashes falling on my face? Into my eyes? I narrowed my gaze, confused. Had we gone back to Majdanek? Was I an American boy, an orphan, or a fevered prisoner behind an electrified barbed-wire fence?

1943

THE NEEDLE WAS lowered onto the record and the cheerful music began. Music for a dance. The dance floor an open field outside the camps, surrounded by dirt piled from the digging of the days before. The prisoners, a warren of the condemned, short dark hair on skeletal heads, stood in front of the ditches. Shifting on weary feet. Knowing. The order to begin was given.

Heinrich Scherer raised his pistol to one of the heads and fired. Found another head and fired. The bodies fell into the ditches as the music played through loudspeakers and the screams and concussions of the shots were buried under scratchy symphonic sound. The bodies spasmed down. A dance, yes, but not one intended by the composer. And when the music paused while the soldiers changed the records, the shooting did not pause. Nor did the screams.

All day until 4 p.m. when the music was permanently silenced. Followed by a shot here. A shot there. On this crisp November day in 1943 in eastern Poland. Heinrich Scherer shook out a wrist and hand sore from the constant firing. A blister on his index finger.

He would rest his hand when he returned to his barracks. Ice his wrist, bandage his finger. Have a stiff drink. Thinking of this as he walked away from the 18,000 corpses of Majdanek and the silence that fell with the setting of the sun. The soldiers closed the lid on the record player and packed up the speakers and took them in.

Then he saw the child. The boy. The blood had mixed with the dirt and painted his face a gruesome mask out of which stared two jaundiced eyes.

Heinrich approached him and the boy slowly, mechanically, lifted his head. His mouth hung open. He drew ragged breath.

Heinrich pressed the pistol to the boy's temple.

The child didn't move. Those eyes, they stared into Heinrich.

He shivered, and then pulled the trigger. Nothing happened.

"Out of bullets," he said, almost apologetic, and trudged on. He needed to sit.

The bodies were left uncovered. The prisoners would work late burying them. Then they would also fall on the dance floor. But without music. Unless the percussion of gunshots could be considered a waltz.

VI
Offertory

Chapter 1

"WHERE AM I?"

My head on a soft lap. Flora's. I looked up at her.

"Relax," she whispered, stroking my forehead. "It's going to be okay."

"My uncle," I said, trying to sit up.

"No." She put her palm on my chest. "My grandma's there. The paramedics are there. He'll be okay."

"Where am I?"

A cattle car? A lorry?

"Mr. Charles's car."

"I'm here, Marius," he said. "You're going to be okay. We're almost there."

Almost where?

"I saw smoke."

Flora patted my chest again.

Chapter 2

BEING WHEELED ON a gurney and staring up at white fluorescent lights. The laundered smell of crisp hospital sheets. A warm blanket dropped onto me. Stopping. In a room. A nurse. Heavy perfume. I cringed. Cold alcohol on my arm then the sharp jab of a needle and I nearly threw up.

"Get a pan," she said in a distant voice.

"It's okay, Marius," Flora, her hand on my shoulder.

"Get a pan," again and I threw up.

Chapter 3

I WOKE UP in a dim room. An IV dripped fluid and a blood pressure cuff tightened and then let go and lights rose and fell on a computer monitor. Night had fallen.

"Flora?" I said. My throat burned.

"She went to get dinner with Mr. Charles. It's Emily."

"I'm happy you're here," I whispered. "Are we in Ohio?"

"I think you're still delusional," she said, but she was near the bed, and she took my hand.

"I'm not d…"

And then I was asleep again.

Chapter 4

IN THE MORNING my senses made their return. The cold, the dehydration, had taken their toll on me, and the doctor kept me another day. Flora, Emily, and Mr. Charles kept me company and told me little.

I was well enough to leave the hospital the following day.

Mr. Charles drove us to a small ranch house near town.

"Why are we here?" I asked.

"This is my home," Mr. Charles said. "You're going to stay here for a while. Until we get things figured out. Mrs. Moira is working on the arrangements as we speak."

"I don't understand."

"Let's get inside first. It's not luxury, but…"

Bookshelves lined the walls of nearly every room. Stained and lacquered oak. Floor to ceiling and full of the major works of literature and more than a few histories.

Mr. Charles had to lift Emily at the front door because there was no ramp. He set her on the sofa next to me in the living room. She didn't complain.

It was late afternoon and a single lamp lit the room as the sky darkened.

"How are you?" Emily asked.

"It's good to see you."

"The drugs are working, I see."

"I'm serious."

She grinned and looked away. "I know."

"So can you tell me now?" I asked.

Mr. Charles and Flora came back into the room chatting quietly and sat on the loveseat. I felt the stab of jealousy and remembered the things I'd heard in the library.

"There was a bad fire at the house," Emily said. I wasn't used to seeing her outside her room. I could see how pale she was, white skin, blue veins, black hair and calm hands resting on her lap. Yet she didn't seem afraid. She'd crossed the threshold of her room and hadn't looked back.

"A fire?"

"Arson, they're pretty sure. If the power hadn't gone out..."

"My grandma and I went to check on her when the storm knocked the power out. We noticed the smoke."

"He was trying to kill us," Emily said.

"Who?"

"My father."

"No."

"What do you mean, no?" There was anger in her voice.

"Emily," said Mr. Charles, trying to calm her.

"No. Did you and my father become friends, Marius? Did he persuade you he's a good guy, a pleasant chum?"

"Emily..." Flora.

"No," I said. "He didn't persuade me he's a good guy."

She shook her head in anger.

"Why don't we save this for another day?" said Mr. Charles.

I ignored him. "He's not a good guy."

"Wasn't a good guy," Emily said. "He's dead."

I took in a deep breath.

"He killed himself," she continued.

"No," I whispered, but it sounded right.

"Yes. He cut open his inner thigh and bled out. That damn dog was whimpering next to him when they found him."

"He saved my life."

"Or tried to end it."

"No," I said. "No."

I told them what had happened in the garden. As much as I could remember. Being locked in the shed. Being freed. Finding the grave and the birch trees and the metal box. Ben finding us, dying. The ladder. All of it.

"If anyone set fire to the house, it was Ben," I said.

"It makes sense," said Mr. Charles, quietly.

"Why would he do it?" said Emily, not wanting to give up her theory.

"A lot of things happened after Marius and Mr. Bracciolini made their little trip down south," said Mr. Charles. "Ben's son—"

"Mr. Charles, maybe—" Flora.

"Tell me, please," I said.

"Michael Padrick killed himself sometime after your visit," said Mr. Charles. "Ben learned about it. He went to town asking questions. Apparently his son had left behind a letter. He said he was glad to finally get things off of his chest. He must have mentioned Mr. Bracciolini by name…"

Flora sighed and looked away.

"Don't tell me," I said.

Mr. Charles sighed and shook his head.

"Jesus Christ," I said.

"The fire at the estate wasn't the only fire that night," Mr. Charles continued. "The Paper World… Someone threw a Molotov cocktail through the window. Jerry was in the basement. He didn't have a chance."

I was quiet for a while as I thought about him. His kindness and intelligence, despite all his faults. I couldn't imagine a more horrible way to go. Fire. So much fire.

"Who else?" I whispered.

"Who else?" Mr. Charles, confused.

"Who else is going to die? There aren't many of us left."

"Marius," chided Flora.

"He's right," said Emily. She'd seemed lost in her own world ever since I'd shared the story of what happened in the garden. "This family is damned."

"We're here," said Flora. "We're not going anywhere. Ben's dead."

"And my dad," said Emily. "Maybe we have a chance."

"He…" I closed my eyes and saw him. The warmth in him at the end. The love for her. The sorrow. Those eyes had begged for forgiveness, hadn't they? And I'd said nothing. "He came to see you, Emily."

She shook her head and scowled. "Don't."

"I think he loved you."

"Don't," more sharply like she might hit me. "Don't you dare. He never even spoke to me. Not once in my life. If he loved me he had the most peculiar fucking way of showing it."

"Like my mother," I said.

Emily and I stared at each other for a long time. Hard stares. Challenging. Then she looked away. We sat in silence for a long time as a grandfather clock ticked in another room and the light from the sun disappeared. Nothing more was said about it that night.

"What now?" I asked after a while.

"Rest," said Flora. "Please." She looked at Emily who hadn't looked up in a long time. "You just got out of the hospital."

"I'm okay."

"Rest. All of us. We're all worn out."

"What about the box?"

"We have it," said Mr. Charles. "You pushed it over the wall."

"I don't remember."

"We haven't opened it."

"It's his confession."

"I told them that," Emily muttered. "We've been waiting for you."

"Let's read it."

***

Mr. Charles cut away at the plastic and pulled out a small metal cashier's box.

"Did you ever find your answers about your grandmother?" I asked as he set the plastic aside.

He shook his head.

"It's a cold case, Marius, and I'm not much of a detective. I tried. I scoured the archives. But, no. That doesn't change what I know in my heart. There's not enough evidence to prosecute. And he's dead now anyway. But I know."

He pulled on the latch and lifted the lid.

"Well?"

"There's no writing in here."

"What?" Emily and I said more or less at the same time. "It's empty?"

"I didn't say that," he said. He pulled out a small tape reel. "And believe it or not, as old as you think I am, I have no way of playing this."

I stared at the reel, the shiny brown tape. Had it even survived its years of burial? Were we about to hear the voices of the dead?

"We can figure it out tomorrow," said Flora. "Rest."

We did.

Chapter 5

WHEN I CAME out of my room the next morning to the smell of coffee and eggs and bacon, Mr. Charles was standing at the kitchen counter with a portable silver reel-to-reel player.

"He's awake," he said.

"Can he have breakfast first?" Flora asked.

"Marius?"

I looked at Flora. She was still in her pajamas. She was beautiful.

"Just toast," I said. "It won't take me long to eat it."

She smiled. I remembered what she felt like.

After I ate we sat at the kitchen table as Mr. Charles mounted the tape.

"I don't know if it'll even work," he said.

He pressed play.

There was a click. A man cleared his throat. Then they spoke.

EDWARD: You said you had some things to tell me.

HEINRICH: [*voice weary, old, interrupted by frequent, violent coughing*] Yeah.

EDWARD: Well? What? What things did you want to tell me?

HEINRICH: [*chuckles*] About life.

EDWARD: Life?

HEINRICH: Life. Death. Yeah.

EDWARD: What happened to Elizabeth, Peter?

HEINRICH: Heinrich. No use to pretend. Not anymore.

EDWARD: What happened to her?

[*There's a long pause. The hum of the tape cycling over the heads. A chair creaks. There's coughing.*]

I looked around the room. Flora glanced towards the hall back to the bedrooms. Emily, deep in thought, watched the tape reels rotate. Mr. Charles held a pen to his lips, a legal pad on the table in front of him.

HEINRICH: I killed her.

[*Pause.*]

EDWARD: Killed her?

HEINRICH: Yeah. Pushed her. Down into that well. Broke her neck. It was easy.

[*Silence. A cough.*]

EDWARD: You don't sound sorry.

HEINRICH: Another face I see. When I dream. These things. You know.

EDWARD: I don't know.

HEINRICH: At Majdanek it was the fevers. So many... They all got sick.

EDWARD: Who all got sick?

HEINRICH: Them, you know. The Jews. The Soviets. Poles. The prisoners. Fevers.

EDWARD: Typhoid?

HEINRICH: Diarrhea. Vomiting. Weeks. Three,

four, before there was some relief.

EDWARD: You said you dream about them.

HEINRICH: Yeah. I don't want to kill, you know. But you get sick. You see these people getting off the train. Sneezing little kids, you know, crying for their moms and dads. We didn't want to touch them. Not with our hands. That's why we used our...

EDWARD: What happened to the people getting off the train?

HEINRICH: There was a cafe, a club, in Lublin. Called the *Deutsches Haus.*

EDWARD: What happened to them, Heinrich?

HEINRICH: I was having a drink, you know, and with a lady. And the music. I start to feel sick. A gnawing, gnawing, like—*fh, fh, fh*—rats, in my, in my intestines. Who put them there? Hmm? Weeks. I thought, ah, I'm going to die. And while I'm lying there, you know, on the bed, I see these people, masses of them, filthy. They... One train we unloaded, these people, they shit at the door, and they froze the door shut, with their shit, and we had to shoot the door open. You see children come out, and their parents, yeah, and I... I... lying there with fever and I see them going by and going by down the hill to the showers. And I see—

EDWARD: Your hands are shaking.

HEINRICH: I see the face of a boy. He's lost, yeah. Jerking his head round. Here. Here. [*In a child's voice*] 'Where's my mommy? Where's my daddy?' Ach. I... They were so dirty.

EDWARD: [*voice nearly a whisper*] What happened to the boy?

HEINRICH: Him? Yeah. Another guard, Hermann. He... It was like he was looking at a mouse, you know? And he raised his rifle. The butt of it. *Bop!* And he hit that kid. I saw. I saw the blood. I saw him drop like... Just drop. But they were all around me. We had the dogs. Screaming. 'Get in line! Get in line!' And... Someone shot. And more shot. And just screams, you know. They scatter and we, we herded them, yeah. And we shoot. I saw it. Lying there with fever just burning, burning through my head. That boy's face. He's, he's calling for his mom. His dad. I had a mom, you know. But...

EDWARD: It didn't stop you, though, did it?

HEINRICH: There was a day. November. It was 1943.

EDWARD: The Harvest Festival? Your hands are shaking.

HEINRICH: And we... You could see the crematorium. The chimney, yeah, smoke rising. And we played music. Because of the screams. So loud. And there were so many.

EDWARD: How many?

HEINRICH: There were so many. And just, just, *pah-pah-pah.* Just shooting and shooting. Like, this is hard work. But I see, I see these faces. I close my eyes now and I see this boy.

EDWARD: The boy the other soldier hit?

HEINRICH: The boy, like a...

EDWARD: Why didn't you try to stop it?

HEINRICH: Before the war, you know, my mom, she had her hands on my collar, on my uniform. And she has tears falling from her eyes. She told me I looked like such a gentleman. That my father, he would be proud of me. But I never knew him. He died in the trenches before I was born. I had a stepfather. You would not have wanted to meet him [*grainy laugh and coughing*]. The back of his hand, yeah? Fast.

EDWARD: You didn't try to stop it.

HEINRICH: She wouldn't have been proud of what I did. I'm not, I'm not proud of it. But the, the germs they carried. The disease. Weeks in bed with a fever and diarrhea and rats gnawing through my stomach.

EDWARD: What happened, after the Harvest Festival?

HEINRICH: The festival?

EDWARD: All those Jews murdered in one day. Executed by firing squad. Mass graves. You made them bury their own and then you killed them too.

HEINRICH: There were public baths in Lublin—

EDWARD: Heinrich—

HEINRICH: For the Germans only. Let me talk. We were treated well. Extra liquor, cigarettes for going east. To the East. The end of the world to us. Full of savages, yeah? The goddamn frontier. You worship here, your West. Ach. The frontier. It wasn't worth it.

EDWARD: What happened after the Harvest Festival?

HEINRICH: There I'm at the bath one day and I'm

sitting there and the hot water, it's like... My arm, hand, they're sore. They hurt. From all of the shooting. And I look down. I look down at my hands and I'm in the bath and I know they're empty. I know I'm not holding anything. But I see a Luger pistol. I see a gun in my hand and I open my hand to drop it because it's on fire. It's overheating. It's... It's on fire. And I...

EDWARD: Heinrich?

HEINRICH: Maybe I should have shot myself then, yeah? I think, maybe, that it's easier to be dead, than to see the dead when I close my eyes.

EDWARD: I'm sure they'd have preferred it that way. How many people did you kill?

HEINRICH: Here?

EDWARD: Here? What do—

Mr. Charles's head jerked up.

HEINRICH: Five, I think.

We looked at each other.

EDWARD: What?

HEINRICH: Five. Here.

EDWARD: Here?

HEINRICH: In America.

EDWARD: What are you—

HEINRICH: But no more with a gun. No. I— Not after Majdanek.

EDWARD: You've killed in America?

HEINRICH: I pushed her down the well.

EDWARD: Who else, Heinrich?

HEINRICH: They... They all had something to say to me, you know? And who doesn't think, sometimes, you know you're bad to me, well, I won't take that. I'll... But the difference with me is, now I don't have control. I—I'm afraid, you know? That...

EDWARD: Afraid of what?

HEINRICH: I couldn't shoot anymore so I used a knife. And I didn't want to see their faces. So I... I cut them off.

EDWARD: You cut off their faces?

HEINRICH: Their... Right here. And their eyes. *Pop.* And I put them, their face down, in the dirt, and put dirt over top. Not rational, I know, right?

EDWARD: You're shaking.

HEINRICH: It was the only way I didn't feel afraid. They couldn't look at me.

EDWARD: Afraid of what, Heinrich?

HEINRICH: They knew who I was.

EDWARD: What?

HEINRICH: And they would... They'd tell. I can see, in that gymnasium, the short rope. They used short rope. Just, '*Ah, ah,*' gasping, you know? For a long time. Short rope. They should have broken their necks, yeah? A long drop and, and an end to it [*soft chuckling*].

EDWARD: What's funny about that?

HEINRICH: I didn't want to end up like them. The ones I... The boy...

EDWARD: I need to know who these people were,

Heinrich.

HEINRICH: Women, mostly. And Jews.

EDWARD: Heinrich—

HEINRICH: But they're dead now. You don't need to worry.

EDWARD: That's—

HEINRICH: You don't need to worry. Listen to me. And me too. Soon. You know? Dead.

EDWARD: That doesn't excuse any of it.

HEINRICH: It's sad, hmm, that in the end, the killing, the killing. That's the only thing that made the fear go away. The killing. But not with a gun.

The tape clicked and was silent for a while and Mr. Charles stood up to turn it off, but then it clicked again.

EDWARD: He was not conscious much after that and I didn't know what to do. He'd given me no names. He was delirious. He could have made it all up. The murders here. But something told me no, that wasn't right. And there was Elizabeth.

I haven't mentioned any of this to Victoria. And I won't. But I will look. And if I find any evidence, anything to corroborate what he claimed he's done, I will have no choice but to report it. Right? Families out there are seeking answers, and I can provide them. Some of them. But what will that mean for my family? Are these hallucinations? If not, what will it mean, for Laurence, for Hannah? I… Forgive me if I'm wrong about this.

There was another click and that was it. Indefinite grainy silence.

Chapter 6

WHAT CAN I say? They were not hallucinations, of course. He was afraid that they would turn him in and he would be taken to Europe or taken to Israel and hanged. For some reason, that scared him beyond anything else, the fact the condemned weren't given more rope.

Mr. Charles acted as messenger and went to the police with the tape and went to the families with compassion—his family had suffered as well, of course—and at the very least brought closure to people who'd long given up on knowing what had happened to those they'd loved and lost. The families of Sara Feld, David Pensak, and Mary Leiber had not forgotten.

Chapter 7

IN MY UNCLE'S will, updated after he became my guardian, he stated his intention to have Emily and I live with Mrs. Moira if we so chose. We did. He also gave us the option of choosing to go to boarding schools in New England. We both declined.

We inherited what remained of the wealth. Enough for each of us to live a lifetime without worry, but apparently, there had once been much more, and no one seemed to know where all of it had gone.

We lived in a simple house in town. Flora, Emily, and I each had our own rooms. Mrs. Moira took care of us but seemed in a state of perpetual shock. The price for ending a curse can be steep. What else can I say?

We went to the local high school and I found a new form of torture among the crass and the simple-minded and the sports-obsessed. In the locker room, another realm of hell, they saw a reed of a boy and at best I wasn't noticed and at worst I was put inside of lockers or had my backpack thrown over my shoulder as I walked down the stairs, forcing me to fall with it. But I also found a friend or two who shared a love of books and who didn't mind driving out to a field late at night to look through a telescope.

Sometimes Flora drove. We discovered much of the pleasures of life in each other but there came the point where the familiarity, where my injured self-esteem and stubbornness and harsh statements, breathed in anger or frustration, separated us. The greatest pain came when she was a senior and I was a junior and she started to date a young college student seriously. It's hard to admit it now, but I think I might have killed myself at that point if not for Emily. It hurt that much. Fortunately she helped me see the fault in such a permanent solution.

Emily had her own trials, of course. She went from isolation in a room in a vast estate to a small house in town and a public high school. She was absent a lot from school. She saw a psychologist a few times a week—I fought it but eventually went to counseling as well. The irony is that Emily seems to have turned out better than I did. I still prefer to be alone. I don't care for people very much. She lives in New York City and stays busy with her friends—artists and writers and professors. And she wrote a book, *The Winter Garden* (a garden she never did go into, ironically enough), fictionalizing our lives. Trying to make sense of her father and our family. She didn't get it all right—who could? But I think she trapped the essence of it. And she's made some money, gained some attention.

"The Fates owe us," she told me when it started to sell.

The Fates do owe us.

Chapter 8

ALL OF MY possessions went up in smoke when the house burned. I've been able to replace Arthur C. Clarke and the other books, but not my computer or camera and the pictures I'd taken. Nor my mother's ashes, which I never saw or held or whatever it is a person does with ashes.

Since the death of my uncle I've woken up many times in the middle of the night thinking about the names written on his legal pad, the names he wouldn't discuss with me. I can remember one or two of them and some of the cities—the cities are easier—and finally sat down at the computer to try to figure out what the names were all about.

I typed combinations of names and cities, perhaps all wrong, into Google. It was Ira Berkovich who provided the key.

Ira Berkovich was born in Lodz, Poland, in 1929. He died in Helena, Montana in 2003. He was a Holocaust survivor, and he was survived by three children and seven grandchildren.

***

Standing in my kitchen on a warm summer evening. Helena. Berkovich. The white pages. Names.

It's the second person I call, Adam, who answers on the fourth ring.

"Hello," he says. His voice is warm.

"Hello. Is this Adam Berkovich?"

"Speaking, yes."

"Hi—"

"You're not selling something, are you?"

"Selling something? No, no. I'm looking for information, about a person I think may have been a relative of yours."

"My father, Ira, I'm going to guess."

"Yes. That's right."

"It's all available, you know, at the Holocaust Memorial Museum in D.C. I don't know that I can tell you anything you won't find there. You are?"

"Marius. Marius Besshaven. I… I don't know that I can find the information I'm looking for at the Holocaust Memorial Museum."

"I see." A pause. I hear a TV turned down low in the background, a woman's voice. "Well, ask away. I have a few minutes."

"Does the name Laurence Frost sound familiar to you?"

"Laurence Frost? No, nope, I don't think I've ever heard the name Laurence Frost."

"Hmm."

"Is that all? Was he someone who knew my father?"

"He, Laurence, he was my uncle, and I've been going through his papers," a lie, because those papers had trailed away into the sky like crematory smoke long ago. "He passed away."

"I'm sorry to hear that."

"And he has… he took some notes, and your father's name, along with some others, are listed. Along with cities. Travel plans, I think. I'm… There was nothing suspicious about the way your father died, was there?" I close my eyes and wait. His tone will turn. Grow hard. My uncle's words a lie that will cause much of the last decade of my life to crumble away on incorrect assumptions, a foundation of naïveté.

"Suspicious? No, no, not unless you call old age suspicious. He had a weak heart. We knew for years. He had a hard life."

I exhale.

"I understand. I'm sorry."

"What are the other names?"

"Pardon?"

"You said there are other names, names your uncle wrote down. Along with my father's. What are they?"

"Oh, right. Yeah. Well. Um." I wrote down everything I could remember and plucked a name off the list. "Elijah Wechsler. He was from—"

"San Francisco. We knew Elijah. Go on."

"Ah, Neta…" I couldn't come up with her surname.

"Hirsch."

He can't see the wrinkled brow, the pursed lips, the confusion. He's filling in the blanks. It's like he sees the original list. I don't know whether to go on.

"I'll be damned," he says. There's still warmth there. "And let me see if I can guess some of the others.

Sara Levine. Eli Cohen."

"Yes." I can't remember, not for sure, if all of the names were there. But they sound right. Like they belong.

"Ari Silverstein. And… Oh, I know there are others. Wow. I'll be damned."

"What—How do you know… How do you know all of these names?"

"You're trying to solve a mystery, I gather. And I'm going to tell you right now, you've solved one. Your uncle was a rather short man. With some stand-out gray eyes. Kind of hard to forget. Like a wolf's eyes."

He's described him perfectly.

"Is that him?" he asks.

"Yes. Yeah—"

"Well, your uncle knocked on the doors of our families shortly after the funerals. We always figured he read about them in the obituaries, saw that they were Holocaust survivors and felt obliged to… In every instance, he apologized, and then made donations. Rather large ones. To the Holocaust Memorial Museum in the name of our parents. Not long after he departed, another check showed up with substantial funds meant for our children. For their education. A few of us know each other from the interviews our parents have done and we've talked and we've been trying to find out for the longest time who that man was. I'll be damned. So that's your uncle. Laurence…"

"Frost."

"Laurence Frost. And your name again?"

"Marius. Marius Besshaven."

"I see. Well, Marius Besshaven. Since I can't thank him, unfortunately, I guess I'm going to tell you. Thank you."

"I…"

"He could have just mailed those checks in and been done with it if that's what he wanted to do. We all thought it a bit strange, until the checks cleared and we were contacted by the Memorial. I guess… I don't know. He came to see all of us. I guess he wanted it to be personal. Without being too personal."

"That sounds… like him."

"Do you have any idea why he did it?"

"I…" Yes. Yes I did. "I can't say for sure."

"Did your family lose loved ones during the Holocaust?"

Not exactly. "I don't know."

He chuckles.

"Well, Marius, if you ever have questions, if you ever need anything, you feel free to give me a call. And if you don't mind, I have your number here, and I might share it with a few others who might have questions and thanks of their own. What do you think?"

"That's not a problem."

"Marius, is there anything else I can do for you?"

"No, sir. No, I think—"

"Well, you have yourself a fine evening."

There's a click and I hear the wonder in his voice

echoing across the plains and river valleys.

Forgiveness. Years and years of wandering, trying to buy forgiveness. Not for himself, I don't think. He knew it was too late. But for Emily. And me.

Chapter 9

"YES, MARIUS."

EMILY'S not always pleased when I call, but she always answers the phone.

"I discovered something," I say.

"A black hole? A nebula? A life-bearing planet?"

"About your father."

Long silence.

"Emily?"

"What is it?" Like she doesn't want to hear it. Like she doesn't have a choice.

I tell her what I discovered in my call to Adam Berkovich.

"How kind of him," she responds, heavy on sarcasm. And who can blame her. He gave money in memory of others. He gave her money. He gave her nothing else of value.

"I've been writing, Emily."

"About what?"

"What happened."

She laughs. "Going to challenge my account of it all?"

"No. No, it's just for me. But—"

"But you're still not over her."

"No."

"Marius, that was ten years ago. Those were the discoveries of a child. For both of you. You need to move on."

"Do you still talk to her?"

"Marius—"

"How is she?"

A deep sigh. "She's fine, Marius."

I close my eyes. Flora's married or a mother or otherwise has moved on. Emily's trying to spare my feelings.

"She'd want you to be happy," Emily continues.

"Thanks."

"And you're going to hang up and go drink and mope and—"

"Stop."

"When are you coming to New York again to see me?"

"I don't like the city."

"I'm here."

"Emily—"

"I'm here, Marius."

"I know you are."

"Don't forget it."

"No. I won't."

My eyes are out of focus. I'm going to open a bottle of wine the second I hang up the phone. I think she knows that.

"Think about it. I'd love to see you. Okay?"

"Okay."

"Good night, Marius."

"Good night."

When I hang up the phone, I don't go for the wine.

Not right away. I go to my study instead, and take the cap off of my telescope. It's a clear night, and the city lights are faint enough that I might just have a chance of seeing something new.

Yes. For once, I look up without thinking of Miriam Reis, Sara Feld, David Pensak, Mary Leiber, and the faces of Majdanek.

Instead I see stars, and the resolution is good.

A Note on Ruin's Entrance and The Secret Garden

RUIN'S WASTEFUL ENTRANCE is a result of the author's lifelong love of *The Secret Garden* by Frances Hodgson Burnett. It was not my intention to simply write a 21st century version of Burnett's great novel, but to explore thematic areas of particular interest to me, including the causes of family downfall and ruin. This necessitated going in some drastically different directions than the great Burnett.

If stories about dark houses, ghostly cries, and family secrets fascinate you as much as they fascinate me, I strongly recommend you read *The Secret Garden*.

Thank you for reading *Ruin's Entrance*. If you enjoyed it, I would be most grateful if you would take a moment to leave me a review at Goodreads or your favorite retailer.

Thanks!
Ray Stickle

About the Author

RAY STICKLE IS the author of *The Footnotes*, *Ruin's Entrance*, and *Stay, Illusion*. He lives in Ohio with his wife and three children.

Connect with Ray

Website: www.raystickle.com

Goodreads:
www.goodreads.com/author/show/7423147.Ray_Stickle

Twitter: @RayStickle

Other Books by Ray Stickle

Stay, Illusion (Marius Besshaven #2)

I brought the branch down on his head and he fell in a heap, unconscious. But breathing. Who was I?

Two bodies found by the banks of a flooded river. The authorities call it murder-suicide, but Marius Besshaven doesn't agree. The man they're blaming had too much to live for. And there's the burned man. A man whose past--shadow and flame, abduction and torture--may hold the key to the investigation.

Marius is obsessed with finding the truth--driven by the traumas of youth, the pathological need for definitive answers. His quest will plunge him into a deadly game of cat and mouse with a killer more isolated and sadistic than anyone ever suspected, a madman who may take from him all he holds dear.

The Footnotes

There was the thin man up the beach walking with a noticeable limp, pinched eyeglasses perched on his nose, a pair of white slacks and a billowing white shirt, his Korean face further hidden by a low-worn white sun hat. Galden had been following the man for more than a week. An easy job for a beach bum.

But a trip to South Korea soon changes things. Because the thin man on the beach has a history steeped in the shadows of the country he served, the country he fled: North Korea. Galden soon finds himself involved with a sociopathic gangster hell-bent on uncertain ends, an ex-military elite on a mission of vengeance spurred on by his traumatized wife, a beautiful woman who hides her identity behind a slowly crumbling façade, and, perhaps most threatening of all, his own alcohol-addled conscience's attempt to grapple with hard decisions. How Galden navigates the kidnappings, explosions, and betrayals will determine whether he has an impact on the outcome or becomes nothing more than just a footnote to the affair.

Lightning Source UK Ltd.
Milton Keynes UK
UKHW022158300519
343634UK00005B/126/P

9 781364 747930